F
KEROUAC

Kerouac, Jack, 1922-
1969.

The Dharma bums.

$24.95

219884

DATE		
988		

BAKER & TAYLOR

The Dharma Bums

JACK KEROUAC

50TH ANNIVERSARY EDITION

Introduction by ANN DOUGLAS

VIKING

VIKING
Published by the Penguin Group
Penguin Group (USA) Inc., 375 Hudson Street,
New York, New York 10014, U.S.A.
Penguin Group (Canada), 90 Eglinton Avenue East, Suite 700,
Toronto, Ontario, Canada M4P 2Y3
(a division of Pearson Penguin Canada Inc.)
Penguin Books Ltd, 80 Strand, London WC2R 0RL, England
Penguin Ireland, 25 St. Stephen's Green, Dublin 2, Ireland
(a division of Penguin Books Ltd)
Penguin Books Australia Ltd, 250 Camberwell Road, Camberwell,
Victoria 3124, Australia
(a division of Pearson Australia Group Pty Ltd)
Penguin Books India Pvt Ltd, 11 Community Centre, Panchsheel Park,
New Delhi – 110 017, India
Penguin Group (NZ), 67 Apollo Drive, Rosedale, North Shore 0632,
New Zealand (a division of Pearson New Zealand Ltd)
Penguin Books (South Africa) (Pty) Ltd, 24 Sturdee Avenue,
Rosebank, Johannesburg 2196, South Africa

Penguin Books Ltd, Registered Offices:
80 Strand, London WC2R 0RL, England

This edition published in 2008 by Viking Penguin,
a member of Penguin Group (USA) Inc.

1 3 5 7 9 10 8 6 4 2

Copyright © John Sampas, Literary Representative of the Estate of Jack Kerouac; John Lash, Executor of the Estate of Jan Kerouac; Nancy Bump; and Anthony M. Sampas, 1958
Introduction copyright © Ann Douglas, 2006
All rights reserved

A brief excerpt from this book appeared in *Chicago Review* under the title "Meditation in the Woods."

Letter from Henry Miller to Pascal Covici used by permission of the Estate of Henry Miller.

Library of Congress Cataloging-in-Publication Data

Kerouac, Jack, 1922–1969.
The Dharma bums / Jack Kerouac ; introduction by Ann Douglas. — 50th anniversary ed.
p. cm.
ISBN 978-0-670-01993-9
1. Beat generation—Fiction. I. Title.
PS3521.E735D48 2008
813'.54—dc22
2008022159

Printed in the United States of America

Contents

Letter from Henry Miller regarding The Dharma Bums,
October 5, 1958   VI

Introduction by Ann Douglas   IX

The Dharma Bums   I

Mr. Pascal Covici
The Viking Press
New York, N.Y.

Dear Pat Covici:

I owe you great thanks for sending me The Dharma Bums by the inimitable Jack Kerouac. I had been wanting to read him for some time but somehow never got the chance. If his other books are anything like this one, then I want to read them too. From the moment I began reading the book I was intoxicated. It's not only joyous, reckless, carefree kind of writing but highly poetic, sensitive and meaningful. Even when he is nonsensical he makes great sense.

A few weeks before the book came I had read his text on writing in the Evergreen Review. I was thoroughly elated and I meant to write him, Kerouac, at once to tell him so. But then some one borrowed the Review and has never returned it. Now, reading The Dharma Bums, I have the feeling that he is one of those rare birds who can not only tell us what writing is and should be like but who can do it. In this he differs from his criticasters.

He is the first contemporary American writer who makes me feel optimistic about the future of American letters. Whether he is a liberated individual I don't know, but he certainly is a liberated writer. No man can write with that delicious freedom and abandonment who has not practised severe discipline. The way he plays havoc with syntax is an inspiration. He says exactly what he wants, in his own way, and he has a thousand ways of doing it. He has no fear, no inhibitions, no spite, no malice. He has a pure warm heart big enough to include the creature world, plants, rocks, even worms. It is even big enough to include the idea of a God. What a marvelous thing it is to read, on the last page of this novel – "I have fallen in love with you, God. Take care of us all, one way or the other." And this from a man of the so-called Beat Generation.

Kerouac could and probably will exert tremendous influence upon our contemporary writers young and old. He points the way out of the present impasse. "Be yourself!" he says in effect. "Do that and you will enjoy your work; do that and you will be read." That is how I read him. And I want to thank him for reminding me of this simple truth. I want to thank him for making me laugh. I want to thank him for taking me up in the XXX High Sierras and for showing me how to come down a mountain as well as go up it. I love the verbs he has created and all the poetry with which he has loaded his prose. I like the way he shrugs off our cock-eyed American behavior, hardly bothering to thumb his nose, but you get it, you know what he stands for and you want to bless him for being so kind, so considerate, so gentle and forgiving.

Here plays good magic too. White magic. What's real comes through, and though it may be empty it's never unreal. Where other writers use whitewash he uses space. Others run out of "material" sooner or later. Kerouac can't. He's all there is, because he's identified himself with everything, material or non-material, and with the silence and the space between. We've had all kinds of bums heretofore but never a Dharma bum, like this Kerouac. He doesn't throw dust in your eyes . . he sings. "God, I love." Take hope, you lost ones – Jack's here!

Sincerely,

(signed) Henry Miller

Introduction

"A Hoop for the Lowly"

When Gary Snyder, the Zen poet immortalized as "Japhy Ry-der" in *The Dharma Bums,* first met Jack Kerouac in San Fran-cisco in the fall of 1955, he sensed about him "a palpable aura of fame and death." Snyder, then twenty-five, was eight years younger than Kerouac and virtually unpublished. Though far from famous, Kerouac had a novel, *The Town and the City,* which came out in 1950 to generally good reviews if tepid sales, behind him; several of his more recent and experimental pieces, whose energy and "evocation of people" impressed Snyder im-mensely, were beginning to find their way into the small literary magazines of the day. But Snyder did not know that Kerouac had "already accomplished," in his words, "a huge life work"; outside his original Beat circle in New York City, no one did. After his breakthrough into the all-out confessional and bebop-inspired style he named "spontaneous prose," in a creative feat seldom matched in American letters, Kerouac had written five major novels between 1951 and 1955 that no publisher would touch—*On the Road,* Kerouac's first venture in the new style, had itself been rejected a half dozen times. The signature avant-garde works of the other charter members of the Beat Genera-tion, Ginsberg's *Howl* (1956) and William Burroughs's *Naked Lunch* (1959), both heavily influenced by Kerouac's spon-taneous prose method, were in print within months of their completion. Only Kerouac had to endure the sickening, heart-breaking wait, "turning out manuscripts," he wrote his agent Sterling Lord on February 24, 1956, which "keep flying away into the void." "Why," he wondered, "don't they realize I'm good?"

Snyder was right that fame was in the wings. *On the Road,* even today the best-known of Kerouac's works, was finally published in September 1957. Still young in years and handsome as any movie star—Salvador Dali pronounced him "more beautiful than Marlon Brando"—blessed with a voice that was in itself a musical instrument, a lightning-swift mind, and an uncanny instinct for absurdist comic timing and impromptu gloom-and-glee drama, Kerouac became an overnight sensation, the first literary figure of the full-fledged media age, interviewed on TV talk shows and reading his work to jazz accompaniment at the Village Vanguard. But attention was not respect.

In advocating spontaneous composition with little or no revision, Kerouac was demanding more discipline, not less; the writer, like the athlete or the jazz musician, was to commit himself to daily and endless practice in letters, journals, and "sketching," as Kerouac called his fast-as-hands-can-print transcriptions of his immediate surroundings, all training for the moment of performance. The skills of improvisation, devalued in the modern industrial West, were to be laboriously unlocked, like prisoners buried in a cave led by a perilous route back into the light. Nor did the fact that Kerouac's work was openly, unabashedly autobiographical, that he staked everything on an ethos of almost physical intimacy in which the somatic self's fluctuations defy the censorship of the mind, bringing the narrative "I" as close to himself as possible and abolishing the traditional distance between author and reader, mean the result was life, not art. Kerouac was indeed compiling in his novels what he called a "contemporary history record" of his times, but he may have been the first American writer to self-consciously discover, as the critic William Crawford Woods puts it, that "history becomes fiction in the . . . act of being written down," a discovery that would underpin the work of contemporaries as diverse as Robert Lowell, Norman Mailer, Philip Roth, and Hunter S. Thompson. The true story of postwar America in all its speed, tomfoolery, and sorrowfulness, Kerouac believed, could only be told as interior monologue and confession. Once unleashed by "one hundred percent personal honesty," in Kerouac's now-famous phrase, the inner self would discover its own art form; it had taken him fifteen years, he estimated, to tap and train his own "voice."

Kerouac, as the poet Robert Creeley instantly understood, was if anything more professional than his peers, not less, an artist "old-fashioned [and] devoted," in his own words, but for most critics and reviewers, subscribers to then fashionable if spurious notions of authorial objectivity, avowed vulnerability and spontaneity spelled amateur; Kerouac had declared open season on himself, and they welcomed the sport, calling him a "know-nothing Bohemian," "the latrine laureate of Hobohemia," and "a slob running a temperature." Truman Capote, who later created his own form of the nonfiction novel, publicly dismissed Kerouac's method as "typing," not "writing." By nature painfully sensitive and self-conscious, the least well-protected of men, capable in his cups of rage but never of malice and utterly devoid of media smarts, Kerouac was helpless before the onslaught. Foolishly, he took advantage of his new visibility to rush his huge backlog of manuscripts into print, strengthening the misapprehension that he tossed off a book every few days.

If his discerning readers were few, Kerouac didn't lack for groupies, and they terrified him too. "You're twenty-one and I'm twenty-nine," one avid fan told Kerouac's girlfriend, the writer Joyce Johnson, pushing her aside at a party. "I have to fuck him now." Perfect strangers felt free to pound on his door. He had finally "popped" into view, Kerouac lamented, only "to be slashed down" by critics and torn apart "limb from limb" by his uncomprehending followers. And by his own reckoning a problem drinker since his late teens, by 1957 Kerouac had burnt his way through several lifetimes. Norman Mailer, an uneasy rival, liked him when they met, but marked his air of fatigue, an exhaustion not surprising, Mailer said, in a pioneer, "the first figure for a new generation," who had traveled in realms where "the adrenaline devours the blood." A critic's darling himself, Mailer was too astute to miss the obvious contrast between them: Kerouac had spent the better part of a decade hitchhiking and jumping freights across America and Mexico, "out there living it," while he stayed home, "an intellectual, writing about it."

Kerouac's creative outpouring continued between 1955 and

1957, the years of his closest friendship with Snyder, but *The Dharma Bums,* written in late 1957 and published the following fall, had no successor for four years. *Big Sur* (1962), set like *The Dharma Bums* in northern California, a gorgeously written tale of despair, was Kerouac's last masterpiece, though not his last book, before his hideous, bitter death of alcoholism in Florida on October 21, 1969. By then, most of his work was out of print. Critical contempt, compounded by Kerouac's naïveté, had translated into consistently poor returns. Mailer got $35,000 for the paperback rights to *The Naked and the Dead* (1948), James Jones $100,000 for *From Here to Eternity* (1951), but Kerouac received only $1,000 for the rights to *On the Road,* a bestseller in hardback. Kerouac's two Hollywood sales (for *On the Road* and *The Subterraneans*) were no better. In the mid-1960s, he calculated his income at $65 a week.

Kerouac himself was agonizingly aware of his decline and honest enough not to put the blame entirely on abusive critics or carnivorous fans. He dated what he described as his "complete turning about from a youthful brave sense of adventure to a complete nausea concerning experience in the world, . . . a *revulsion,*" not to the time of *On the Road*'s publication, but to the period right after Snyder's departure for Japan to study Zen in May 1956. That summer, following (at Snyder's suggestion) in Snyder's footsteps, Kerouac spent two months in complete isolation as a lookout on Desolation Peak in the Mount Baker National Forest in Washington state just south of the Canadian border, an experience covered in *The Dharma Bums* and treated in greater detail and depth in *Desolation Angels* (1965). Snyder remained in Japan on and off for more than a decade; though they corresponded frequently at first, with Kerouac continuing to put in the occasional drunken phone call, followed by an apology, till the mid-sixties, the two men never met again. But Snyder, in Kerouac's eyes the embodiment of the truest, least self-serving form of American optimism, and Kerouac's tumbling, lyrical homage to him are at the dead center of Kerouac's career, the moment when he was poised between protracted obscurity and a notoriety still more destructive, before "the authority of failure," to borrow a line from F. Scott

Fitzgerald, forever eclipsed what chances he had had to obtain "the authority of success." Synder, Kerouac sometimes believed, was his last hope. "I need some of your gaity and natural bikkhu openness," Jack wrote him in February 1956. In early 1959, he felt too "ashamed" to see Synder; "I'm so decadent and drunk and dontgiveashit." Ten months later he was telling Ginsberg, "I need Gary's way now for a while, a long while. This is serious."

No writer ever traveled farther while staying so close to home. Though he married three times and had a child, the late writer Jan Kerouac, the first two marriages were brief, and he met his daughter only once; when he wasn't on the road, he spent most of his time with his shrewd and tenacious mother, Gabrielle (his father, Leo, died in 1946), who helped to support Jack by working in shoe factories until he was well into his thirties. Others might join the Cold War ranks of Organization Men as nine-to-five employees heading up suburban nuclear families; Kerouac preferred dependence to the sham of enforced maturity. "Infancy," Kerouac said, quoting Emerson, "conforms to nobody." Even after *On the Road* had given him enough money to put down the purchase price, Kerouac always thought of whatever house he shared with Gabrielle as hers and not his. Being born, in Kerouac's lexicon, was sin enough; at least he hadn't made the same mistake twice. As a writer, Kerouac's models were Thomas Wolfe, Herman Melville, James Joyce, Louis-Ferdinand Céline, and Fyodor Dostoyevsky; as a persona and even as a person, he saw himself as Boswell, Sancho Panza, and Pip, the child who accompanies Ahab on his doomed quest for the white whale, and goes mad in the process. Kerouac's job was to "shamble after," as Sal Paradise does in *On the Road,* to record rather than precipitate, to watch the fabulous, divinely inexplicable doings of a world he never made. Kerouac always played the "straight guy," Snyder observed, the one who gets set up and tripped up in the vaudeville routine, the second fiddle, not the star. It was a role he was born to.

The Kerouacs were working-class immigrant French-Canadians with a touch of Iroquois blood, "Canucks," in the local pejorative term. Though Leo and Gabrielle had migrated to Lowell,

Massachusetts, before Jack's birth on March 12, 1922, "Ti-Jean," as he was called, grew up outside looking in, part of an alternative culture, intensely Catholic and entirely French-speaking, and not even proper French at that. The Kerouacs spoke a regional, largely oral dialect called joual; Kerouac didn't master English until his late teens, and he failed French in high school. When he went to France in 1965 in a vain and drunken attempt to trace his genealogy, he was outraged to discover that all such records were labeled, accurately enough, *"les affaires Colonielles."* In his family circle too, Kerouac was, if hardly the subaltern, the acolyte; however great his gifts, he could never be the equal of his older brother, Gerard, who died of rheumatic fever at nine in 1926 after a lifetime's worth of pain. In family and local lore, Gerard was not only an artist in embryo but a saint, visited by the Madonna in visions and preaching eloquent little sermons to the obstreperously healthy Ti-Jean about the suffering and sacredness of even the lowliest of God's creatures. Jack prayed to Gerard for the rest of his own life—all his expeditions doubled as retrieval missions, a search for what he described as his lost "mysterious brother . . . across the ages." Gerard also stood as an eloquent argument for the virtues, practical as well as spiritual, of death, of being, in Kerouac's words in *Mexico City Blues* (1959), "free of that slaving meat wheel . . . safe in heaven dead." This was an argument for which, though his beginnings were auspicious, even spectacular, Kerouac never found an adequate rebuttal.

An honor student and a three-sport athletic star in high school, Kerouac went to Columbia on a scholarship in 1941. His commitment to writing, conceived early, never faltered, but when it came to upward mobility, his attention span was short. Dropping out, as he did during World War II, first from Columbia, then from the U.S. Navy, became his vocation, dropping out and *down:* into Harlem's jumping jazz joints where bebop, as Langston Hughes put it, was letting midnight out on bail, into the honky-tonks and all-night cafeterias of Times Square populated by a subterranean throng of hustlers, drug addicts, pimps, and visionary losers exploring the perils and power of obscurity. In July 1947, Kerouac began bumming his way west, determined to rediscover the continent, learning its secrets from those seldom caught by the camera's eye. Kerouac brought to the task of chronicling his age his own extraordinary cultural ESP, an ability to be "right on top of things" at which Snyder marveled. He caught the first signs of pop trends reflecting subtle shifts in historical reality, like the vogue of black leather jackets and T-shirts for men or the raised public profile of high-fashion models right after the war. From the moment he met Gary Snyder, he knew, as he had when Neal Cassady, the real-life original for Dean Moriarty, the Denver "jailkid," exuberant con man, desperate Lothario, and hot-rod hero of *On the Road,* first knocked on his door almost a decade earlier, that Synder represented the new, the next thing; like Neal, he was subject matter as well as soul mate.

Both Cassady and Snyder were rebels, pointing not to the broad thoroughfares of American life but to the detours and exits, the places where the Depression, sacred ground to Kerouac, Cassady, and Snyder alike, still lingered amid the staggering prosperity of the richest, most successful nation in history. At one moment in *On the Road* as Sal Paradise is trying to hitch a ride, a car full of teenagers yelling "We won! We won!" whizzes by. "I hated every one of them," Sal says. It is still hardly surprising that Snyder and Cassady, despite the overlapping circles they moved in, never became friends. If both were ahead of their times, Cassady anticipated the delinquent hipster who flashed across innumerable screens in the teen-exploitation films of the fifties; Snyder, the ecologically minded Woodstock nation of the 1960s, refusing to be "imprisoned," in Japhy Ryder's words, "in a system of work, produce, consume, work, produce, consume."

Like Kerouac, Cassady was a Catholic who could quote Biblical chapter and verse, while Snyder, a Buddhist who had moved beyond theism, held the Bible and its anthropomorphic view of creation partly responsible for the damage man had wreaked upon the earth. An autodidact, Cassady's politics didn't go much beyond dodging and outwitting any law that impeded his prodigious motion; Snyder was a well-educated and articulate intellectual who had tangled with the sterile

communism-versus-capitalism debate of the times to emerge an
anarchist. To him the world's dominant major nation-states
were "monstrous protection rackets," emblems of "greed made
legal with a monopoly of violence." Born Skid-Row poor, Cassady worked hard, if intermittently, on the Southern-Pacific
railroad to provide for his family; Snyder was proud to be one
of the small band whose members had "freely chosen to disaf-
filiate [themselves] from the 'American standard of living.'"
Cassady was impulse incarnate; Snyder thought that excess desire, whether for material goods or epistemological certainties,
was the source of suffering. A lifelong victim of violent mood-
swings now deranged by the uppers to which he was addicted,
Cassady died of exposure on a train track in Mexico in February 1968 just short of his forty-second birthday; he had long
since abandoned the autobiography that Kerouac had hoped
would bring about a new age in American letters. Snyder, who
knew how to capture complex contradictions in an ethos of
crystal-hard clarity, is still writing today.

By 1955, the days of Kerouac's closest friendship with Cassady were over. That spring he wrote Cassady's wife Caroline
of the "good times when Neal respected me"; "something has
happened and everybody has changed," he said sadly. At the
legendary Six Gallery poetry reading on October 13, 1955,
chronicled in *The Dharma Bums,* which inaugurated the San
Francisco Renaissance, the occasion on which Ginsberg first
presented *Howl* and Snyder followed with "A Berry Feast,"
Kerouac, too shy to take the stage himself, supplied the ecstatic
audience with jugs of wine and led it in chanting "Go!" Everyone present knew a new age had dawned. "We had gone beyond a point of no return," Michael McClure, another young
West Coast poet introduced at Six Gallery (he's Ike O'Shay in
The Dharma Bums), said, "and we were ready for it." Cassady
was there too; he would later play muse to Ken Kesey and the
Merry Pranksters, but on that night he asked a friend if he could
stand near him. "I don't know anybody here," he explained.
Though Cassady appears in *The Dharma Bums* (as Cody Pom-
eroy), he's a minor character.

If Cassady, a son of Missouri and Colorado, had opened to

Kerouac the gates of the West, Snyder, bred in Oregon, ushered him through them to places Cassady lacked the patience to seek and taught him the skills to survive there—among the lakes, rocks, and woods, the northwestern mountain fortresses as yet untouched by America's headlong material progress. Cassady, whose automotive frenzies mimicked what they outpaced, always "wrapped up," in Kerouac's words about Dean Moriarty in *On the Road*, "in a fast car, a coast to reach, and a woman at the end of the road," was a sorcerer's apprentice; once set in motion, he couldn't stop. All Snyder's activities were purposeful; a scholar of Native American lore, he laid bare the foundations of earthly being in places which were American sheerly by accident. Growing up in Oregon, Japhy, the descendant of pioneers and Wobblies, tells Ray Smith, Kerouac's stand-in in *The Dharma Bums*, "I didn't feel American at all"; parting from him and heading for Desolation Peak, Ray senses Siberia in the northernmost reaches of America. What matters are latitudes and landmasses, not the countries that claim and dispute them. Citizenship here is potentially global; Dean Moriarty could only be American but Japhy appears in Ray's visions as a mischievous Chinese sage.

Time magazine's summation of *The Dharma Bums* as "On the Trail" held more than a grain of truth. After crisscrossing the country half a dozen times by car with Dean Moriarty, Sal feels like a traveling salesman watching the landscape speed by in a blur—he has missed "the pearl" he sought. Next time, he will make a "pilgrimage on foot." *The Dharma Bums* recounts the sequel. Climbing Matterhorn Mountain with Japhy, an episode that forms the climax of the first part of the novel, hopeful he is now leaving his "recent years of drinking and disappointment" behind, Ray vows to tramp "all over the West and . . . the East, and the desert," "mak[ing] it the purer way" at last, and Japhy will be his patron saint. On Desolation Peak, Ray sees not mountains and lakes but "Japhy's mountains" and "Japhy's lake"—"Japhy had been right," he concludes happily, "about everything." It's not coincidence that Kerouac wrote *Visions of Gerard*, a tribute to his dead brother published in 1959, not long after his hike up Matterhorn; both books are free-form acts of modern hagiography and prayer. One brother had summoned up thoughts of the other.

The meeting of Kerouac and Snyder held reverberations beyond their personal or even artistic collaboration. As Ginsberg, the PR genius of the Beat Generation who had moved to Berkeley the year before, realized, a fusion was taking place of the "San Francisco West Coast Bohemian-Anarchist-Modernist tradition" and "the New York impulse or energy," with "Kerouac's obvious genius" as catalyst—it was America's first truly bicoastal literary movement, and the shared excitement was electric. "I thought [the East Coast] was dead," Japhy tells Ray and Alvah Goldbook (Ginsberg) in *The Dharma Bums.* "We thought the *West Coast* was dead!," they chorus back. It made sense that, despite the eastern metropolis' unrivaled artistic resources, the place of rendezvous was San Francisco, not New York City, the Beat Generation's launching pad. In Kerouac's words, "all the . . . loose American elements" were voyaging in that direction, leaving the "brown and holy" East for the "great dry West," a region "white like washlines and empty-headed." California's population increased seventy percent between 1940 and 1950, while for the first time in its history, New York lost more people than it gained. The fact that the destination of the westward migrants was usually Los Angeles, a suburban "jungle," in Kerouac's hostile description, the "most brutal of American cities," not Frisco, its older neighbor to the north, was part of the city's charm.

A century past its Gold Rush boom, free of the grotesqueries of constant gestation, San Francisco had the same feeling of "whacky comradeship" Kerouac loved in New York. Made largely of wood, its steep houses and steep hills piling conversationally upon one another, San Francisco, unlike L.A., the world's car capital, was a pedestrian's city scaled to the human being. Sprawling landlocked L.A. had to hack an outlet to the sea; Frisco perched atop its own bay, a tuning fork of East-West vibrations, with nothing between it and China or Japan save the vast glittering waters of the Pacific. Chinese workers arrived in the area in the 1850s to build the railroads, bringing their Buddhist temples with them, and the Japanese followed in the 1890s. When Kerouac, who had immersed himself in solitary studies of Buddhism at the start of 1954, arrived on the scene and expressed his surprised delight that there were other Buddhists in America, Kenneth Rexroth, the elder statesman of the West Coast poetry scene, satirized in *The Dharma Bums* as Reinhold Cacoethes, promptly put him down. "Everybody in San Francisco is a Buddhist, Kerouac. Didn't you know that?"

San Francisco, of course, whatever its edge, had no monopoly on things Buddhist. Interest in the East had been building since the late 1940s, part of what the historian Robert Ellwood calls "the spiritual underground" of Cold War America. *The Seven-Storied Mountain,* an autobiography by the Trappist monk Thomas Merton, whose career Kerouac at moments thought might be a model for his own, was a surprise bestseller in 1948; Merton began studying Buddhism in the early 1950s. Joseph Campbell's *The Hero with a Thousand Faces* (1949) popularized the idea of the quest as the core of mythology, religion, and literature in the East as well as the West; Morey Bernstein documented a purportedly real-life case of reincarnation in America in *The Search for Bridey Murphy,* a bestseller in 1956. D. T. Suzuki, who had arrived from Japan decades earlier, began lecturing on Buddhism at Columbia University in 1950; Japhy Ryder has Suzuki's books on his orange crate shelves in *The Dharma Bums,* and Kerouac himself went to visit the sage in New York in the fall of 1958. Suzuki took one look at Jack's flushed face and advised him to stick to green tea. As Kerouac was leaving, he asked Suzuki if he could stay with him always. Suzuki replied enigmatically, "Sometime." In July 1958, three months before *The Dharma Bums* was published, *Time* remarked that "Zen Buddhism is growing more chic by the moment," and *Mademoiselle* ran a surprisingly intelligent article on it around the same time.

In fact, Kerouac's turn East had been prompted by rereading *Walden* (1854), an impeccably New England source. Thoreau, a hero to Snyder as well, called the Hindu *Bhagavad Gita* a summit of wisdom and art that made the "modern world and its literature seem puny and trivial"; he published the first sutra, a poetic rendering of Buddha's teachings, to appear in English in the United States in *The Dial* in 1844. Like the transcendentalist movement in its day, from its inception the Beat Generation had marked a crisis and renewal of belief: "beat," Kerouac said, meant "beatific." Ginsberg and Kerouac's original template came as much from Eurasia as Europe, from Holy Rus and Dostoyevsky's anguished, absurdist portraits of Slavic madmen, fools, and saints; given the spiritual bankruptcy of the Western tradition as they saw it, a move farther East was almost preordained. With *The Dharma Bums,* Kerouac hoped to "crash open whole scene to sudden Buddhism boom . . . everybody reading Suzuki on Madison Avenue," paving the way for Snyder's poetry. "Gary, this is your year," he promised. To Kerouac's disappointment, *The Dharma Bums* didn't make the bestseller lists, but it did indeed, as he later claimed, "turn certain types on [to] Dharma."

Snyder, however, though he had initially professed himself "amazed and touched" by the "many nice things" Jack had said about him in his "beautiful book," was not happy. "I told you I liked it," Snyder wrote an apprehensive Kerouac in March 1959, "but that doesn't make it right. . . . Do *you* think you understand [Buddhism]?" Snyder referred darkly to a hell "where they pull out the writer's tongue with red-hot pliers." Though the two patched up their quarrel, Snyder always believed that Jack had taken little more from Buddhism than its emphasis on compassion and its sense of the vastness of time and space—both of which were already present in Kerouac's version of Catholicism and evident in his work as far back as *The Town and the City.* Echoing mainstream reviewers, Alan Watts ("Arthur Whane" in *The Dharma Bums*), who popularized Buddhism in several bestsellers, said Kerouac had "Zen flesh but no Zen bones"; he had confused Zen's " 'anything goes' at the existential level with 'anything goes' on the artistic and social levels."

But it was Buddhism's comparative lack of dogma that attracted Kerouac in the first place. Snyder might see Buddhism as a chance to move past the confines imposed by notions of an all-powerful God; Buddhism itself does not require its converts to renounce their former faith. From the start Kerouac was skeptical about the Zen branch of Buddhism to which Snyder gave his allegiance, a set of practices structured as a stringently disciplined ascent to ever greater degrees of enlightenment. In *The Dharma Bums,* Ray Smith openly scorns "those silly Zen masters throwing young kids in the mud because they can't answer their silly questions"—it's just plain "mean." Kerouac preferred the older all-embracing Indian Mahayana Buddhism to the Japanese Zen model, which to his mind could breed self-righteousness; "righteousness," Ray realizes, is itself the greatest sin, one to which he himself is far from immune. Ray almost perversely refuses to climb all the way up Matterhorn Mountain, though the last stretch is within his sight and within his capability. Clinging to his "protective nook" instead, he momentarily wonders if Japhy, however admirable, is not insane. If Japhy's Buddhism is about action, Ray is "Buddha the Quitter." Kerouac wanted to go further; he didn't want to be tested or pushed. It may be as significant not to reach the peak as to scale it.

Japhy's role as master to Ray's disciple is never fundamentally challenged, nor do we ever doubt the profound camaraderie between them. Still, a subtle current of antagonism between its two main figures runs throughout *The Dharma Bums.* Snyder had a number of good reasons to be uncomfortable with Kerouac's portrait of him. A private man with a healthy sense of his own limitations, he didn't want to be held up as the model for his times, nor, as a neo-imagist poet very influenced by Ezra Pound—"that pretentious nut," scoffs Ray—a style in many ways antithetical to Kerouac's, did he wish to be forever associated with the Beat Generation. Though both writers were fascinated by the three-line Japanese haiku form, "a sentence that's short and sweet with a sudden jump of thought," in Kerouac's definition, "a whole vision of life" free of "poetic trickery," a test of the artist's ability to resist projection and anthropomorphization, in *The Dharma Bums* Ray wants to make haikus up "real fast as you go along, spontaneously," while Japhy believes "you never can be too careful about haiku." But surely another reason for Snyder's displeasure was that Japhy, Ray's guide to Buddhism and backwoods alike, at moments seems annoyingly didactic, even priggish, a charge that can also be brought against Gerard as Kerouac portrayed him—everyone is inferior to a saint, and sometimes they resent it.

"Comparisons are odious," Japhy likes to say, but he lives on them, prefacing his remarks with phrases like "the trouble with you" or "you don't realize." "It'll do you good" passes for an explanation. Climbing Matterhorn, the irrepressibly loquacious Henry Morley (based on the Berkeley librarian John Montgomery and one of Kerouac's greatest comic portraits), a master of dadaist feats of free association and a charmingly feckless hiker, lets out a yodel. Japhy corrects him, explaining that the Native American "hoo!" is "much nicer," though once he's reached the summit, naked save for his jockstrap, he starts yodeling himself. Again and again, Japhy condemns middle-class America, its "grooming school" colleges, "white-tiled toilets," and general "fuggup with appearances"; he wants to start a printing press that will turn out "icy bombs for the booby public." But Ray demurs—"Ah, the public aren't so bad, they suffer too." He understands why his mother loves her kitchen appliances; he even sympathizes with his hardworking brother-in-law and his growing impatience with Ray's apparently shiftless ways. However frightened he is at the prospect of a world "electrified to the Master Switch," Ray can't forget that the people sitting in front of their TV sets—an activity in which he occasionally indulges himself—are also individuals, and "they're not hurting anyone." Ray knows that his own demand for unconditional acceptance means that he must accept others unconditionally too.

Nor do Japhy and Ray respond to nature in quite the same way. Coming down Matterhorn, Ray is ecstatic because, he says, he's learned from Japhy that "you can't fall off a mountain." He's also thrilled to "begin to smell people" again; returning to civilization is like "waking up from an endless nightmare." As Ray's first forebodings approaching the isolated bleakness of Desolation Peak again reveal, nature unadorned by human inventiveness can look premeditated to Kerouac, like a plot or a crime. In the far darker account he gives in *Desolation Angels,* Kerouac can't wait to leave Desolation Peak for the city, where there will be "rumpled couches with women on them" and "drama rag[ing] all unthinking," the world that, after all, birthed Kerouac's own spontaneous prose. In his hikes in *Dharma Bums,* Ray is happiest when he has a sense that he already knows this wilderness, when he feels "something inexpressibly broken in my heart as though I'd lived before and walked this trail." To activate his deepest imagination, Kerouac needed a doublefold of memory on place that nature unaided does not supply—not someone else's memories but *his* memories, if need be from another life. Ideas can't interpret landscapes for Kerouac as they sometimes did for Snyder; he could never write, as Snyder did, that "the most / Revolutionary consciousness is to be found / Among the most ruthlessly exploited classes: /Animals, trees, water, air, grasses." Only people, or ghosts, can populate Kerouac's world.

Kerouac's real Buddhist period was over by the late 1950s, but at no time did he pretend that Christ had lost the dominant place in his heart. In an interview with *The Paris Review* in the last year of his life, when questioned as to why he had written about Buddha and not Christ, Kerouac retorted angrily, "All I write about is Jesus!" For Kerouac, there was no real difference between the two religious leaders; the story of Siddhartha, later known as the Buddha, born in India in the fifth century BCE, a tale Kerouac retells in *The Dharma Bums,* who leaves the wealth and privilege to which he was born for the ascetic life of a religious wanderer, finally discovering the Four Noble Truths that form the core of Buddhism, paralleled Christ's renunciation of his divinity to take on human form. But Buddhism did offer Kerouac a literal selflessness, a profound kind of anonymity, that Catholicism could not; Buddhism abolished, in Alan Watts's phrase, the "Good I—Bad Me" dichotomy endemic to Western thought. If all was really "the Void" upon which men merely project their illusions, all labels are meaningless, all bets off. "What a horror it would have been if the world was real," Ray reflects in one of the book's most haunting lines, "because if the world was real it would be immortal."

The no-nonsense William Burroughs, chastising Kerouac for his new faith in 1954, said that in the West, Buddhism could only be part of "history, . . . a subject for understanding"; the "California Buddhists" were "trying to sit on the sidelines." But the sidelines were just where Kerouac wanted to be. Unlike the creeds and ideologies of the West, or Russia for that matter, Buddhism wasn't responsible for the insane atrocities of human history as Kerouac named them in a catalogue of nightmares in *Desolation Angels:* not for the guillotine or the burning stake, the concentration camps, gas ovens, and barbed wire, nor for the ruinations of Genghis Khan or Tamerlane. If no Westerner, and certainly not Kerouac, could fully understand Buddhism, Buddhism served the West, in Kerouac's words, as a "form of heresy," "gentle" and "goofy," but heresy all the same. Kerouac's political views insofar as he formulated them were increasingly reactionary, but he feared the "America-lovers" as much as the "America-haters." At a time when Americans were routinely told they had only two choices—Soviet-style communism or American capitalist democracy and all that went with it—Buddhism offered a third way. In *The Dharma Bums,* in a characteristically unflappable bit of apparent illogic, Henry Morley remarks of Buddhism, "I'm not much interested in the belief part of it." "I'm neutral," he says, and Japhy gives his imprimatur, shouting, "Neutral is what Buddhism is!" Buddhism was a recovery program for the West, "a hospital," Kerouac wrote in *Mexico City Blues,* "for the sick, / Lying high in crystal."

Buddhism promised Kerouac a world where wanderers could fashion their own religious order, one more ecumenical than Christianity ever devised, a special form of the gathered church, "big wild bands of holy men," in Kerouac's words in *The Dharma Bums,* "Zen lunatics" bringing the "vision of freedom of eternity" to all creatures and sanctifying a way of life fast disappearing in America: the way of the vagrant, the hobo, the bum. The "Dharma" in Kerouac's title meant "truth," but the word "Bums" held an older and deeper resonance. It summoned up the Depression images of his boyhood Kerouac loved, men traveling "with nothing but a paper bag for lug-

gage," as he put it in *Desolation Angels,* "waiting in line for
coffee and donuts . . . forag[ing] in riverside dumps looking for
junk to sell," an image with a long pedigree in American life
and popular culture from the Wobblies' songs and Charlie
Chaplin's tramp to *Sullivan's Travels* (1941), a movie Kerouac
cited fondly in *On the Road,* and the Judy Garland-Fred Astaire
number "A Couple of Swells" in *Easter Parade* (1948). In
"The Vanishing American Hobo," a tidal-wave jeremiad against
the ever-stepped-up surveillance operations of the postwar
United States published in *Holiday*'s March 1960 issue, Kerouac widened the category further, putting Christ and Buddha
at the head of a line that included Ben Franklin, the Russian
poet Sergei Yesenin, and Teddy Roosevelt.

The bum has always had a mixed reputation in American
life. Often frowned upon, at other times, he was idealized as
"The Happy Hooligan," in the title of one old ballad, the em-
blem of what Kerouac called a very American "special idea of
footwalking freedom," never a criminal, yet living by his wits in
the best tradition of American ingenuity. Jack London, whose
travelogue *The Road* (1907) was of incalculable importance to
Kerouac, thought it was his own early life as a mendicant hobo,
compelled to improvise a story from what he saw on "the face
of the person who opened the door," that had made him a
writer. Sometimes, most notably during the Depression, the
hobo served as a reminder that anyone caught in an economic
system rigged to deliver profits largely to the powerful could
fall between the cracks; in 1933, FDR installed a federal program to aid "transients," whose poverty was now considered
neither their fault nor their choice. But once World War II had
jump-started the economy, the pendulum swung back the other
way. New York cracked down on chronic drunkards in public
places; the nation's Skid Rows, where Kerouac had often found
lodgings and friends in his cross-country journeys, would soon
be tagged "blighted areas" ripe for "urban renewal." In San
Francisco by 1956, cops were stopping Kerouac and his friends
simply for walking on the streets late at night or loitering on
corners to talk in the daytime. Systematic police raids plagued
North Beach, the city's bohemian quarter; Neal Cassady, en-

trapped by an undercover agent, was arrested for drug trafficking in 1958 and spent two years in San Quentin. By then Kerouac had returned east for good.

In *The Dharma Bums,* Ray wants nothing to do with "Japhy's ideas about society." His plan is to just "avoid it altogether, walk around it," but that proves harder to do than he expects; cops are as plentiful here as in a Chaplin movie. Hitching his way west, Ray learns that it's illegal for him to camp out anywhere within or near a town. Border patrolmen, even the rangers he joins at Desolation Peak, observe rules just as narrow and expect him to, while uranium prospectors looking to make a buck out of the United States' ballooning nuclear weapons program comb the apparently unspoiled northwest. The fat, maliciously grinning cowboy in a gravel truck who deliberately tries to run over Ray's backpack in northern California anticipates the vigilantes of *Easy Rider* (1969), and Cody's girlfriend, Rosie (drawn directly from Natalie Jackson, Cassady's real-life lover), an artist's model and "a real gone chick," rapidly turns into a proto-sixties burnout, skeletal and deranged, raving about an imminent "big new revolution of police"—"they'll have *everybody* in jail!" Before she commits suicide, Ray tries to tell her that all of life is "just a dream," that a "rucksack revolution" is coming instead, but she doesn't believe him, and she almost, he admits, convinces him.

By the time he wrote his essay on the American hobo for *Holiday,* Kerouac had joined Rosie's camp. The "thousand and one hiding places of industrial night" are being boarded up; cops in five-thousand-dollar patrol cars "pick on the first human being they see . . . anything that seems to be moving independently of gasoline, power, Army, or police." Kerouac's heart is with the homeless, the people outside the new nuclear family and the state that rewards and patrols it, but most of America is sitting home "watching the cop heroes on TV"; *Dragnet,* a huge hit, had just ended its eight-year run, and *Naked City,* another police series, stayed on the air until 1963. Even in the wilderness places he and Snyder had explored together, Kerouac notes, there's always a helicopter "snooping around." It's bad enough that the tramp is all but obsolete—the hobo never

lived who could snag a free ride atop a jet—he's pathologized
too, as a "rapist, . . . strangler, child-eater." Kerouac went off
the road, he announces, for good in 1956, the year Snyder left
the United States. "The only thing to do [now] is to sit alone in
a room and get drunk." Bordering Kerouac's essay on *Holiday*'s pages are ads for "Comfy Slippers" and packaged tours of
Scandinavia. Of course, even as Kerouac wrote, the rucksack
revolution he had predicted in *The Dharma Bums* was in the
wings; public camping sites and hippie communes would soon
dot the landscape. But there was one thing Kerouac never did,
and that was fake it. The hippies, he wrote in "After Me the
Deluge," an essay published posthumously in 1969, were hyp-
ocrites, organizing their own fund-raising dinners, "parasites
feeding on their juicy national host," a far cry from those who
a decade or two earlier had tried to make a new life on America's margins.

Ginsberg thought *The Dharma Bums* flattering, less personal
and "wild" than Kerouac's other major works, and Kerouac was
aware that he had caught the moment's optimism while playing
down its darker side. Natalie Jackson's suicide occupies only a
few pages, yet in his first plan for the book, sketched out in
March 1957, Kerouac described it as the novel's culmination;
Neal Cassady, not Snyder, was to take center stage. The night of
the Six Gallery reading, Kerouac confided to a friend, he'd gone
on "the worst binge of my life," coming to with scabs on his
face. Yet the alcoholism that did so much in real life to destroy
his relationship with Snyder is treated in *The Dharma Bums* as a
relatively minor sore point between friends. In late 1961, Kerouac assured Snyder that he'd like *Big Sur,* in which a drunken
Kerouac is patently unable to endure either solitude or society,
better than *The Dharma Bums;* it's "honester."

Kerouac's holdback on personal revelations in *The Dharma
Bums* has costs, starting with its jarring tone of misogyny. Although Kerouac was always more interested in his male charac-
ters, in his other books, most notably *The Subterraneans*
(1958), he compensates by exposing his own troubled mas-
culinity, homosexual impulses and all; the reader is invited to
understand a fear, a belittling of women Kerouac himself does

not entirely condone. But no such self-examination takes place in *The Dharma Bums*. Princess, one of Japhy's several girl-friends, sleeps with all the men she meets, Ray casually informs us, because she knows that as a woman she can never become a Boddhisattva herself. Ray, vacillating between vows of celibacy and envy of Japhy's easy sexual prowess, says "pretty girls make graves," meaning that the cause of death is birth or procreation, but we don't really learn how it feels to believe this. The ethnically bland name "Ray Smith," though it was the name Kerouac originally gave Sal Paradise, his alter ego in *On the Road,* is an exception in Kerouac's work after *The Town and the City*. As a French-Canadian-Iroquois-American, Kerouac considered himself part of a minority group, and he didn't want to pass. Even Sal is of Italian descent; if Ray is anything other than a mainstream Euro-American, we don't know it. Nor, a true anomaly, do we learn much about Ray's childhood.

Yet this curtailment of subjectivity and the curious narrator-ial vacancy it sometimes entails are also part of the special and vast charm of *The Dharma Bums*. In Kerouac's other books, childhood is the inescapable theme precisely because the narra-tor is avowedly an adult, enraged that the time of innocence is over. No one expects children to hold coherent political and philosophical views or to conduct self-analysis. Children aren't asked to support themselves, to make permanent commitments or to have sex, much less marry. And children by and large don't habitually get drunk. Indeed, adults who force children into such activities are held to be committing crimes, against nature as well as the state. Kerouac novels such as *Visions of Gerard* (1963), *Maggie Cassidy* (1959), and *Vanity of Duluoz* (1967), self-consciously told from the perspective of the alco-holic and disillusioned adult man, are murder mysteries in disguise—who killed Ti-Jean, and why? In assessing the dam-age done, the grown-up Jack is the prosecutor's Exhibit A. In *The Dharma Bums,* however, Ray actually does for a few pre-cious moments regain childhood's bliss. His fears, his drinking, even the tensions that occasionally surface between Ray and Japhy can, at least for now, under the magic spell of Japhy's sheer lively health, be contained. All spells will eventually be broken but disillusion here is postponed, not courted. Kerouac's popping and parenthesizing persona has been pruned back, emptied out, to let Japhy, and joy, in.

The visions that come to Ray are large, all-encompassing—"Everything is all right forever and forever," he realizes—but the novel's language and imagery often suggest the close-up, the near, intimate, and dear: the "petrified rabbit" listening to the sounds of their approach, the "little creek, shallow as your hand." And the universe is not only vast but elastic, "everlastingly loose and responsive . . . beyond empty space blue." All large gifts are made up here of small pleasures—"a rainbow," Ray says, in one of Kerouac's most perfect haikus, capturing both the leap and modesty of the book, is "a hoop / for the lowly." The solution, he decides, is to pray in solitude "for all living creatures . . . it was the only decent activity left in the world."

If the real-life Kerouac found Desolation Peak more ordeal than inspiration, if he could not possibly have stuck it out in Japan as Snyder did or spent years living in Tangier à la William Burroughs, what he did have was curiosity at depth, a willingness to enter other people's worlds and live there on their terms, not his, no matter how foolish he looked, no matter how many mistakes he made. It's difficult to imagine Burroughs signing up for a lookout job in the northwest or Snyder exploring New York's underworld, or indeed any other contemporary writer willing and able to do both. Unlike Snyder or Ginsberg, Kerouac sustained very few intimate relationships over the course of his life, yet it's exhausting even to contemplate the extraordinary amount of time this "strange solitary crazy Catholic mystic," in his own description, spent at close quarters with other and very diverse people: driving cross-country with Cassady or later the photographer Robert Frank, living in their various homes with the Cassadys, Ginsberg, Burroughs, Snyder, and others. Nor were such visits usually passed in drunken stupors or made up of superficial contacts. Locke McCorkle, the original of Sean Monahan in *The Dharma Bums,* remembers that Kerouac was the only one of his friends his wife would let babysit their children.

Children live in other people's worlds because they have to;

to do so voluntarily as an adult can be the mark of a special and courageous kind of artist. This openness, this almost miraculous adaptiveness, the complete receptivity of his sensorium, was Kerouac's greatest gift, what made him count as a leader, in Michael McClure's words, in our "longterm biopolitics, . . . our effect on everything." Japhy Ryder was the last of the mythological figures Kerouac would add to the American pantheon. After *The Dharma Bums,* he centered his narratives on himself, now a castaway on the island of adulthood ever less sure of rescue.

Dedicated to Han Shan

The Dharma Bums

I

Hopping a freight out of Los Angeles at high noon one day in late September 1955 I got on a gondola and lay down with my duffel bag under my head and my knees crossed and contemplated the clouds as we rolled north to Santa Barbara. It was a local and I intended to sleep on the beach at Santa Barbara that night and catch either another local to San Luis Obispo the next morning or the firstclass freight all the way to San Francisco at seven p.m. Somewhere near Camarillo where Charlie Parker'd been mad and relaxed back to normal health, a thin old little bum climbed into my gondola as we headed into a siding to give a train right of way and looked surprised to see me there. He established himself at the other end of the gondola and lay down, facing me, with his head on his own miserably small pack and said nothing. By and by they blew the highball whistle after the eastbound freight had smashed through on the main line and we pulled out as the air got colder and fog began to blow from the sea over the warm valleys of the coast. Both the little bum and I, after unsuccessful attempts to huddle on the cold steel in wraparounds, got up and paced back and forth and jumped and flapped arms at each our end of the gon. Pretty soon we headed into another siding at a small railroad town and I figured I needed a poorboy of Tokay wine to complete the cold dusk run to Santa Barbara. "Will you watch my pack while I run over there and get a bottle of wine?"

"Sure thing."

I jumped over the side and ran across Highway 101 to the store, and bought, besides wine, a little bread and candy. I ran

back to my freight train which had another fifteen minutes to
wait in the now warm sunny scene. But it was late afternoon
and bound to get cold soon. The little bum was sitting crosslegged at his end before a pitiful repast of one can of sardines. I
took pity on him and went over and said, "How about a little
wine to warm you up? Maybe you'd like some bread and cheese
with your sardines."

"Sure thing." He spoke from far away inside a little meek
voice-box afraid or unwilling to assert himself. I'd bought the
cheese three days ago in Mexico City before the long cheap bus
trip across Zacatecas and Durango and Chihuahua two thousand long miles to the border at El Paso. He ate the cheese and
bread and drank the wine with gusto and gratitude. I was
pleased. I reminded myself of the line in the Diamond Sutra that
says, "Practice charity without holding in mind any conceptions about charity, for charity after all is just a word." I was
very devout in those days and was practicing my religious devo-
tions almost to perfection. Since then I've become a little hypo-
critical about my lip-service and a little tired and cynical.
Because now I am grown so old and neutral. . . . But then I really believed in the reality of charity and kindness and humility
and zeal and neutral tranquillity and wisdom and ecstasy, and I
believed that I was an oldtime bhikku in modern clothes wandering the world (usually the immense triangular arc of New
York to Mexico City to San Francisco) in order to turn the
wheel of the True Meaning, or Dharma, and gain merit for myself as a future Buddha (Awakener) and as a future Hero in Paradise. I had not met Japhy Ryder yet, I was about to the next
week, or heard anything about "Dharma Bums" although at
this time I was a perfect Dharma Bum myself and considered
myself a religious wanderer. The little bum in the gondola solidified all my beliefs by warming up to the wine and talking
and finally whipping out a tiny slip of paper which contained a
prayer by Saint Teresa announcing that after her death she will
return to the earth by showering it with roses from heaven, forever, for all living creatures.

"Where did you get this?" I asked.

"Oh, I cut it out of a reading-room magazine in Los Angeles couple of years ago. I always carry it with me."

"And you squat in boxcars and read it?"

"Most every day." He talked not much more than this, didn't amplify on the subject of Saint Teresa, and was very modest about his religion and told me little about his personal life. He is the kind of thin quiet little bum nobody pays much attention to even in Skid Row, let alone Main Street. If a cop hustled him off, he hustled, and disappeared, and if yard dicks were around in bigcity yards when a freight was pulling out, chances are they never got a sight of the little man hiding in the weeds and hopping on in the shadows. When I told him I was planning to hop the Zipper firstclass freight train the next night he said, "Ah you mean the Midnight Ghost."

"Is that what you call the Zipper?"

"You musta been a railroad man on that railroad."

"I was, I was a brakeman on the S.P."

"Well, we bums call it the Midnight Ghost cause you get on it at L.A. and nobody sees you till you get to San Francisco in the morning the thing flies so fast."

"Eighty miles an hour on the straightaways, pap."

"That's right but it gits mighty cold at night when you're flyin up that coast north of Gavioty and up around Surf."

"Surf that's right, then the mountains down south of Margarita."

"Margarity, that's right, but I've rid that Midnight Ghost more times'n I can count I guess."

"How many years been since you've been home?"

"More years than I care to count I guess. Ohio was where I was from."

But the train got started, the wind grew cold and foggy again, and we spent the following hour and a half doing everything in our power and will power not to freeze and chatterteeth too much. I'd huddle and meditate on the warmth, the actual warmth of God, to obviate the cold; then I'd jump up and flap my arms and legs and sing. But the little bum had more patience than I had and just lay there most of the time chewing

his cud in forlorn bitterlipped thought. My teeth were chatter-
ing, my lips blue. By dark we saw with relief the familiar mountains of Santa Barbara taking shape and soon we'd be stopped
and warm in the warm starlit night by the tracks.

I bade farewell to the little bum of Saint Teresa at the crossing, where we jumped off, and went to sleep the night in the
sand in my blankets, far down the beach at the foot of a cliff
where cops wouldn't see me and drive me away. I cooked hotdogs on freshly cut and sharpened sticks over the coals of a big
wood fire, and heated a can of beans and a can of cheese macaroni in the redhot hollows, and drank my newly bought wine,
and exulted in one of the most pleasant nights of my life. I
waded in the water and dunked a little and stood looking up at
the splendorous night sky, Avalokitesvara's ten-wondered universe of dark and diamonds. "Well, Ray," sez I, glad, "only a
few miles to go. You've done it again." Happy. Just in my swim
shorts, barefooted, wild-haired, in the red fire dark, singing,
swigging wine, spitting, jumping, running—that's the way to
live. All alone and free in the soft sands of the beach by the sigh
of the sea out there, with the Ma-Wink fallopian virgin warm
stars reflecting on the outer channel fluid belly waters. And if
your cans are redhot and you can't hold them in your hands,
just use good old railroad gloves, that's all. I let the food cool a
little to enjoy more wine and my thoughts. I sat crosslegged in
the sand and contemplated my life. Well, there, and what difference did it make? "What's going to happen to me up ahead?"
Then the wine got to work on my taste buds and before long
I had to pitch into those hotdogs, biting them right off the
end of the stick spit, and chomp chomp, and dig down into the
two tasty cans with the old pack spoon, spooning up rich bites
of hot beans and pork, or of macaroni with sizzling hot sauce,
and maybe a little sand thrown in. "And how many grains of
sand are there on this beach?" I think. "Why, as many grains of
sand as there are stars in that sky!" (chomp chomp) and if so
"How many human beings have there been, in fact how many
living creatures have there been, since before the *less* part of beginningless time? Why, oy, I reckon you would have to calcu-
late the number of grains of sand on this beach and on every

star in the sky, in every one of the ten thousand great chili-cosms, which would be a number of sand grains uncomputable by IBM and Burroughs too, why boy I don't rightly know" (swig of wine) "I don't rightly know but it must be a couple umpteen trillion sextillion infideled and busted up unnumberable num-ber of roses that sweet Saint Teresa and that fine little old man are now this minute showering on your head, with lilies."

Then, meal done, wiping my lips with my red bandana, I washed up the dishes in the salt sea, kicked a few clods of sand, wandered around, wiped them, put them away, stuck the old spoon back in the salty pack, and lay down curled in my blanket for a night's good and just rest. Waking up in the middle of the night, "Wa? Where am I, what is the basketbally game of eter-nity the girls are playing here by me in the old house of my life, the house isn't on fire is it?" but it's only the banding rush of waves piling up higher closer high tide to my blanket bed. "I be as hard and old as a conch shell," and I go to sleep and dream that while sleeping I use up three slices of bread breathing. . . . Ah poor mind of man, and lonely man alone on the beach, and God watching with intent smile I'd say. . . . And I dreamed of home long ago in New England, my little kitkats trying to go a thousand miles following me on the road across America, and my mother with a pack on her back, and my father running af-ter the ephemeral uncatchable train, and I dreamed and woke up to a gray dawn, saw it, sniffed (because I had seen all the hori-zon shift as if a sceneshifter had hurried to put it back in place and make me believe in its reality), and went back to sleep, turn-ing over. "It's all the same thing," I heard my voice say in the void that's highly embraceable during sleep.

2

The little Saint Teresa bum was the first genuine Dharma Bum I'd met, and the second was the number one Dharma Bum of them all and in fact it was he, Japhy Ryder, who coined the phrase. Japhy Ryder was a kid from eastern Oregon brought up in a log cabin deep in the woods with his father and mother and sister, from the beginning a woods boy, an axman, farmer, interested in animals and Indian lore so that when he finally got to college by hook or crook he was already well equipped for his early studies in anthropology and later in Indian myth and in the actual texts of Indian mythology. Finally he learned Chinese and Japanese and became an Oriental scholar and discovered the greatest Dharma Bums of them all, the Zen Lunatics of China and Japan. At the same time, being a Northwest boy with idealistic tendencies, he got interested in oldfashioned I.W.W. anarchism and learned to play the guitar and sing old worker songs to go with his Indian songs and general folksong interests. I first saw him walking down the street in San Francisco the following week (after hitchhiking the rest of the way from Santa Barbara in one long zipping ride given me, as though anybody'll believe this, by a beautiful darling young blonde in a snow-white strapless bathing suit and barefooted with a gold bracelet on her ankle, driving a next-year's cinnamon-red Lincoln Mercury, who wanted benzedrine so she could drive all the way to the City and when I said I had some in my duffel bag yelled "Crazy!")—I saw Japhy loping along in that curious long stride of the mountainclimber, with a small knapsack on his back filled with books and toothbrushes and whatnot which was his small "goin-to-the-city" knapsack as apart from his big full rucksack complete with sleeping bag, poncho, and cookpots. He wore a little goatee, strangely Oriental-looking with his somewhat slanted green eyes, but he didn't look like a Bohemian at all, and was far from being a Bohemian (a hanger-onner around the arts). He was wiry, suntanned, vigorous, open, all howdies and glad talk and even yelling hello to bums on the street and when asked a question answered right off the bat from the top or bottom of his mind I don't know which and always in a sprightly sparkling way.

"Where did you meet Ray Smith?" they asked him when we walked into The Place, the favorite bar of the hepcats around the Beach.

"Oh I always meet my Bodhisattvas in the street!" he yelled, and ordered beers.

It was a great night, a historic night in more ways than one.

He and some other poets (he also wrote poetry and translated Chinese and Japanese poetry into English) were scheduled to give a poetry reading at the Gallery Six in town. They were all meeting in the bar and getting high. But as they stood and sat around I saw that he was the only one who didn't look like a poet, though poet he was indeed. The other poets were either hornrimmed intellectual hepcats with wild black hair like Alvah Goldbook, or delicate pale handsome poets like Ike O'Shay (in a suit), or out-of-this-world genteel-looking Renaissance Italians like Francis DaPavia (who looks like a young priest), or bow-tied wild-haired old anarchist fuds like Rheinhold Cacoethes, or big fat bespectacled quiet booboos like Warren Coughlin. And all the other hopeful poets were standing around, in various costumes, worn-at-the-sleeves corduroy jackets, scuffly shoes, books sticking out of their pockets. But Japhy was in rough workingman's clothes he'd bought secondhand in Goodwill stores to serve him on mountain climbs and hikes and for sitting in the open at night, for campfires, for hitchhiking up and down the Coast. In fact in his little knapsack he also had a funny green alpine cap that he wore when he got to the foot of a mountain, usually with a yodel, before starting to tromp up a few thousand feet. He wore mountain-climbing boots, expensive ones, his pride and joy, Italian make, in which he clomped around over the sawdust floor of the bar like an oldtime lumberjack. Japhy wasn't big, just about five foot seven, but strong and wiry and fast and muscular. His face was a mask of woeful bone, but his eyes twinkled like the eyes of old giggling sages of China, over that little goatee, to offset the rough look of his handsome face. His teeth were a little brown, from early backwoods neglect, but you never noticed that and he opened his mouth wide to guffaw at jokes. Sometimes he'd quiet down and just stare sadly at the floor, like a man whittling. He was merry at times. He showed great sympathetic interest in me and in the story about the little Saint Teresa bum and the stories I told him about my own experiences hopping freights or hitchhiking or hiking in woods. He claimed at once that I was a great "Bodhisattva," meaning "great wise being" or "great wise angel," and that I was ornamenting this world with my sincerity. We had the same favorite Buddhist saint, too: Avalokitesvara, or, in Japanese, Kwannon the Eleven-Headed. He knew all the details of Tibetan, Chinese, Mahayana, Hinayana, Japanese and even Burmese Buddhism but I warned him at once I didn't give a goddamn about the mythology and all the names and national flavors of Buddhism, but was just interested in the first of Sakyamuni's four noble truths, *All life is suffering.* And to an extent interested in the third, *The suppression of suffering can be achieved,* which I didn't quite believe was possible then. (I hadn't yet digested the Lankavatara Scripture which eventually shows you that there's nothing in the world but the mind itself, and therefore all's possible including the suppression of suffering.) Japhy's buddy was the aforementioned booboo big old goodhearted Warren Coughlin a hundred and eighty pounds of poet meat, who was advertised by Japhy (privately in my ear) as being more than meets the eye.

"Who is he?"

"He's my big best friend from up in Oregon, we've known each other a long time. At first you think he's slow and stupid but actually he's a shining diamond. You'll see. Don't let him cut you to ribbons. He'll make the top of your head fly away, boy, with a choice chance word."

"Why?"

"He's a great mysterious Bodhisattva I think maybe a reincarnation of Asagna the great Mahayana scholar of the old centuries."

"And who am I?"

"I dunno, maybe you're Goat."

"Goat?"

"Maybe you're Mudface."

"Who's Mudface?"

"Mudface is the mud in your goatface. What would you say if someone was asked the question 'Does a dog have the Buddha nature?' and said 'Woof!' "

"I'd say that was a lot of silly Zen Buddhism." This took Japhy back a bit. "Lissen Japhy," I said, "I'm not a Zen Buddhist, I'm a serious Buddhist, I'm an oldfashioned dreamy Hinayana coward of later Mahayanism," and so forth into the

night, my contention being that Zen Buddhism didn't concentrate on kindness so much as on confusing the intellect to make
it perceive the illusion of all sources of things. "It's *mean*," I
complained. "All those Zen Masters throwing young kids in
the mud because they can't answer their silly word questions."

"That's because they want them to realize mud is better than
words, boy." But I can't recreate the exact (will try) brilliance
of all Japhy's answers and come-backs and come-ons with
which he had me on pins and needles all the time and did eventually stick something in my crystal head that made me change
my plans in life.

Anyway I followed the whole gang of howling poets to the
reading at Gallery Six that night, which was, among other important things, the night of the birth of the San Francisco Poetry Renaissance. Everyone was there. It was a mad night. And
I was the one who got things jumping by going around collect-
ing dimes and quarters from the rather stiff audience standing
around in the gallery and coming back with three huge gallon
jugs of California Burgundy and getting them all piffed so that
by eleven o'clock when Alvah Goldbook was reading his, wailing his poem "Wail" drunk with arms outspread everybody was
yelling "Go! Go! Go!" (like a jam session) and old Rheinhold
Cacoethes the father of the Frisco poetry scene was wiping his
tears in gladness. Japhy himself read his fine poems about Coyote the God of the North American Plateau Indians (I think), at
least the God of the Northwest Indians, Kwakiutl and what-all.
"Fuck you! sang Coyote, and ran away!" read Japhy to the dis-
tinguished audience, making them all howl with joy, it was so
pure, fuck being a dirty word that comes out clean. And he had
his tender lyrical lines, like the ones about bears eating berries,
showing his love of animals, and great mystery lines about oxen
on the Mongolian road showing his knowledge of Oriental literature even on to Hsuan Tsung the great Chinese monk who
walked from China to Tibet, Lanchow to Kashgar and Mongo-
lia carrying a stick of incense in his hand. Then Japhy showed
his sudden barroom humor with lines about Coyote bringing
goodies. And his anarchistic ideas about how Americans don't
know how to live, with lines about commuters being trapped in

living rooms that come from poor trees felled by chainsaws (showing here, also, his background as a logger up north). His voice was deep and resonant and somehow brave, like the voice of oldtime American heroes and orators. Something earnest and strong and humanly hopeful I liked about him, while the other poets were either too dainty in their aestheticism, or too hysterically cynical to hope for anything, or too abstract and indoorsy, or too political, or like Coughlin too incomprehensible to understand (big Coughlin saying things about "unclarified processes" though where Coughlin did say that revelation was a personal thing I noticed the strong Buddhist and idealistic feeling of Japhy, which he'd shared with goodhearted Coughlin in their buddy days at college, as I had shared mine with Alvah in the Eastern scene and with others less apocalyptical and straighter but in no sense more sympathetic and tearful).

Meanwhile scores of people stood around in the darkened gallery straining to hear every word of the amazing poetry reading as I wandered from group to group, facing them and facing away from the stage, urging them to glug a slug from the jug, or wandered back and sat on the right side of the stage giving out little wows and yesses of approval and even whole sentences of comment with nobody's invitation but in the general gaiety nobody's disapproval either. It was a great night. Delicate Francis DaPavia read, from delicate onionskin yellow pages, or pink, which he kept flipping carefully with long white fingers, the poems of his dead chum Altman who'd eaten too much peyote in Chihuahua (or died of polio, one) but read none of his own poems—a charming elegy in itself to the memory of the dead young poet, enough to draw tears from the Cervantes of Chapter Seven, and read them in a delicate Englishy voice that had me crying with inside laughter though I later got to know Francis and liked him.

Among the people standing in the audience was Rosie Buchanan, a girl with a short haircut, red-haired, bony, handsome, a real gone chick and friend of everybody of any consequence on the Beach, who'd been a painter's model and a writer herself and was bubbling over with excitement at that time because she was in love with my old buddy Cody. "Great, hey Rosie?" I yelled, and she took a big slug from my jug and shined eyes at me. Cody just stood behind her with both arms around her waist. Between poets, Rheinhold Cacoethes, in his bow tie and shabby old coat, would get up and make a little funny speech in his snide funny voice and introduce the next reader; but as I say come eleven-thirty when all the poems were read and everybody was milling around wondering what had happened and what would come next in American poetry, he was wiping his eyes with his handkerchief. And we all got together with him, the poets, and drove in several cars to Chinatown for a big fabulous dinner off the Chinese menu, with chopsticks, yelling conversation in the middle of the night in one of those free-swinging great Chinese restaurants of San Francisco. This happened to be Japhy's favorite Chinese restaurant, Nam Yuen, and he showed me how to order and how to eat with chopsticks and told anecdotes about the Zen Lunatics of the Orient and had me going so glad (and we had a bottle of wine on the table) that finally I went over to an old cook in the doorway of the kitchen and asked him "Why did Bodhidharma come from the West?" (Bodhidharma was the Indian who brought Buddhism eastward to China.)

"I don't care," said the old cook, with lidded eyes, and I told Japhy and he said, "Perfect answer, absolutely perfect. Now you know what I mean by Zen."

I had a lot more to learn, too. Especially about how to handle girls—Japhy's incomparable Zen Lunatic way, which I got a chance to see firsthand the following week.

3

In Berkeley I was living with Alvah Goldbook in his little rose-covered cottage in the backyard of a bigger house on Milvia Street. The old rotten porch slanted forward to the ground, among vines, with a nice old rocking chair that I sat in every morning to read my Diamond Sutra. The yard was full of tomato plants about to ripen, and mint, mint, everything smelling of mint, and one fine old tree that I loved to sit under and meditate

on those cool perfect starry California October nights un-
matched anywhere in the world. We had a perfect little kitchen
with a gas stove, but no icebox, but no matter. We also had a
perfect little bathroom with a tub and hot water, and one main
room, covered with pillows and floor mats of straw and mat-
tresses to sleep on, and books, books, hundreds of books everything from Catullus to Pound to Blyth to albums of Bach and
Beethoven (and even one swinging Ella Fitzgerald album with
Clark Terry very interesting on trumpet) and a good three-
speed Webcor phonograph that played loud enough to blast the
roof off: and the roof nothing but plywood, the walls too,
through which one night in one of our Zen Lunatic drunks I
put my fist in glee and Coughlin saw me and put his head
through about three inches.

About a mile from there, way down Milvia and then upslope
toward the campus of the University of California, behind another big old house on a quiet street (Hillegass), Japhy lived in
his own shack which was infinitely smaller than ours, about
twelve by twelve, with nothing in it but typical Japhy appurte-
nances that showed his belief in the simple monastic life—no
chairs at all, not even one sentimental rocking chair, but just
straw mats. In the corner was his famous rucksack with
cleaned-up pots and pans all fitting into one another in a compact unit and all tied and put away inside a knotted-up blue
bandana. Then his Japanese wooden pata shoes, which he never
used, and a pair of black inside-pata socks to pad around softly
in over his pretty straw mats, just room for your four toes on
one side and your big toe on the other. He had a slew of orange
crates all filled with beautiful scholarly books, some of them in
Oriental languages, all the great sutras, comments on sutras,
the complete works of D. T. Suzuki and a fine quadruple-volume
edition of Japanese haikus. He also had an immense collection
of valuable general poetry. In fact if a thief should have broken
in there the only things of real value were the books. Japhy's
clothes were all old hand-me-downs bought secondhand with a
bemused and happy expression in Goodwill and Salvation
Army stores: wool socks darned, colored undershirts, jeans,
workshirts, moccasin shoes, and a few turtleneck sweaters that

he wore one on top the other in the cold mountain nights of the High Sierras in California and the High Cascades of Washington and Oregon on the long incredible jaunts that sometimes lasted weeks and weeks with just a few pounds of dried food in his pack. A few orange crates made his table, on which, one late sunny afternoon as I arrived, was steaming a peaceful cup of tea at his side as he bent his serious head to the Chinese signs of the poet Han Shan. Coughlin had given me the address and I came there, seeing first Japhy's bicycle on the lawn in front of the big house out front (where his landlady lived) then the few odd boulders and rocks and funny little trees he'd brought back from mountain jaunts to set out in his own "Japanese tea garden" or "tea-house garden," as there was a convenient pine tree soughing over his little domicile.

A peacefuller scene I never saw than when, in that rather nippy late red afternoon, I simply opened his little door and looked in and saw him at the end of the little shack, sitting crosslegged on a Paisley pillow on a straw mat, with his spectacles on, making him look old and scholarly and wise, with book on lap and the little tin teapot and porcelain cup steaming at his side. He looked up very peacefully, saw who it was, said, "Ray, come in," and bent his eyes again to the script.

"What you doing?"

"Translating Han Shan's great poem called 'Cold Mountain' written a thousand years ago some of it scribbled on the sides of cliffs hundreds of miles away from any other living beings."

"Wow."

"When you come into this house though you've got to take your shoes off, see those straw mats, you can ruin 'em with shoes." So I took my softsoled blue cloth shoes off and laid them dutifully by the door and he threw me a pillow and I sat crosslegged along the little wooden board wall and he offered me a cup of hot tea. "Did you ever read the Book of Tea?" said he.

"No, what's that?"

"It's a scholarly treatise on how to make tea utilizing all the knowledge of two thousand years about tea-brewing. Some of the descriptions of the effect of the first sip of tea, and the second, and the third, are really wild and ecstatic."

"Those guys got high on nothing, hey?"

"Sip your tea and you'll see; this is good green tea." It was good and I immediately felt calm and warm. "Want me to read you parts of this Han Shan poem? Want me to tell you about Han Shan?"

"Yeah."

"Han Shan you see was a Chinese scholar who got sick of the big city and the world and took off to hide in the mountains."

"Say, that sounds like you."

"In those days you could really do that. He stayed in caves not far from a Buddhist monastery in the T'ang Hsing district of T'ien Tai and his only human friend was the funny Zen Lunatic Shih-te who had a job sweeping out the monastery with a straw broom. Shih-te was a poet too but he never wrote much down. Every now and then Han Shan would come down from Cold Mountain in his bark clothing and come into the warm kitchen and wait for food, but none of the monks would ever feed him because he didn't want to join the order and answer the meditation bell three times a day. You see why in some of his utterances, like—listen and I'll look here and read from the Chinese," and I bent over his shoulder and watched him read from big wild crowtracks of Chinese signs: "Climbing up Cold Mountain path, Cold Mountain path goes on and on, long gorge choked with scree and boulders, wide creek and mist-blurred grass, moss is slippery though there's been no rain, pine sings but there's no wind, who can leap the world's ties and sit with me among white clouds?"

"Wow."

"Course that's my own translation into English, you see there are five signs for each line and I have to put in Western prepositions and articles and such."

"Why don't you just translate it as it is, five signs, five words? What's those first five signs?"

"Sign for climbing, sign for up, sign for cold, sign for mountain, sign for path."

"Well then, translate it 'Climbing up Cold Mountain path.'"

"Yeah, but what do you do with the sign for long, sign for gorge, sign for choke, sign for avalanche, sign for boulders?"

"Where's that?"

"That's the third line, would have to read 'Long gorge choke avalanche boulders.' "

"Well that's even better!"

"Well yeah, I thought of that, but I have to have this pass the approval of Chinese scholars here at the university and have it clear in English."

"Boy what a great thing this is," I said looking around at the little shack, "and you sitting here so very quietly at this very quiet hour studying all alone with your glasses. . . ."

"Ray what you got to do is go climb a mountain with me soon. How would you like to climb Matterhorn?"

"Great! Where's that?"

"Up in the High Sierras. We can go there with Henry Morley in his car and bring our packs and take off from the lake. I could carry all the food and stuff we need in my rucksack and you could borrow Alvah's small knapsack and carry extra socks and shoes and stuff."

"What's these signs mean?"

"These signs mean that Han Shan came down from the mountain after many years roaming around up there, to see his folks in town, says, 'Till recently I stayed at Cold Mountain, et cetera, yesterday I called on friends and family, more than half had gone to the Yellow Springs,' that means death, the Yellow Springs, 'now morning I face my lone shadow, I can't study with both eyes full of tears.' "

"That's like you too, Japhy, studying with eyes full of tears."

"My eyes aren't full of tears!"

"Aren't they going to be after a long, long time?"

"They certainly will, Ray . . . and look here, 'In the mountains it's cold, it's always been cold not just this year,' see, he's real high, maybe twelve thousand or thirteen thousand feet or more, way up there, and says, 'Jagged scarps always snowed in, woods in the dark ravines spitting mist, grass is still sprouting at the end of June, leaves begin to fall in early August, and here am I high as a junkey—' "

"As a junkey!"

"That's my own translation, he actually says here am I as

high as the sensualist in the city below, but I made it modern and high translation."

"Great." I wondered why Han Shan was Japhy's hero.

"Because," said he, "he was a poet, a mountain man, a Buddhist dedicated to the principle of meditation on the essence of all things, a vegetarian too by the way though I haven't got on that kick from figuring maybe in this modern world to be a vegetarian is to split hairs a little since all sentient beings eat what they can. And he was a man of solitude who could take off by himself and live purely and true to himself."

"That sounds like you too."

"And like you too, Ray, I haven't forgotten what you told me about how you made it in the woods meditating in North Carolina and all." Japhy was very sad, subdued, I'd never seen him so quiet, melancholy, thoughtful his voice was as tender as a mother's, he seemed to be talking from far away to a poor yearning creature (me) who needed to hear his message he wasn't putting anything on he was in a bit of a trance.

"Have you been meditating today?"

"Yeah I meditate first thing in the morning before breakfast and I always meditate a long time in the afternoon unless I'm interrupted."

"Who interrupts you?"

"Oh, people. Coughlin sometimes, and Alvah came yesterday, and Rol Sturlason, and I got this girl comes over to play yabyum."

"Yabyum? What's that?"

"Don't you know about yabyum, Smith? I'll tell you later." He seemed to be too sad to talk about yabyum, which I found out about a couple of nights later. We talked a while longer about Han Shan and poems on cliffs and as I was going away his friend Rol Sturlason, a tall blond goodlooking kid, came in to discuss his coming trip to Japan with him. This Rol Sturlason was interested in the famous Ryoanji rock garden of Shokokuji monastery in Kyoto, which is nothing but old boulders placed in such a way, supposedly mystically aesthetic, as to cause thousands of tourists and monks every year to journey there to stare at the boulders in the sand and thereby gain peace of mind. I have never met such weird yet serious and earnest people. I never saw Rol Sturlason again, he went to Japan soon after, but I can't forget what he said about the boulders, to my question, "Well who placed them in that certain way that's so great?"

"Nobody knows, some monk, or monks, long ago. But there is a definite mysterious form in the arrangement of the rocks. It's only through form that we can realize emptiness." He showed me the picture of the boulders in well-raked sand, looking like islands in the sea, looking as though they had eyes (declivities) and surrounded by a neatly screened and architectural monastery patio. Then he showed me a diagram of the stone arrangement with the projection in silhouette and showed me the geometrical logics and all, and mentioned the phrases "lonely individuality" and the rocks as "bumps pushing into space," all meaning some kind of koan business I wasn't as much interested in as in him and especially in good kind Japhy who brewed more tea on his noisy gasoline primus and gave us added cups with almost a silent Oriental bow. It was quite different from the night of the poetry reading.

4

But the next night, about midnight, Coughlin and I and Alvah got together and decided to buy a big gallon jug of Burgundy and go bust in on Japhy in his shack.

"What's he doing tonight?" I asked.

"Oh," says Coughlin, "probably studying, probably screwing, we'll go see." We bought the jug on Shattuck Avenue way down and went over and once more I saw his pitiful English bicycle on the lawn. "Japhy travels around on that bicycle with his little knapsack on his back all up and down Berkeley all day," said Coughlin. "He used to do the same thing at Reed College in Oregon. He was a regular fixture up there. Then we'd throw big wine parties and have girls and end up jumping out of windows and playing Joe College pranks all up and down town."

"Gee, he's strange," said Alvah, biting his lip, in a mood of marvel, and Alvah himself was making a careful interested study of our strange noisy-quiet friend. We came in the little door again, Japhy looked up from his crosslegged study over a book, American poetry this time, glasses on, and said nothing but "Ah" in a strangely cultured tone. We took off our shoes and padded across the little five feet of straw to sit by him, but I was last with my shoes off, and had the jug in my hand, which I turned to show him from across the shack, and from his cross-legged position Japhy suddenly roared "Yaaaaah!" and leaped up into the air and straight across the room to me, landing on his feet in a fencing position with a sudden dagger in his hand the tip of it just barely stabbing the glass of the bottle with a small distinct "clink." It was the most amazing leap I ever saw in my life, except by nutty acrobats, much like a mountain goat, which he was, it turned out. Also it reminded me of a Japanese samurai warrior—the yelling roar, the leap, the position, and his expression of comic wrath his eyes bulging and making a big funny face at me. I had the feeling it was really a complaint against our breaking in on his studies and against wine itself which would get him drunk and make him miss his planned evening of reading. But without further ado he uncapped the bottle himself and took a big slug and we all sat crosslegged and spent four hours screaming news at one another, one of the funniest nights. Some of it went like this:

JAPHY: Well, Coughlin, you old fart, what you been doin?
COUGHLIN: Nothin.
ALVAH: What are all these strange books here? Hm, Pound, do you like Pound?
JAPHY: Except for the fact that that old fartface flubbed up the name of Li Po by calling him by his Japanese name and all such famous twaddle, he was all right—in fact he's my favorite poet.
RAY: Pound? Who wants to make a favorite poet out of that pretentious nut?
JAPHY: Have some more wine, Smith, you're not making sense. Who is your favorite poet, Alvah?

RAY: Why don't somebody ask me *my* favorite poet, I know
   more about poetry than all of you put together.
JAPHY: Is that true?
ALVAH: It might be. Haven't you seen Ray's new book of poems
   he just wrote in Mexico—"the wheel of the quivering meat
   conception turns in the void expelling tics, porcupines, ele-
   phants, people, stardusts, fools, nonsense . . ."
RAY: That's not it!
JAPHY: Speaking of meat, have you read the new poem of . . .

Etc., etc., then finally disintegrating into a wild talkfest and
yellfest and finally songfest with people rolling on the floor in
laughter and ending with Alvah and Coughlin and I going staggering up the quiet college street arm in arm singing "Eli Eli" at
the top of our voices and dropping the empty jug right at our
feet in a crash of glass, as Japhy laughed from his little door.
But we'd made him miss his evening of study and I felt bad
about that, till the following night when he suddenly appeared
at our little cottage with a pretty girl and came in and told her
to take her clothes off, which she did at once.

5

This was in keeping with Japhy's theories about women and
lovemaking. I forgot to mention that the day the rock artist had
called on him in the late afternoon, a girl had come right after,
a blonde in rubber boots and a Tibetan coat with wooden buttons, and in the general talk she'd inquired about our plan to
climb Mount Matterhorn and said "Can I come with ya?" as
she was a bit of a mountainclimber herself.
   "Shore," said Japhy, in his funny voice he used for joking, a
big loud deep imitation of a lumberjack he knew in the Northwest, a ranger actually, old Burnie Byers, "shore, come on with
us and we'll all screw ya at ten thousand feet" and the way he
said it was so funny and casual, and in fact serious, that the girl
wasn't shocked at all but somewhat pleased. In this same spirit
he'd now brought this girl Princess to our cottage, it was about

eight o'clock at night, dark, Alvah and I were quietly sipping
tea and reading poems or typing poems at the typewriter and
two bicycles came in the yard: Japhy on his, Princess on hers.
Princess had gray eyes and yellow hair and was very beautiful
and only twenty. I must say one thing about her, she was sex
mad and man mad, so there wasn't much of a problem in per-
suading her to play yabyum. "Don't you know about yabyum,
Smith?" said Japhy in his big booming voice striding in in his
boots holding Princess's hand. "Princess and I come here to
show ya, boy."

"Suits me," said I, "whatever it is." Also I'd known Princess
before and had been mad about her, in the City, about a year
ago. It was just another wild coincidence that she had happened
to meet Japhy and fallen in love with him and madly too, she'd
do anything he said. Whenever people dropped in to visit us at
the cottage I'd always put my red bandana over the little wall
lamp and put out the ceiling light to make a nice cool red dim
scene to sit and drink wine and talk in. I did this, and went to
get the bottle out of the kitchen and couldn't believe my eyes
when I saw Japhy and Alvah taking their clothes off and throwing them every whichaway and I looked and Princess was stark
naked, her skin white as snow when the red sun hits it at dusk,
in the dim red light. "What the hell," I said.

"Here's what yabyum is, Smith," said Japhy, and he sat crosslegged on the pillow on the floor and motioned to Princess, who
came over and sat down on him facing him with her arms about
his neck and they sat like that saying nothing for a while. Japhy
wasn't at all nervous and embarrassed and just sat there in perfect form just as he was supposed to do. "This is what they do in
the temples of Tibet. It's a holy ceremony, it's done just like this
in front of chanting priests. People pray and recite Om Mani
Pahdme Hum, which means Amen the Thunderbolt in the Dark
Void. I'm the thunderbolt and Princess is the dark void, you
see."

"But what's she thinking?" I yelled almost in despair, I'd had
such idealistic longings for that girl in that past year and had
conscience-stricken hours wondering if I should seduce her because she was so young and all.

"Oh this is lovely," said Princess. "Come on and try it."

"But I can't sit crosslegged like that." Japhy was sitting in the full lotus position, it's called, with both ankles over both thighs. Alvah was sitting on the mattress trying to yank his ankles over his thighs to do it. Finally Japhy's legs began to hurt and they just tumbled over on the mattress where both Alvah and Japhy began to explore the territory. I still couldn't believe it.

"Take your clothes off and join in, Smith!" But on top of all that, the feelings about Princess, I'd also gone through an entire year of celibacy based on my feeling that lust was the direct cause of birth which was the direct cause of suffering and death and I had really no lie come to a point where I regarded lust as offensive and even cruel.

"Pretty girls make graves," was my saying, whenever I'd had to turn my head around involuntarily to stare at the incomparable pretties of Indian Mexico. And the absence of active lust in me had also given me a new peaceful life that I was enjoying a great deal. But this was too much. I was still afraid to take my clothes off; also I never liked to do that in front of more than one person, especially with men around. But Japhy didn't give a goddamn hoot and holler about any of this and pretty soon he was making Princess happy and then Alvah Had a turn (with his big serious eyes staring in the dim light, and him reading poems a minute ago). So I said "How about me startin to work on her arm?"

"Go ahead, great." Which I did, lying down on the floor with all my clothes on and kissing her hand, then her wrist, then up, to her body, as she laughed and almost cried with delight everybody everywhere working on her. All the peaceful celibacy of my Buddhism was going down the drain. "Smith, I distrust any kind of Buddhism or *any* kinda philosophy or social system that puts down sex," said Japhy quite scholarly now that he was done and sitting naked crosslegged rolling himself a Bull Durham cigarette (which he did as part of his "simplicity" life). It ended up with everybody naked and finally making gay pots of coffee in the kitchen and Princess on the kitchen floor naked with her knees clasped in her arms, lying on her side, just for nothing, just to do it, then finally she and I took a warm bath together in the bathtub and could hear Alvah and Japhy discussing Zen Free Love Lunacy orgies in the other room.

"Hey Princess we'll do this every Thursday night, hey?" yelled Japhy. "It'll be a regular function."

"Yeah," yelled Princess from the bathtub. I'm telling you she was actually glad to do all this and told me "You know, I feel like I'm the mother of all things and I have to take care of my little children."

"You're such a young pretty thing yourself."

"But I'm the old mother of earth. I'm a Bodhisattva." She was just a little off her nut but when I heard her say "Bodhisattva" I realized she wanted to be a big Buddhist like Japhy and being a girl the only way she could express it was this way, which had its traditional roots in the yabyum ceremony of Tibetan Buddhism, so everything was fine.

Alvah was immensely pleased and was all for the idea of "every Thursday night" and so was I by now.

"Alvah, Princess says she's a Bodhisattva."

"Of course she is."

"She says she's the mother of all of us."

"The Bodhisattva women of Tibet and parts of ancient India," said Japhy, "were taken and used as holy concubines in temples and sometimes in ritual caves and would get to lay up a stock of merit and they meditated too. All of them, men and women, they'd meditate, fast, have balls like this, go back to eating, drinking, talking, hike around, live in viharas in the rainy season and outdoors in the dry, there was no question of what to do about sex which is what I always liked about Oriental religion. And what I always dug about the Indians in our country . . . You know when I was a little kid in Oregon I didn't feel that I was an American at all, with all that suburban ideal and sex repression and general dreary newspaper gray censorship of all our real human values but and when I discovered Buddhism and all I suddenly felt that I had lived in a previous lifetime innumerable ages ago and now because of faults and sins in that lifetime I was being degraded to a more grievous domain of existence and my karma was to be born in America where nobody has any fun or believes in anything, especially freedom. That's why I was always sympathetic to freedom movements, too, like anarchism in the Northwest, the oldtime heroes of Everett Massacre and all. . . ." It ended up with long earnest discussions about all these subjects and finally Princess got dressed and went home with Japhy on their bicycles and Alvah and I sat facing each other in the dim red light.

"But you know, Ray, Japhy is really sharp—he's really the wildest craziest sharpest cat we've ever met. And what I love about him is he's the big hero of the West Coast, do you realize I've been out here for two years now and hadn't met anybody worth knowing really or anybody with any truly illuminated intelligence and was giving up hope for the West Coast? Besides all the background he has, in Oriental scholarship, Pound, taking peyote and seeing visions, his mountainclimbing and bhikkuing, wow, Japhy Ryder is a great new hero of American culture."

"He's mad!" I agreed. "And other things I like about him, his quiet sad moments when he don't say much. . . ."

"Gee, I wonder what will happen to him in the end."

"I think he'll end up like Han Shan living alone in the mountains and writing poems on the walls of cliffs, or chanting them to crowds outside his cave."

"Or maybe he'll go to Hollywood and be a movie star, you know he said that the other day, he said 'Alvah you know I've never thought of going to the movies and becoming a star, I can do anything you know, I haven't tried that yet,' and I believe him, he *can* do anything. Did you see the way he had Princess all wrapped around him?"

"Aye indeed" and later that night as Alvah slept I sat under the tree in the yard and looked up at the stars or closed my eyes to meditate and tried to quiet myself down back to my normal self.

Alvah couldn't sleep and came out and lay flat on his back in the grass looking up at the sky, and said "Big steamy clouds going by in the dark up there, it makes me realize we live on an actual planet."

"Close your eyes and you'll see more than that."

"Oh I don't know what you mean by all that!" he said pettishly. He was always being bugged by my little lectures on

Samadhi ecstasy, which is the state you reach when you stop everything and stop your mind and you actually with your eyes closed see a kind of eternal multiswarm of electrical Power of some kind ululating in place of just pitiful images and forms of objects, which are, after all, imaginary. And if you don't believe me come back in a billion years and deny it. For what is time? "Don't you think it's much more interesting just to be like Japhy and have girls and studies and good times and really be doing something, than all this silly sitting under trees?"

"Nope," I said, and meant it, and I knew Japhy would agree with me. "All Japhy's doing is amusing himself in the void."

"I don't think so."

"I bet he is. I'm going mountainclimbing with him next week and I'll find out and tell you."

"Well" (sigh), "as for me, I'm just going to go on being Alvah Goldbook and to hell with all this Buddhist bullshit."

"You'll be sorry some day. Why don't you ever understand what I'm trying to tell you: it's with your six senses that you're fooled into believing not only that you have six senses, but that you contact an actual outside world with them. If it wasn't for your eyes, you wouldn't see me. If it wasn't for your ears, you wouldn't hear that airplane. If it wasn't for your nose, you wouldn't smell the midnight mint. If it wasn't for your tongue taster, you wouldn't taste the difference between A and B. If it wasn't for your body, you wouldn't feel Princess. There is no me, no airplane, no mind, no Princess, no nothing, you for krissakes do you want to go on being fooled every damn minute of your life?"

"Yes, that's all I want, I thank God that something has come out of nothing."

"Well, I got news for you, it's the other way around, nothing has come out of something, and that something is Dharmakaya, the body of the True Meaning, and that nothing is this and all this twaddle and talk. I'm going to bed."

"Well sometimes I see a flash of illumination in what you're trying to say but believe me I get more of a satori out of Princess than out of words."

"It's a satori of your foolish flesh, you lecher."

"I know my redeemer liveth."

"What redeemer and what liveth?"

"Oh let's cut this out and just live!"

"Balls, when I thought like you, Alvah, I was just as miserable and graspy as you are now. All you want to do is run out there and get laid and get beat up and get screwed up and get old and sick and banged around by samsara, you fucking eternal meat of comeback you you'll deserve it too, I'll say."

"That's not nice. Everybody's tearful and trying to live with what they got. Your Buddhism has made you mean Ray and makes you even afraid to take your clothes off for a simple healthy orgy."

"Well, I did finally, didn't I?"

"But you were coming on so hincty about—Oh let's forget it."

Alvah went to bed and I sat and closed my eyes and thought "This thinking has stopped" but because I had to think it no thinking had stopped, but there did come over me a wave of gladness to know that all this perturbation was just a dream already ended and I didn't have to worry because I wasn't "I" and I prayed that God, or Tathagata, would give me enough time and enough sense and strength to be able to tell people what I knew (as I can't even do properly now) so they'd know what I know and not despair so much. The old tree brooded over me silently, a living thing. I heard a mouse snoring in the garden weeds. The rooftops of Berkeley looked like pitiful living meat sheltering grieving phantoms from the eternality of the heavens which they feared to face. By the time I went to bed I wasn't taken in by no Princess or no desire for no Princess and nobody's disapproval and I felt glad and slept well.

6

Now came the time for our big mountain climb. Japhy came over in late afternoon on his bike to get me. We took out Alvah's knapsack and put it in his bike basket. I took out socks and sweaters. But I had no climbing shoes and the only things that could serve were Japhy's tennis sneakers, old but firm. My own shoes were too floppy and torn. "That might be better, Ray, with sneakers your feet are light and you can jump from boulder to boulder with no trouble. Of course we'll swap shoes at certain times and make it."

"What about food? What are you bringing?"

"Well before I tell you about food, R-a-a-y" (sometimes he called me by my first name and always when he did so, it was a long-drawn-out sad "R-a-a-a-y" as though he was worried about my welfare), "I've got your sleeping bag, it's not a duck down like my own, and naturally a lot heavier, but with clothes on and a good big fire you'll be comfortable up there."

"Clothes on yeah, but why a big fire, it's only October."

"Yeah but it's below freezing up there, R-a-a-y, in October," he said sadly.

"At night?"

"Yeah at night and in the daytime it's real warm and pleasant. You know old John Muir used to go up to those mountains where we're going with nothing but his old Army coat and a paper bag full of dried bread and he slept in his coat and just soaked the old bread in water when he wanted to eat, and he roamed around like that for months before tramping back to the city."

"My goodness he musta been tough!"

"Now as for food, I went down to Market Street to the Crystal Palace market and bought my favorite dry cereal, bulgur, which is a kind of a Bulgarian cracked rough wheat and I'm going to stick pieces of bacon in it, little square chunks, that'll make a fine supper for all three of us, Morley and us. And I'm bringing tea, you always want a good cup of hot tea under those cold stars. And I'm bringing real chocolate pudding, not that instant phony stuff but good chocolate pudding that I'll bring to a boil and stir over the fire and then let it cool ice cold in the snow."

"Oh boy!"

"So insteada rice this time, which I usually bring, I thought I'd make a nice delicacy for you, R-a-a-y, and in the bulgur too I'm going to throw in all kinds of dried diced vegetables I bought at the Ski Shop. We'll have our supper and breakfast outa this, and for energy food this big bag of peanuts and raisins and another bag with dried apricot and dried prunes oughta fix us for the rest." And he showed me the very tiny bag in which all this important food for three grown men for twenty-four hours or more climbing at high altitudes was stored. "The main thing in going to mountains is to keep the weight as far down as possible, those packs get heavy."

"But my God there's not enough food in that little bag!"

"Yes there is, the water swells it up."

"Do we bring wine?"

"No it isn't any good up there and once you're at high altitude and tired you don't crave alcohol." I didn't believe this but said nothing. We put my own things on the bike and walked across the campus to his place pushing the bike along the edge of the sidewalk. It was a cool clear Arabian Night dusk with the tower clock of University of Cal a clean black shadow against a backdrop of cypress and eucalyptus and all kinds of trees, bells ringing somewhere, and the air crisp. "It's going to be cold up there," said Japhy, but he was feeling fine that night and laughed when I asked him about next Thursday with Princess. "You know we played yabyum twice more since that last night, she comes over to my shack any day or night any minute and man she won't take no for an answer. So I satisfy the Bodhisattva." And Japhy wanted to talk about everything, his boyhood in Oregon. "You know my mother and father and sister were living a real primitive life on that logcabin farm and on cold winter mornings we'd all undress and dress in front of the fire, we had to, that's why I'm not like you about undressing, I mean I'm not bashful or anything like that."

"What'd you use to do around college?"

"In the summers I was always a government fire lookout— that's what you oughta do next summer, Smith—and in the winters I did a lot of skiing and used to walk around the campus on crutches real proud. I climbed some pretty big mountains up there, including a long haul up Rainier almost to the top where you sign your name. I finally made it one year. There are only a few names up there, you know. And I climbed all around the Cascades, off season and in season, and worked as a

logger. Smith, I gotta tell you all about the romance of Northwest logging, like you keep talking about railroading, you
shoulda seen the little narrow-gauge railways up there and those
cold winter mornings with snow and your belly fulla pancakes
and syrup and black coffee, boy, and you raise your doublebitted
ax to your morning's first log there's nothing like it."

"That's just like my dream of the Great Northwest. The
Kwakiutl Indians, the Northwest Mounted Police. . . ."

"Well, there in Canada they got them, over in British Columbia, I used to meet some on the trail." We pushed the bike
down past the various college hangouts and cafeterias and
looked into Robbie's to see if we knew anybody. Alvah was in
there, working his part-time job as busboy. Japhy and I were
kind of outlandish-looking on the campus in our old clothes in
fact Japhy was considered an eccentric around the campus,
which is the usual thing for campuses and college people to
think whenever a real man appears on the scene—colleges being nothing but grooming schools for the middle-class non-
identity which usually finds its perfect expression on the
outskirts of the campus in rows of well-to-do houses with
lawns and television sets in each living room with everybody
looking at the same thing and thinking the same thing at the
same time while the Japhies of the world go prowling in the
wilderness to hear the voice crying in the wilderness, to find
the ecstasy of the stars, to find the dark mysterious secret of the
origin of faceless wonderless crapulous civilization. "All these
people," said Japhy, "they all got white-tiled toilets and take
big dirty craps like bears in the mountains, but it's all washed
away to convenient supervised sewers and nobody thinks of
crap any more or realizes that their origin is shit and civet and
scum of the sea. They spend all day washing their hands with
creamy soaps they secretly wanta eat in the bathroom." He
had a million ideas, he had 'em all.

We got to his little shack as it grew dark and you could smell
woodsmoke and smoke of leaves in the air, and packed everything up neat and went down the street to meet Henry Morley
who had the car. Henry Morley was a bespectacled fellow of
great learning but an eccentric himself, more eccentric and

outré than Japhy on the campus, a librarian, with few friends,
but a mountainclimber. His own little one-room cottage in a
back lawn of Berkeley was filled with books and pictures of
mountainclimbing and scattered all over with rucksacks, climbing boots, skis. I was amazed to hear him talk, he talked exactly
like Rheinhold Cacoethes the critic, it turned out they'd been
friends long ago and climbed mountains together and I couldn't
tell whether Morley had influenced Cacoethes or the other way
around. I felt it was Morley who had done the influencing—he
had the same snide, sarcastic, extremely witty, well-formulated
speech, with thousands of images, like, when Japhy and I
walked in and there was a gathering of Morley's friends in there
(a strange outlandish group including one Chinese and one German from Germany and several other students of some kind)
Morley said "I'm bringing my air mattress, you guys can sleep
on that hard cold ground if you want but I'm going to have
pneumatic aid besides I went and spend sixteen dollars on it
in the wilderness of Oakland Army Navy stores and drove
around all day wondering if with rollerskates or suction cups
you can technically call yourself a vehicle" or some such to-me-
incomprehensible (to everybody else) secret-meaning joke of his
own, to which nobody listened much anyway, he kept talking
and talking as though to himself but I liked him right away. We
sighed when we saw the huge amounts of junk he wanted to
take on the climb: even canned goods, and besides his rubber
air mattress a whole lot of pickax and whatnot equipment we'd
really never need.

"You can carry that ax, Morley, but I don't think we'll need
it, but canned goods is just a lot of water you have to lug on
your back, don't you realize we got all the water we want
waitin for us up there?"

"Well I just thought a can of this Chinese chop suey would be
kinda tasty."

"I've got enough food for all of us. Let's go."

Morley spent a long time talking and fishing around and getting together his unwieldy packboard and finally we said goodbye to his friends and got into Morley's little English car and
started off, about ten o'clock, toward Tracy and up to Bridgeport

from where we would drive another eight miles to the foot of the trail at the lake.

I sat in the back seat and they talked up front. Morley was an actual madman who would come and get me (later) carrying a quart of eggnog expecting me to drink that, but I'd make him drive me to a liquor store, and the whole idea was to go out and see some girl and he'd have me come along to act as pacifier of some kind: we came to her door, she opened it, when she saw who it was she slammed the door and we drove back to the cottage. "Well what was this?" "Well it's a long story," Morley would say vaguely, I never quite understood what he was up to. Also, seeing Alvah had no spring bed in the cottage, one day he appeared like a ghost in a doorway as we were innocently getting up and brewing coffee and presented us with a huge double-bed spring that, after he left, we struggled to hide in the barn. And he'd bring odd assorted boards and whatnot, and impossible bookshelves, all kinds of things, and years later I had further Three Stooges adventures with him going out to his house in Contra Costa (which he owned and rented) and spending impossible-to-believe afternoons when he paid me two dollars an hour for hauling out bucket after bucket of mudslime which he himself was doling out of a flooded cellar by hand, black and mudcovered as Tartarilouak the King of the Mudslimes of Paratioalaouakak Span, with a secret grin of elfish delight on his face; and later, returning through some little town and wanting ice-cream cones, we walked down Main Street (had hiked on the highway with buckets and rakes) with ice-cream cones in our hands knocking into people on the little sidewalks like a couple of oldtime Hollywood silent film comedians, whitewash and all. An extremely strange person anyway, in any case, any old way you looked at, and drove the car now out toward Tracy on the busy fourlaner highway and did most of the talking, at everything Japhy said he had twelve to say, and it went like this: Japhy would say something like "By God I feel real studious lately, I think I'll read some ornithology next week." Morley would say, "Who doesn't feel studious when he doesn't have a girl with a Riviera suntan?"

Every time he said something he would turn and look at

Japhy and deliver these rather brilliant inanities with a complete
deadpan; I couldn't understand what kind of strange secret
scholarly linguistic clown he really was under these California
skies. Or Japhy would mention sleeping bags, and Morley
would ramble in with "I'm going to be the possessor of a pale
blue French sleeping bag, light weight, goose down, good buy I
think, find 'em in Vancouver—good for Daisy Mae. Completely
wrong type for Canada. Everyone wants to know if her grand-
father was an explorer who met an Eskimo. I'm from the North
Pole myself."

"What's he talking about?" I'd ask from the back seat, and
Japhy: "He's just an interesting tape recorder."

I'd told the boys I had a touch of thrombophlebitis, blood
clots in the veins in my feet, and was afraid about tomorrow's
climb, not that it would hobble me but would get worse when
we came down. Morley said "Is thrombophlebitis a peculiar
rhythm for piss?" Or I'd say something about Westerners and
he'd say, "I'm a dumb Westerner . . . look what preconceptions
have done to England."

"You're crazy, Morley."

"I dunno, maybe I am, but if I am I'll leave a lovely will anyway." Then out of nowhere he would say "Well I'm very
pleased to go climbing with two poets, I'm going to write a
book myself, it'll be about Ragusa, a late medieval maritime
city state republic which solved the class problem, offered the
secretaryship to Machiavelli and for a generation had its language used as the diplomatic one for the Levant. This was because of pull with the Turks, of course."

"Of course," we'd say.

So he'd ask himself the question out loud: "Can you secure
Christmas with an approximation only eighteen million sec-
onds left of the original old red chimney?"

"Sure," says Japhy laughing.

"Sure," says Morley wheeling the car around increasing
curves, "they're boarding reindeer Greyhound specials for a
pre-season heart-to-heart Happiness Conference deep in Sierra
wilderness ten thousand five hundred and sixty yards from a
primitive motel. It's newer than analysis and deceptively simple."

If you lost the roundtrip ticket you can become a gnome, the outfits are cute and there's a rumor that Actors Equity conventions sop up the overflow bounced from the Legion. Either way, of course, Smith" (turning to me in the back) "and in finding your way back to the emotional wilderness you're bound to get a present from . . . someone. Will some maple syrup help you feel better?"

"Sure, Henry."

And that was Morley. Meanwhile the car began climbing into the foothills somewhere and we came to sundry sullen towns where we stopped for gas and nothing but bluejeaned Elvis Presleys in the road, waiting to beat somebody up, but down beyond them the roar of fresh creeks and the feel of the high mountains not far away. A pure sweet night, and finally we got out on a real narrow tar country road and headed up toward the mountains for sure. Tall pine trees began to appear at the side of the road and occasional rock cliffs. The air felt nippy and grand. This also happened to be the opening eve of the hunting season and in a bar where we stopped for a drink there were many hunters in red caps and wool shirts looking silly getting loaded, with all their guns and shells in their cars and eagerly asking us if we'd seen any deer or not. We had, certainly, seen a deer, just before we came to the bar. Morley had been driving and talking, saying, "Well Ryder maybe you'll be Alfred Lord Tennyson of our little tennis party here on the Coast, they'll call you the New Bohemian and compare you to the Knights of the Round Table minus Amadis the Great and the extraordinary splendors of the little Moorish kingdom that was sold round to Ethiopia for seventeen thousand camels and sixteen hundred foot soldiers when Caesar was sucking on his mammy's teat," and suddenly the deer was in the road, looking at our headlamps, petrified, before leaping into the shrubbery by the side of the road and disappearing into the sudden vast diamond silence of the forest (which we heard as Morley cut the motor) and just the scuffle of its hoofs running off to the haven of the raw fish Indian up there in the mists. It was real country we were in, Morley said about three thousand feet now. We could hear creeks rushing coldly below on cold starlit rocks without seeing them. "Hey little deer," I'd yelled to the animal, "don't worry, we won't shoot you." Now in the bar, where we'd stopped at my insistence ("In this kinda cold northern up-mountain country ain't nothin better for a man's soul at midnight but a good warm glass of warmin red port heavy as the syrups of Sir Arthur")—

"Okay Smith," said Japhy, "but seems to me we shouldn't drink on a hiking trip."

"Ah who gives a damn?"

"Okay, but look at all the money we saved by buying cheap dried foods for this weekend and all you're gonna do is drink it right down."

"That's the story of my life rich or poor and mostly poor and truly poor." We went in the bar, which was a roadhouse all done up in the upcountry mountain style, like a Swiss chalet, with moose heads and designs of deer on the booths and the people in the bar itself an advertisement for the hunting season but all of them loaded, a weaving mass of shadows at the dim bar as we walked in and sat at three stools and ordered the port. The port was a strange request in the whisky country of hunters but the bartender rousted up an odd bottle of Christian Brothers port and poured us two shots in wide wineglasses (Morley a teetotaler actually) and Japhy and I drank and felt it fine.

"Ah," said Japhy warming up to his wine and midnight, "soon I'm going back north to visit my childhood wet woods and cloudy mountains and old bitter intellectual friends and old drunken logger friends, by God, Ray you ain't lived till you been up there with me, or without. And then I'm going to Japan and walk all over that hilly country finding ancient little temples hidden and forgotten in the mountains and old sages a hundred and nine years old praying to Kwannon in huts and meditating so much that when they come out of meditation they laugh at everything that moves. But that don't mean I don't love America, by God, though I hate these damn hunters, all they wanta do is level a gun at a helpless sentient being and murder it, for every sentient being or living creature these actual pricks kill they will be reborn a thousand times to suffer the horrors of samsara and damn good for 'em too."

"Hear, that, Morley, Henry, what you think?"

"My Buddhism is nothing but a mild unhappy interest in some of the pictures they've drawn though I must say sometimes Cacoethes strikes a nutty note of Buddhism in his mountainclimbing poems though I'm not much interested in the belief part of it." In fact it didn't make a goddamn much of a difference to him. "I'm neutral," said he, laughing happily with a kind of an eager slaking leer, and Japhy yelled:

"Neutral is what Buddishm is!"

"Well, that port'll make you have to swear off yogurt. You know I am *a fortiori* disappointed because there's no Benedictine or Trappist wine, only Christian Brothers holy waters and spirits around here. Not that I feel very expansive about being here in this curious bar anyway, it looks like the home-plate for Ciardi and Bread Loaf writers, Armenian grocers all of 'em, well-meaning awkward Protestants who are on a group excursion for a binge and want to but don't understand how to insert the contraception. These people must be assholes," he added in sudden straight revelation. "The milk around here must be fine but more cows than people. This must be a different race of Anglos up here, I don't particularly warm up to their appearance. The fast kids around here must go thirty-four miles. Well, Japhy," said he, concluding, "if you ever get an official job I hope you get a Brooks Brothers suit . . . hope you don't wind up in artsfartsy parties where it would—Say," as some girls walked in, "young hunters . . . must be why the baby wards are open all year."

But the hunters didn't like us to be huddled there talking close and friendly in low voices about sundry personal topics and joined us and pretty soon it was a long funny harangue up and down the oval bar about deer in the locality, where to go climb, what do do, and when they heard we were out in this country not to kill animals but just to climb mountains they took us to be hopeless eccentrics and left us alone. Japhy and I had two wines and felt fine and went back in the car with Morley and we drove away, higher and higher, the trees taller, the air colder, climbing, till finally it was almost two o'clock in the morning and they said we had a long way to go yet to Bridgeport and the foot of the trail so we might as well sleep out in these woods in our sleeping bags and call it a day.

"We'll get up at dawn and take off. Meanwhile we have this good brown bread and cheese too," said Japhy producing it, brown bread and cheese he'd thrown in at the last minute in his little shack, "and that'll make a fine breakfast and we'll save the bulgur and goodies for our breakfast tomorrow morning at ten thousand feet." Fine. Still talking and all, Morley drove the car a little way over some hard pine needles under an immense spread of natural park trees, firs and ponderosas a hundred feet high some of them, a great quiet starlit grove with frost on the ground and dead silence except for occasional little ticks of sound in the thickets where maybe a rabbit stood petrified hearing us. I got out my sleeping bag and spread it out and took off my shoes and just as I was sighing happily and slipping my stockinged feet into my sleeping bag and looking around gladly at the beautiful tall trees thinking "Ah what a night of true sweet sleep this will be, what meditations I can get into in this intense silence of Nowhere" Japhy yelled at me from the car: "Say, it appears Mr. Morley has forgotten his sleeping bag!"

"What . . . well now what?"

They discussed it awhile fiddling with flashlights in the frost and then Japhy came over and said "You'll have to crawl outa there Smith, all we have is two sleeping bags now and gotta zip 'em open and spread 'em out to form a blanket for three, goddammit that'll be cold."

"What? And the cold'll slip in around the bottoms!"

"Well Henry can't sleep in that car, he'll freeze to death, no heater."

"But goddammit I was all ready to enjoy this so much," I whined getting out and putting on my shoes and pretty soon Japhy had fixed the two sleeping bags on top of ponchos and was already settled down to sleep and on toss it was me had to sleep in the middle, and it was way below freezing by now, and the stars were icicles of mockery. I got in and lay down and Morley, I could hear the maniac blowing up his ridiculous air mattress so he could lay beside me, but the moment he'd done so, he started at once to turn over and heave and sigh, and around the other side, and back toward me, and around the other side, all under the ice-cold stars and loveliness, while Japhy snored, Japhy who wasn't subjected to all the mad wiggling. Finally Morley couldn't sleep at all and got up and went to the car probably to talk to himself in that mad way of his and I got a wink of sleep, but in a few minutes he was back, freezing, and got under the sleeping-bag blanket but started to turn and turn again, even curse once in a while, or sigh, and this went on for what seemed to be eternities and the first thing I knew Aurora was paling the eastern hems of Amida and pretty soon we'd be getting up anyway. That mad Morley! And this was only the beginning of the misadventures of that most remarkable man (as you'll see now), that remarkable man who was probably the only mountainclimber in the history of the world who forgot to bring his sleeping bag. "Jesus," I thought, "why didn't he just forget his dreary air mattress instead."

7

From the very first moment we'd met Morley he'd kept emitting sudden yodels in keeping with our venture. This was a simple "Yodelayhee" but it came at the oddest moments and in oddest circumstances, like several times when his Chinese and German friends were still around, then later in the car, sitting with us enclosed, "Yodelayhee!" and then as we got out of the car to go in the bar, "Yodelayhee!" Now as Japhy woke up and saw it was dawn and jumped out of the bags and ran to gather firewood and shudder over a little preliminary fire, Morley woke up from his nervous small sleep of dawn, yawned, and yelled "Yodelayhee!" which echoed toward vales in the distance. I got up too; it was all we could do to hold together; the only thing to do was hop around and flap your arms, like me and my sad bum on the gon on the south coast. But soon Japhy got more logs on the fire and it was a roaring bonfire that we turned our backs to after a while and yelled and talked. A beautiful morning—red pristine shafts of sunlight coming in over the hill and slanting down into the cold trees like cathedral light, and the mists rising to meet the sun, and all the way around the giant secret roar of tumbling creeks probably with films of ice in the pools. Great fishing country. Pretty soon I was yelling "Yodelayhee" myself but when Japhy went to fetch more wood and we couldn't see him for a while and Morley yelled "Yodelayhee" Japhy answered back with a simple "Hoo" which he said was the Indian way to call in the mountains and much nicer. So I began to yell "Hoo" myself.

Then we got in the car and started off. We ate the bread and cheese. No difference between the Morley of this morning and the Morley of last night, except his voice as he rattled on yakking in that cultured snide funny way of his was sorta cute with that morning freshness, like the way people's voices sound after getting up early in the morning, something faintly wistful and hoarse and eager in it, ready for a new day. Soon the sun was warm. The black bread was good, it had been baked by Sean Monahan's wife, Sean who had a shack in Corte Madera we could all go live in free of rent some day. The cheese was sharp Cheddar. But it didn't satisfy me much and when we got out into country with no more houses and anything I began to yearn for a good old hot breakfast and suddenly after we'd gone over a little creek bridge we saw a merry little lodge by the side of the road under tremendous juniper trees with smoke boiling out of the chimney and neon signs outside and a sign in the window advertising pancakes and hot coffee.

"Let's go in there, by God we need a man's breakfast if we're gonna climb all day."

Nobody complained about my idea and we went in, and sat at booths, and a nice woman took our orders with that cheery loquaciousness of people in the backcountry. "Well you boys goin huntin this mornin?"

"No'm," said Japhy, "just climbing Matterhorn."

"*Matterhorn*, why I wouldn't do that if somebody paid me a thousand dollars!"

Meanwhile I went out to the log johns out back and washed from water in the tap which was delightfully cold and made my face tingle, then I drank some of it and it was like cool liquid ice in my stomach and sat there real nice, and I had more. Shaggy dogs were barking in the golden red sunlight slanting down from the hundred-foot branches of the firs and ponderosas. I could see snowcapped mountains glittering in the distance. One of them was Matterhorn. I went in and the pancakes were ready, hot and steaming, and poured syrup over my three pats of butter and cut them up and slurped hot coffee and ate. So did Henry and Japhy—for once no conversation. Then we washed it all down with that incomparable cold water as hunters came in in hunting boots with wool shirts but no giddy drunk hunters but serious hunters ready to go out there after break-fast. There was a bar adjoining but nobody cared about alcohol this morning.

We got in the car, crossed another creek bridge, crossed a meadow with a few cows and log cabins, and came out on a plain which clearly showed Matterhorn rising the highest most awful looking of the jagged peaks to the south. "There she is," said Morley really proud. "Isn't it beautiful, doesn't it remind you of the Alps? I've got a collection of snow covered mountain photos you should see sometime."

"I like the real thing meself," said Japhy, looking seriously at the mountains and in that far-off look in his eyes, that secret self-sigh, I saw he was back home again. Bridgeport is a little sleepy town, curiously New England-like, on that plain. Two restaurants, two gas stations, a school, all sidewalking High-way 395 as it comes through there running from down Bishop way up to Carson City Nevada.

8

Now another incredible delay was caused as Mr. Morley decided to see if he could find a store open in Bridgeport and buy a sleep-ing bag or at least a canvas cover or tarpaulin of some kind for tonight's sleep at nine thousand feet and judging from last night's sleep at four thousand it was bound to be pretty cold. Meanwhile Japhy and I waited, sitting in the now hot sun of ten a.m. on the grass of the school, watching occasional laconic traffic pass by on the not-busy highway and watching to see the fortunes of a

young Indian hitchhiker pointed north. We discussed him
warmly. "That's what I like, hitchhiking around, feeling free,
imagine though being an Indian and doing all that. Dammit
Smith, let's go talk to him and wish him luck." The Indian
wasn't very talkative but not unfriendly and told us he'd been
making pretty slow time on 395. We wished him luck. Meanwhile in the very tiny town Morley was nowhere to be seen.

"What's he doing, waking up some proprietor in his bed
back there?"

Finally Morley came back and said there was nothing avail-
able and the only thing to do was to borrow a couple of blankets at the lake lodge. We got in the car, went back down the
highway a few hundred yards, and turned south toward the glittering trackless snows high in the blue air. We drove along
beautiful Twin Lakes and came to the lake lodge, which was a
big white framehouse inn, Morley went in and deposited five
dollars for the use of two blankets for one night. A woman was
standing in the doorway arms akimbo, dogs barked. The road
was dusty, a dirt road, but the lake was cerulean pure. In it the
reflections of the cliffs and foothills showed perfectly. But the
road was being repaired and we could see yellow dust boiling
up ahead where we'd have to walk along the lake road awhile
before cutting across a creek at the end of the lake and up
through underbrush and up the beginning of the trail.

We parked the car and got all our gear out and arranged it in
the warm sun. Japhy put things in my knapsack and told me I
had to carry it or jump in the lake. He was being very serious
and leaderly and it pleased me more than anything else. Then
with the same boyish gravity he went over to the dust of the
road with the pickax and drew a big circle and began drawing
things in the circle.

"What's that?"

"I'm doin a magic mandala that'll not only help us on our
climb but after a few more marks and chants I'll be able to pre-
dict the future from it."

"What's a mandala?"

"They're the Buddhist designs that are always circles filled
with things, the circle representing the void and the things

illusion, see. You sometimes see mandalas painted over a Bodhisattva's head and can tell his history from studying it. Tibetan
in origin."

I had on the tennis sneakers and now I whipped out my
mountainclimbing cap for the day, which Japhy had consigned
to me, which was a little black French beret, which I put on at a
jaunty angle and hitched the knapsack up and I was ready to
go. In the sneakers and the beret I felt more like a Bohemian
painter than a mountainclimber. But Japhy had on his fine big
boots and his little green Swiss cap with feather, and looked
elfin but rugged. I see the picture of him alone in the mountains
in that outfit: the vision: it's pure morning in the high dry Sierras, far off clean firs can be seen shadowing the sides of rocky
hills, further yet snowcapped pinpoints, nearer the big bushy
forms of pines and there's Japhy in his little cap with a big rucksack on his back, clomping along, but with a flower in his left
hand which is hooked to the strap of the rucksack at his breast;
grass grows out between crowded rocks and boulders; distant
sweeps of scree can be seen making gashes down the sides of
morning, his eyes shine with joy, he's on his way, his heroes are
John Muir and Han Shan and Shih-te and Li Po and John Burroughs and Paul Bunyan and Kropotkin; he's small and has a
funny kind of belly coming out as he strides, but it's not because his belly is big, it's because his spine curves a bit, but
that's offset by the vigorous long steps he takes, actually the
long steps of a tall man (as I found out following him uptrail)
and his chest is deep and shoulders broad.

"Goldangit Japhy I feel great this morning," I said as we
locked the car and all three of us started swinging down the
lake road with our packs, straggling a bit occupying side and
center and other side of the road like straggling infantrymen.
"Isn't this a hell of a lot greater than The Place? Gettin drunk in
there on a fresh Saturday morning like this, all bleary and sick,
and here we are by the fresh pure lake walkin along in this
good air, by God it's a haiku in itself."

"Comparisons are odious, Smith," he sent sailing back to me,
quoting Cervantes and making a Zen Buddhist observation to
boot. "It don't make a damn frigging difference whether you're

in The Place or hiking up Matterhorn, it's all the same old void, boy." And I mused about that and realized he was right, comparisons *are* odious, it's all the same, but it sure felt great and suddenly I realized this (in spite of my swollen foot veins) would do me a lot of good and get me away from drinking and maybe make me appreciate perhaps a whole new way of living.

"Japhy I'm glad I met you. I'm gonna learn all about how to pack rucksacks and what to do and hide in these mountains when I'm sick of civilization. In fact I'm grateful I met you."

"Well Smith I'm grateful I met you too, learnin about how to write spontaneously and all that."

"Ah that's nothing."

"To me it's a lot. Let's go boys, a little faster, we ain't got no time to waste."

By and by we reached the boiling yellow dust where caterpillars were churning around and great big fat sweaty operators who didn't even look at us were swearing and cussing on the job. For them to climb a mountain you'd have to pay them double time and quadruple time today, Saturday.

Japhy and I laughed to think of it. I felt a little embarrassed with my silly beret but the cat operators didn't even look and soon we left them behind and were approaching the final little store lodge at the foot of the trail. It was a log cabin, set right on the end of the lake, and it was enclosed in a V of pretty big foothills. Here we stopped and rested awhile on the steps, we'd hiked approximately four miles but on flat good road, and went in and bought candy and crackers and Cokes and stuff. Then suddenly Morley, who'd not been silent on the four-mile hike, and looked funny in his own outfit which was that immense packboard with air mattress and all (deflated now) and no hat at all, so that he looked just like he does in the library, but with big floppy pants of some kind, Morley suddenly remembered he'd forgotten to drain the crankcase.

"So he forgot to drain the crankcase," I said noticing their consternation and not knowing much about cars, "so he forgot to brain the drankbase."

"No, this means that if it gets below freezing tonight down here the goddamn radiator explodes and we can't drive back home and have to walk twelve miles to Bridgeport and all and get all hung-up."

"Well maybe it won't be so cold tonight."

"Can't take a chance," said Morley and by that time I was pretty mad at him for finding more ways than he could figure to forget, foul up, disturb, delay, and make go round in circles this relatively simple hiking trip we'd undertaken.

"What you gonna do? What we gonna do, walk back four miles?"

"Only thing to do, I'll walk back alone, drain the crankcase, walk back and follow you up the trail and meet you tonight at the camp."

"And I'll light a big bonfire," said Japhy, "and you'll see the glow and just yodel and we'll direct you in."

"That's simple."

"But you've got to step on it to make it by nightfall at camp."

"I will, I'll start back right now."

But then I felt sorry about poor old hapless funny Henry and said "Ah hell, you mean you're not going to climb with us today, the hell with the crankcase come on with us."

"It'd cost too much money if that thing froze tonight, Smith no I think I better go back. I've got plenty of nice thoughts to keep me acquainted with probably what you two'll be talking about all day, aw hell I'll just start back right now. Be sure not to roar at bees and don't hurt the cur and if the tennis party comes on with everybody shirtless don't make eyes at the searchlight or the sun'll kick a girl's ass right back at you, cats and all and boxes of fruit and oranges thrown in" and some such statement and with no ado or ceremony there he went down the road with just a little handwave, muttering and talking on to himself, so we had to yell "Well so long Henry, hurry up" and he didn't answer but just walked off shrugging.

"You know," I said, "I think it doesn't make any difference to him anyway. He's just satisfied to wander around and forget things."

"And pat his belly and look at things as they are, sorta like in

Chuangtse" and Japhy and I had a good laugh watching forlorn Henry swaggering down all that road we'd only just negotiated, alone and mad.

"Well here we go" said Japhy. "When I get tired of this big rucksack we'll swap."

"I'm ready now. Man, come on, give it to me now, I feel like carrying something heavy. You don't realize how *good* I feel, man, come on!" So we swapped packs and started off.

Both of us were feeling fine and were talking a blue streak, about anything, literature, the mountains, girls, Princess, the poets, Japan, our past adventures in life, and I suddenly realized it was a kind of blessing in disguise Morley had forgotten to drain the crankcase, otherwise Japhy wouldn't have got in a word edgewise all the blessed day and now I had a chance to hear his ideas. In the way he did things, hiking, he reminded me of Mike my boyhood chum who also loved to lead the way, real grave like Buck Jones, eyes to the distant horizons, like Natty Bumppo, cautioning me about snapping twigs or "It's too deep here, let's go down the creek a ways to ford it," or "There'll be mud in that low bottom, we better skirt around" and dead serious and glad. I saw all Japhy's boyhood in those eastern Oregon forests the way he went about it. He walked like he talked, from behind I could see his toes pointed slightly inward, the way mine do, instead of out; but when it came time to climb he pointed his toes out, like Chaplin, to make a kind of easier flapthwap as he trudged. We went across a kind of muddy riverbottom through dense undergrowth and a few willow trees and came out on the other side a little wet and started up the trail, which was clearly marked and named and had been recently repaired by trail crews but as we hit parts where a rock had rolled on the trail he took great precaution to throw the rock off saying "I used to work on trail crews, I can't see a trail all mettlesome like that, Smith." As we climbed the lake began to appear below us and suddenly in its clear blue pool we could see the deep holes where the lake had its springs, like black wells, and we could see schools of fish skitter.

"Oh this is like an early morning in China and I'm five years old in beginningless time!" I sang out and felt like sitting by the trail and whipping out my little notebook and writing sketches about it.

"Look over there," sang Japhy, "yellow aspens. Just put me in the mind of a haiku . . .'Talking about the literary life—the yellow aspens.'" Walking in this country you could understand the perfect gems of haikus the Oriental poets had written, never getting drunk in the mountains or anything but just going along as fresh as children writing down what they saw without literary devices or fanciness of expression. We made up haikus as we climbed, winding up and up now on the slopes of brush.

"Rocks on the side of the cliff," I said, "why don't they tumble down?"

"Maybe that's a haiku, maybe not, it might be a little too complicated," said Japhy. "A real haiku's gotta be as simple as porridge and yet make you see the real thing, like the greatest haiku of them all probably is the one that goes 'The sparrow hops along the veranda, with wet feet.' By Shiki. You see the wet footprints like a vision in your mind and yet in those few words you also see all the rain that's been falling that day and almost smell the wet pine needles."

"Let's have another."

"I'll make up one of my own this time, let's see, 'Lake below . . . the black holes the wells make,' no that's not a haiku goddammit, you never can be too careful about haiku."

"How about making them up real fast as you go along, spontaneously?"

"Look here," he cried happily, "mountain lupine, see the delicate blue color those little flowers have. And there's some California red poppy over there. The whole meadow is just powdered with color! Up there by the way is a genuine California white pine, you never see them much any more."

"You sure know a lot about birds and trees and stuff."

"I've studied it all my life." Then also as we went on climbing we began getting more casual and making funnier sillier talk and pretty soon we got to a bend in the trail where it was suddenly gladey and dark with shade and a tremendous cataracting stream was bashing and frothing over scummy rocks and tumbling on down, and over the stream was a perfect bridge formed by a fallen snag, we got on it and lay belly-down and dunked our heads down, hair wet, and drank deep as the water splashed in our faces, like sticking your head by the jet of a dam. I lay there a good long minute enjoying the sudden coolness.

"This is like an advertisement for Rainier Ale!" yelled Japhy.

"Let's sit awhile and enjoy it."

"Boy you don't know how far we got to go yet!"

"Well I'm not tired!"

"Well you'll be, Tiger."

9

We went on, and I was immensely pleased with the way the trail had a kind of immortal look to it, in the early afternoon now, the way the side of the grassy hill seemed to be clouded with ancient gold dust and the bugs flipped over rocks and the wind sighed in shimmering dances over the hot rocks, and the way the trail would suddenly come into a cool shady part with big trees overhead, and here the light deeper. And the way the lake below us soon became a toy lake with those black well holes perfectly visible still, and the giant cloud shadows on the lake, and the tragic little road winding away where poor Morley was walking back.

"Can you see Morl down back there?"

Japhy took a long look. "I see a little cloud of dust, maybe that's him comin back already." But it seemed that I had seen the ancient afternoon of that trail, from meadow rocks and lupine posies, to sudden revisits with the roaring stream with its splashed snag bridges and undersea greennesses, there was something inexpressibly broken in my heart as though I'd lived before and walked this trail, under similar circumstances with a fellow Bodhisattva, but maybe on a more important journey, I felt like lying down by the side of the trail and remembering it all. The woods do that to you, they always look familiar, long lost, like the face of a long-dead relative, like an old dream, like a piece of forgotten song drifting across the water, most of all like golden eternities of past childhood or past manhood and all the living and the dying and the heartbreak that went on a million years ago and the clouds as they pass overhead seem to testify (by their own lonesome familiarity) to this feeling. Ecstasy, even, I felt, with flashes of sudden remembrance, and feeling sweaty and drowsy I felt like sleeping and dreaming in the grass. As we got higher we got more tired and now like two true mountainclimbers we weren't talking any more and didn't have to talk and were glad, in fact Japhy mentioned that, turning to me after a half-hour's silence, "This is the way I like it, when you get going there's just no need to talk, as if we were animals and just communicated by silent telepathy." So huddled in our own thoughts we tromped on, Japhy using that gazotsky trudge I mentioned, and myself finding my own true step, which was short steps slowly patiently going up the mountain at one mile an hour, so I was always thirty yards behind him and when we had any haikus now we'd yell them fore and aft. Pretty soon we got to the top of the part of the trail that was a trail no more, to the incomparable dreamy meadow, which had a beautiful pond, and after that it was boulders and nothing but boulders.

"Only sign we have now to know which way we're going, is ducks."

"What's ducks?"

"See those boulders over there?"

"See those boulders over there! Why God man, I see five miles of boulders leading up to that mountain."

"See the little pile of rocks on that near boulder there by the pine? That's a duck, put up by other climbers, maybe that's one I put up myself in 'fifty-four I'm not sure. We just go from boulder to boulder from now on keeping a sharp eye for ducks then we get a general idea how to raggle along. Although of course we know which way we're going, that big cliff face up there is where our plateau is."

"Plateau? My God you mean that ain't the top of the mountain?"

"Of course not, after that we got a plateau and then scree and

then more rocks and we get to a final alpine lake no biggern
this pond and then comes the final climb over one thousand feet
almost straight up boy to the top of the world where you'll see
all California and parts of Nevada and the wind'll blow right
through your pants."

"Ow . . . How long does it all take?"

"Why the only thing we can expect to make tonight is our
camp up there on that plateau. I call it a plateau, it ain't that at
all, it's a shelf between heights."

But the top and the end of the trail was such a beautiful spot
I said: "Boy look at this . . ." A dreamy meadow, pines at one
end, the pond, the clear fresh air, the afternoon clouds rushing
golden . . . "Why don't we just sleep here tonight, I don't think
I've ever seen a more beautiful park."

"Ah this is nowhere. It's great of course, but we might wake
up tomorrow morning and find three dozen schoolteachers on
horseback frying bacon in our backyard. Where we're going
you can bet your ass there won't be one human being, and if
there is, I'll be a spotted horse's ass. Or maybe just one mountainclimber, or two, but I don't expect so at this time of the
year. You know the snow's about to come here any time now. If
it comes tonight it's goodbye me and you."

"Well goodbye Japhy. But let's rest here and drink some water and admire the meadow." We were feeling tired and great.
We spread out in the grass and rested and swapped packs and
strapped them on and were rarin to go. Almost instantaneously
the grass ended and the boulders started; we got up on the first
one and from that point on it was just a matter of jumping from
boulder to boulder, gradually climbing, climbing, five miles up
a valley of boulders getting steeper and steeper with immense
crags on both sides forming the walls of the valley, till near the
cliff face we'd be scrambling up the boulders, it seemed.

"And what's behind that cliff face?"

"There's high grass up there, shrubbery, scattered boulders,
beautiful meandering creeks that have ice in 'em even in the afternoon, spots of snow, tremendous trees, and one boulder just
about as big as two of Alvah's cottages piled on top the other
which leans over and makes a kind of concave cave for us to

camp at, lightin a big bonfire that'll throw heat against the wall. Then after that the grass and the timber ends. That'll be at nine thousand just about."

With my sneakers it was as easy as pie to just dance nimbly from boulder to boulder, but after a while I noticed how gracefully Japhy was doing it and he just ambled from boulder to boulder, sometimes in a deliberate dance with his legs crossing from right to left, right to left and for a while I followed his every step but then I learned it was better for me to just spontaneously pick my own boulders and make a ragged dance of my own.

"The secret of this kind of climbing," said Japhy, "is like Zen. Don't think. Just dance along. It's the easiest thing in the world, actually easier than walking on flat ground which is monotonous. The cute little problems present themselves at each step and yet you never hesitate and you find yourself on some other boulder you picked out for no special reason at all, just like Zen." Which it was.

We didn't talk much now. It got tiresome on the leg muscles. We spent hours, about three, going up that long, long valley. In that time it grew to late afternoon and the light was growing amber and shadows were falling ominously in the valley of dry boulders and instead, though, of making you feel scared it gave you that immortal feeling again. The ducks were all laid out easy to see: on top of a boulder you'd stand, and look ahead, and spot a duck (usually only two flat rocks on top of each other maybe with one round one on top for decoration) and you aimed in that general direction. The purpose of these ducks, as laid out by all previous climbers, was to save a mile or two of wandering around in the immense valley. Meanwhile our roaring creek was still at it, but thinner and more quiet now, running from the cliff face itself a mile up the valley in a big black stain I could see in the gray rock.

Jumping from boulder to boulder and never falling, with a heavy pack, is easier than it sounds; you just can't fall when you get into the rhythm of the dance. I looked back down the valley sometimes and was surprised to see how high we'd come, and to see farther horizons of mountains now back there. Our beautiful trail-top park was like a little glen of the Forest of Arden. Then the climbing got steeper, the sun got redder, and pretty soon I began to see patches of snow in the shade of some rocks. We got up to where the cliff face seemed to loom over us. At one point I saw Japhy throw down his pack and danced my way up to him.

"Well this is where we'll drop our gear and climb those few hundred feet up the side of that cliff, where you see there it's shallower, and find that camp. I remember it. In fact you can sit here and rest or beat your bishop while I go ramblin around there, I like to ramble by myself."

Okay. So I sat down and changed my wet socks and changed soaking undershirt for dry one and crossed my legs and rested and whistled for about a half-hour, a very pleasant occupation, and Japhy got back and said he'd found the camp. I thought it would be a little jaunt to our resting place but it took almost another hour to jump up the steep boulders, climb around some, get to the level of the cliff-face plateau, and there, on flat grass more or less, hike about two hundred yards to where a huge gray rock towered among pines. Here now the earth was a splendorous thing—snow on the ground, in melting patches in the grass, and gurgling creeks, and the huge silent rock mountains on both sides, and a wind blowing, and the smell of heather. We forded a lovely little creek, shallow as your hand, pearl pure lucid water, and got to the huge rock. Here were old charred logs where other mountainclimbers had camped.

"And where's Matterhorn mountain?"

"You can't see it from here, but"—pointing up the farther long plateau and a scree gorge twisting to the right—"around that draw and up two miles or so and then we'll be at the foot of it."

"Wow, heck, whoo, that'll take us a whole other day!"

"Not when you're travelin with me, Smith."

"Well Ryderee, that's okay with me."

"Okay Smithee and now how's about we relax and enjoy ourselves and cook up some supper and wait for ole Morleree?"

So we unpacked our packs and laid things out and smoked and had a good time. Now the mountains were getting that

pink tinge, I mean the rocks, they were just solid rock covered
with the atoms of dust accumulated there since beginningless
time. In fact I was afraid of those jagged monstrosities all
around and over our heads.

"They're so silent!" I said.

"Yeah man, you know to me a mountain is a Buddha. Think
of the patience, hundreds of thousands of years just sittin there
bein perfectly perfectly silent and like praying for all living
creatures in that silence and just waitin for us to stop all our
frettin and foolin." Japhy got out the tea, Chinese tea, and
sprinkled some in a tin pot, and had the fire going meanwhile, a
small one to begin with, the sun was still on us, and stuck a
long stick tight down under a few big rocks and made himself
something to hang the teapot on and pretty soon the water was
boiling and he poured it out steaming into the tin pot and we
had cups of tea with our tin cups. I myself'd gotten the water
from the stream, which was cold and pure like snow and the
crystal-lidded eyes of heaven. Therefore, the tea was by far the
most pure and thirstquenching tea I ever drank in all my life, it
made you want to drink more and more, it actually quenched
your thirst and of course it swam around hot in your belly.

"Now you understand the Oriental passion for tea," said
Japhy. "Remember that book I told you about the first sip is joy
the second is gladness, the third is serenity, the fourth is mad-
ness, the fifth is ecstasy."

"Just about old buddy."

That rock we were camped against was a marvel. It was
thirty feet high and thirty feet at base, a perfect square almost,
and twisted trees arched over it and peeked down on us. From
the base it went outward, forming a concave, so if rain came
we'd be partially covered. "How did this immense sonumbitch
ever get here?"

"It probably was left here by the retreating glacier. See over
there that field of snow?"

"Yeah."

"That's the glacier what's left of it. Either that or this rock
tumbled here from inconceivable prehistoric mountains we
can't understand, or maybe it just landed here when the friggin

mountain range itself burst out of the ground in the Jurassic up-
heaval. Ray when you're up here you're not sittin in a Berkeley
tea room. This is the beginning and the end of the world right
here. Look at all those patient Buddhas lookin at us saying
nothing."

"And you come out here by yourself . . ."

"For weeks on end, just like John Muir, climb around all by
myself following quartzite veins or making posies of flowers for
my camp, or just walking around naked singing, and cook my
supper and laugh."

"Japhy I gotta hand it to you, you're the happiest little cat in
the world and the greatest by God you are. I'm sure glad I'm
learning all this. This place makes me feel devoted, too, I mean,
you know I have a prayer, did you know the prayer I use?"

"What?"

"I sit down and say, and I run all my friends and relatives and
enemies one by one in this, without entertaining any angers or
gratitudes or anything, and I say, like 'Japhy Ryder, equally
empty, equally to be loved, equally a coming Buddha,' then I
run on, say, to 'David O. Selznick, equally empty, equally to be
loved, equally a coming Buddha' though I don't use names like
David O. Selznick, just people I know because when I say the
words 'equally a coming Buddha' I want to be thinking of their
eyes, like you take Morley, his blue eyes behind those glasses,
when you think 'equally a coming Buddha' you think of those
eyes and you really do suddenly see the true secret serenity and
the truth of his coming Buddhahood. Then you think of your
enemy's eyes."

"That's great, Ray," and Japhy took out his notebook and
wrote down the prayer, and shook his head in wonder. "That's
really really great. I'm going to teach this prayer to the monks I
meet in Japan. There's nothing wrong with you Ray, your only
trouble is you never learned to get out to spots like this, you've
let the world drown you in its horseshit and you've been
vexed . . . though as I say comparisons *are* odious, but what
we're sayin now is true."

He took his bulgur rough cracked wheat and dumped a couple of packages of dried vegetables in and put it all in the pot

to be ready to be boiled at dusk. We began listening for the yodels of Henry Morley, which didn't come. We began to worry
about him.

"The trouble about all this, dammit, if he fell off a boulder
and broke his leg there'd be no one to help him. It's dangerous
to . . . I do it all by myself but I'm pretty good, I'm a mountain
goat."

"I'm gettin hungry."

"Me too dammit, I wish he gets here soon. Let's ramble
around and eat snowballs and drink water and wait."

We did this, investigating the upper end of the flat plateau,
and came back. By now the sun was gone behind the western
wall of our valley and it was getting darker, pinker, colder,
more hues of purple began to steal across the jags. The sky was
deep. We even began to see pale stars, at least one or two. Suddenly we heard a distant "Yodelayhee" and Japhy leaped up
and jumped to the top of a boulder and yelled "Hoo hoo hoo!"
The Yodelayhee came back.

"How far is he?"

"My God from the sound of it he's not even started. He's not
even at the beginning of the valley of boulders. He can never
make it tonight."

"What'll we do?"

"Let's go to the rock cliff and sit on the edge and call him an
hour. Let's bring these peanuts and raisins and munch on 'em
and wait. Maybe he's not so far as I think."

We went over to the promontory where we could see the
whole valley and Japhy sat down in full lotus posture crosslegged on a rock and took out his wooden juju prayerbeads and
prayed. That is, he simply held the beads in his hands, the hands
upsidedown with thumbs touching, and stared straight ahead
and didn't move a bone. I sat down as best I could on another
rock and we both said nothing and meditated. Only I meditated
with my eyes closed. The silence was an intense roar. From
where we were, the sound of the creek, the gurgle and slapping
talk of the creek, was blocked off by rocks. We heard several
more melancholy Yodelayhees and answered them but it seemed
farther and farther away each time. When I opened my eyes the

pink was more purple all the time. The stars began to flash. I fell into deep meditation, felt that the mountains were indeed Buddhas and our friends, and I felt the weird sensation that it was strange that there were only three men in this whole immense valley: the mystic number three. Nirmanakaya, Sambhogakaya, and Dharmakaya. I prayed for the safety and in fact the eternal happiness of poor Morley. Once I opened my eyes and saw Japhy sitting there rigid as a rock and I felt like laughing he looked so funny. But the mountains were mighty solemn, and so was Japhy, and for that matter so was I, and in fact laughter is solemn.

It was beautiful. The pinkness vanished and then it was all purple dusk and the roar of the silence was like a wash of diamond waves going through the liquid porches of our ears, enough to soothe a man a thousand years. I prayed for Japhy, for his future safety and happiness and eventual Buddhahood. It was all completely serious, all completely hallucinated, all completely happy.

"Rocks are space," I thought, "and space is illusion." I had a million thoughts. Japhy had his. I was amazed at the way he meditated with his eyes open. And I was mostly humanly amazed that this tremendous little guy who eagerly studied Oriental poetry and anthropology and ornithology and everything else in the books and was a tough little adventurer of trails and mountains should also suddenly whip out his pitiful beautiful wooden prayerbeads and solemnly pray there, like an oldfashioned saint of the deserts certainly, but so amazing to see it in America with its steel mills and airfields. The world ain't so bad, when you got Japhies, I thought, and felt glad. All the aching muscles and the hunger in my belly were bad enough, and the surroundant dark rocks, the fact that there is nothing there to soothe you with kisses and soft words, but just to be sitting there meditating and praying for the world with another earnest young man—'twere good enough to have been born just to die, as we all are. Something will come of it in the Milky Ways of eternity stretching in front of all our phantom unjaundiced eyes, friends. I felt like telling Japhy everything I thought but I knew it didn't matter and moreover he knew it anyway and silence is the golden mountain.

"Yodelayhee," sang Morley, and now it was dark, and Japhy said "Well, from the looks of things he's still far away. He has enough sense to pitch his own camp down there tonight so let's go back to our camp and cook supper."

"Okay." And we yelled "Hoo" a couple of times reassuringly and gave up poor Morl for the night. He did have enough sense, we knew. And as it turned out he did, and pitched his camp, wrapped up in his two blankets on top of the air mattress, and slept the night out in that incomparably happy meadow with the pond and the pines, telling us about it when he finally reached us the next day.

10

I rousted about and got a lot of little pieces of wood to make kindling for the fire and then I went around gathering bigger pieces and finally I was hunting out huge logs, easy to find all over the place. We had a fire that Morley must have seen from five miles away, except we were way up behind the cliff face, cut off from his view. It cast mighty blasts of heat against our cliff, the cliff absorbed it and threw it back, we were in a hot room except that the ends of our noses were nippy from sticking them out of that area to get firewood and water. Japhy put the bulgur in the pot with water and started it boiling and stirred it around and meanwhile busied himself with the mixings for the chocolate pudding and started boiling that in a separate smaller pot out of my knapsack. He also brewed a fresh pot of tea. Then he whipped out his double set of chopsticks and pretty soon we had our supper ready and laughed over it. It was the most delicious supper of all time. Up out of the orange glow of our fire you could see immense systems of uncountable stars, either as individual blazers, or in low Venus droppers, or vast Milky Ways incommensurate with human understanding, all cold, blue, silver, but our food and our fire was pink and goodies. And true to what Japhy had predicted, I had absolutely not a jot of appetite for alcohol, I'd forgotten all about it, the altitude was too high, the exercise too heavy, the air too brisk, the air itself was enough to get your drunk ass drunk. It was a tremendous supper, food is always better eaten in doleful little pinchfuls off the ends of chopsticks, no gobbling, the reason why Darwin's law of survival applies best to China: if you don't know how to handle a chopstick and stick it in that family pot with the best of 'em, you'll starve. I ended up flupping it all up with my forefinger anyhow.

Supper done, Japhy assiduously got to scraping the pots with a wire scraper and got me to bring water, which I did dipping a leftover can from other campers into the fire pool of stars, and came back with a snowball to boot, and Japhy washed the dishes in preboiled water. "Usually I don't wash my dishes, I just wrap 'em up in my blue bandana, cause it really doesn't matter . . . though they don't appreciate this little bit of wisdom in the horse-soap building thar on Madison Avenue, what you call it, that English firm, Urber and Urber, whatall, damn hell and upsidedown boy I'll be as tight as Dick's hatband if I don't feel like takin out my star map and seein what the lay of the pack is tonight. That houndsapack up there more uncountable than all your favorite Surangamy sutries, boy." So he whips out his star map and turns it around a little, and adjusts, and looks, and says, "It's exactly eight-forty-eight p.m."

"How do you know."

"Sirius wouldn't be where Sirius is, if it wasn't eight-forty-eight p.m. . . . You know what I like about you, Ray, you've woke me up to the true language of this country which is the language of the working men, railroad men, loggers. D'yever hear them guys talk?"

"I shore did. I had a guy, an oil rig driver, truck, picked me up in Houston Texas one night round about midnight after some little faggot who owned some motel courts called of all things and rather appropriately my dear, Dandy Courts, had left me off and said if you can't get a ride come on in sleep on my floor, so I wait about an hour in the empty road and here comes this rig and it's driven by a Cherokee he said he was but his name was Johnson or Ally Reynolds or some damn thing and as he talked starting in with a speech like 'Well boy I left my mammy's cabin before you knew the smell of the river and

came west to drive myself mad in the East Texas oilfield' and all
kinds of rhythmic talk and with every bang of rhythm he'd ram
at his clutch and his various gears and pop up the truck and had
her roaring down the road about seventy miles an hour with
momentum only when his story got rolling with him, magnificent, that's what I call poetry."

"That's what I mean. You oughta hear old Burnie Byers talk
up that talk up in the Skagit country, Ray you just gotta go up
there."

"Okay I will."

Japhy, kneeling there studying his star map, leaning forward
slightly to peek up through the overhanging gnarled old rock
country trees, with his goatee and all, looked, with that mighty
grawfaced rock behind him, like, exactly like the vision I had of
the old Zen Masters of China out in the wilderness. He was
leaning forward on his knees, upward looking, as if with a holy
sutra in his hands. Pretty soon he went to the snowbank and
brought back the chocolate pudding which was now ice cold
and absolutely delicious beyond words. We ate it all up.

"Maybe we oughta leave some for Morley."

"Ah it won't keep, it'll melt in the morning sun."

As the fire stopped roaring and just got to be red coals, but
big ones six feet long, the night interposed its icy crystal feel
more and more but with the smell of smoking logs it was as delicious as chocolate pudding. For a while I went on a little walk
by myself, out by the shallow iced creek, and sat meditating
against a stump of dirt and the huge mountain walls on both
sides of our valley were silent masses. Too cold to do this more
than a minute. As I came back our orange fire casting its glow
on the big rock, and Japhy kneeling and peering up at the sky,
and all of it ten thousand feet above the gnashing world, was a
picture of peace and good sense. There was another aspect of
Japhy that amazed me: his tremendous and tender sense of charity. He was always giving things, always practicing what the
Buddhists call the Paramita of Dana, the perfection of charity.

Now when I came back and sat down by the fire he said
"Well Smith it's about time you owned a set of juju beads you
can have these," and he handed me the brown wood beads run

together over a strong string with the string, black and shiny, coming out at the large bead at the end in a pretty loop.

"Aw you can't give me something like this, these things come from Japan don't they?"

"I've got another set of black ones. Smith that prayer you gave me tonight is worth that set of juju beads, but you can have it anyway." A few minutes later he cleaned out the rest of the chocolate pudding but made sure that I got most of it. Then when he laid boughs over the rock of our clearing and the poncho over that he made sure his sleeping bag was farther away from the fire than mine so I would be sure to be warm. He was always practicing charity. In fact he taught me, and a week later I was giving him nice new undershirts I'd discovered in the Goodwill store. He'd turn right around and make me a gift of a plastic container to keep food in. For a joke I'd give him a gift of a huge flower from Alvah's yard. Solemnly a day later he'd bring me a little bouquet of flowers picked in the street plots of Berkeley. "And you can keep the sneakers too," he said. "I've got another pair older than those but just as good."

"Aw I can't be taking all your things."

"Smith you don't realize it's a privilege to practice giving presents to others." The way he did it was charming; there was nothing glittery and Christmasy about it, but almost sad, and sometimes his gifts were old beat-up things but they had the charm of usefulness and sadness of his giving.

We rolled into our sleeping bags, it was freezing cold now, about eleven o'clock, and talked a while more before one of us just didn't answer from the pillow and pretty soon we were asleep. While he snored I woke up and just lay flat back with my eyes to the stars and thanked God I'd come on this mountain climb. My legs felt better, my whole body felt strong. The crack of the dying logs was like Japhy making little comments on my happiness. I looked at him, his head was buried way under inside his duck-down bag. His little huddled form was the only thing I could see for miles of darkness that was so packed and concentrated with eager desire to be good. I thought, "What a strange thing is man . . . like in the Bible it says, Who knoweth the spirit of man that looketh upward? This poor kid ten years younger than I am is making me look like a fool forgetting all the ideals and joys I knew before, in my recent years of drinking and disappointment, what does he care if he hasn't got any money: he doesn't need any money, all he needs is his rucksack with those little plastic bags of dried food and a good pair of shoes and off he goes and enjoys the privileges of a millionaire in surroundings like this. And what gouty millionaire could get up this rock anyhow? It took us all day to climb." And I promised myself that I would begin a new life. "All over the West, and the mountains in the East, and the desert, I'll tramp with a rucksack and make it the pure way." I went to sleep after burying my nose under the sleeping bag and woke up around dawn shivering, the ground cold had seeped through the poncho and through the bag and my ribs were up against a damper damp than the damp of a cold bed. My breath was coming out it steams. I rolled over to the other ribs and slept more: my dreams were pure cold dreams like ice water, happy dreams, no nightmares.

When I woke up again and the sunlight was a pristine orange pouring through the crags to the East and down through our fragrant pine boughs, I felt like I did when I was a boy and it was time to get up and go play all day Saturday, in overalls. Japhy was already up singing and blowing on his hands at a small fire. White frost was on the ground. He rushed out a way and yelled out "Yodelayhee" and by God we heard it come right back at us from Morley, closer than the night before. "He's on his way now. Wake up Smith and have a hot cupa tea, do you good!" I got up and fished my sneakers out of the sleeping bag where they'd been kept warm all night, and put them on, and put on my beret, and jumped up and ran a few blocks in the grass. The shallow creek was iced over except in the middle where a rill of gurgles rolled like tinkly tinkly. I fell down on my belly and took a deep drink, wetting my face. There's no feeling in the world like washing your face in cold water on a mountain morning. Then I went back and Japhy was heating up the remains of last night's supper and it was still good. Then we went out on the edge of the cliff and Hooed at Morley, and suddenly we could see him, a tiny figure two miles down the valley of boulders moving like a little animate being in the immense void. "That little dot down there is our witty friend Morley," said Japhy in his funny resounding voice of a lumberjack.

In about two hours Morley was within talking distance of us and started right in talking as he negotiated the final boulders, to where we were sitting in the now warm sun on a rock waiting.

"The Ladies' Aid Society says I should come up and see if you boys would like to have blue ribbons pinned on your shirts, they say there's plenty of pink lemonade left and Lord Mount-batten is getting mighty impatient. You think they'll investigate the source of that recent trouble in the Mid-East, or learn to ap-preciate coffee better. I should think with a couple of literary gentlemen like you two they should learn to mind their man-ners . . ." and so on and so on, for no reason at all, yakking in the happy blue morning sky over rocks with his slaking grin, sweating a little from the long morning's work.

"Well Morley you ready to climb Matterhorn?"

"I'm ready just as soon as I can change these wet socks."

I I

At about noon we started out, leaving our big packs at the camp where nobody was likely to be till next year anyway, and went up the scree valley with just some food and first-aid kits. The valley was longer than it looked. In no time at all it was two o'clock in the afternoon and the sun was getting that later more golden look and a wind was rising and I began to think "By gosh how we ever gonna climb that mountain, tonight?"

I put it up to Japhy who said: "You're right, we'll have to hurry."

"Why don't we just forget it and go on home?"

"Aw come on Tiger, we'll make a run up that hill and then we'll go home." The valley was long and long and long. And at the top end it got very steep and I began to be a little afraid of falling down, the rocks were small and it got slippery and my ankles were in pain from yesterday's muscle strain anyway. But Morley kept walking and talking and I noticed his tremendous endurance. Japhy took his pants off so he could look just like an Indian, I mean stark naked, except for a jockstrap, and hiked almost a quarter-mile ahead of us, sometimes waiting a while, to give us time to catch up, then went on, moving fast, wanting to climb the mountain today. Morley came second, about fifty yards ahead of me all the way. I was in no hurry. Then as it got later afternoon I went faster and decided to pass Morley and join Japhy. Now we were at about eleven thousand feet and it was cold and there was a lot of snow and to the East we could see immense snowcapped ranges and whooee levels of valleyland below them, we were already practically on top of California. At one point I had to scramble, like the others, on a narrow ledge, around a butte of rock, and it really scared me: the fall was a hundred feet, enough to break your neck, with another little ledge letting you bounce a minute preparatory to a nice goodbye one-thousand-foot drop. The wind was whipping now. Yet that whole afternoon, even more than the other, was filled with old premonitions or memories, as though I'd been there before, scrambling on these rocks, for other purposes more ancient, more serious, more simple. We finally got to the foot of Matterhorn where there was a most beautiful small lake unknown to the eyes of most men in this world, seen by only a handful of mountainclimbers, a small lake at eleven thousand some odd feet with snow on the edges of it and beautiful flowers and a beautiful meadow, an alpine meadow, flat and dreamy, upon which I immediately threw myself and took my shoes off. Japhy'd been there a half-hour when I made it, and it was cold now and his clothes were on again. Morley came up behind us smiling. We sat there looking up at the imminent steep scree slope of the final crag of Matterhorn.

"That don't look much, we can do it!" I said glad now.

"No, Ray, that's more than it looks. Do you realize that's a thousand feet more?"

"That much?"

"Unless we make a run up there, double-time, we'll never make it down again to our camp before nightfall and never make it down to the car at the lodge before tomorrow morning at, well at midnight."

"Phew."

"I'm tired," said Morley. "I don't think I'll try it."

"Well that's right," I said. "The whole purpose of mountain-climbing to me isn't just to show off you can get to the top, it's getting out to this wild country."

"Well I'm gonna go," said Japhy.

"Well if you're gonna go I'm goin with you."

"Morley?"

"I don't think I can make it. I'll wait here." And that wind was strong, too strong, I felt that as soon as we'd be a few hundred feet up the slope it might hamper our climbing.

Japhy took a small pack of peanuts and raisins and said "This'll be our gasoline, boy. You ready Ray to make a double-time run?"

"Ready. What would I say to the boys in The Place if I came all this way only to give up at the last minute?"

"It's late so let's hurry." Japhy started up walking very rapidly and then even running sometimes where the climb had to be to the right or left along ridges of scree. Scree is long landslides of rocks and sand, very difficult to scramble through, always little avalanches going on. At every few steps we took it seemed we were going higher and higher on a terrifying elevator, I gulped when I turned around to look back and see all of the state of California it would seem stretching out in three directions under huge blue skies with frightening planetary space clouds and immense vistas of distant valleys and even plateaus and for all I knew whole Nevadas out there. It was terrifying to look down and see Morley a dreaming spot by the little lake waiting for us. "Oh why didn't I stay with old Henry?" I thought. I now began to be afraid to go any higher from sheer fear of being too high. I began to be afraid of being blown away by the wind. All the nightmares I'd ever had about falling off mountains and precipitous buildings ran through my head in perfect clarity. Also with every twenty steps we took upward we both became completely exhausted.

"That's because of the high altitude now Ray," said Japhy sitting beside me panting. "So have raisins and peanuts and you'll see what kick it gives you." And each time it gave us such a tremendous kick we both jumped up without a word and climbed another twenty, thirty steps. Then sat down again, panting, sweating in the cold wind, high on top of the world our noses sniffling like the noses of little boys playing late Saturday afternoon their final little games in winter. Now the wind began to howl like the wind in movies about the Shroud of Tibet. The steepness began to be too much for me; I was afraid now to look back any more; I peeked: I couldn't even make out Morley by the tiny lake.

"Hurry it up," yelled Japhy from a hundred feet ahead. "It's getting awfully late." I looked up to the peak. It was right there, I'd be there in five minutes. "Only a half-hour to go!" yelled Japhy. I didn't believe it. In five minutes of scrambling angrily upward I fell down and looked up and it was still just as far away. What I didn't like about that peak-top was that the clouds of all the world were blowing right through it like fog.

"Wouldn't see anything up there anyway," I muttered. "Oh why did I ever let myself into this?" Japhy was way ahead of me now, he'd left the peanuts and raisins with me, it was with a kind of lonely solemnity now he had decided to rush to the top if it killed him. He didn't sit down any more. Soon he was a whole football field, a hundred yards ahead of me, getting smaller. I looked back and like Lot's wife that did it. *"This is too high!"* I yelled to Japhy in a panic. He didn't hear me. I raced a few more feet up and fell exhausted on my belly, slipping back just a little. *"This is too high!"* I yelled. I was really scared. Supposing I'd start to slip back for good, these screes might start sliding any time anyway. That damn mountain goat Japhy, I could see him jumping through the foggy air up ahead from rock to rock, up, up, just the flash of his boot bottoms. "How can I keep up with a maniac like that?" But with nutty desperation I followed him. Finally I came to a kind of ledge where I could sit at a level angle instead of having to cling not to slip, and I nudged my whole body inside the ledge just to hold me there tight, so the wind would not dislodge me, and I looked down and around and I had had it. *"I'm stayin here!"* I yelled to Japhy.

"Come on Smith, only another five minutes. I only got a hundred feet to go!"

"I'm staying right here! It's too high!"

He said nothing and went on. I saw him collapse and pant and get up and make his run again.

I nudged myself closer into the ledge and closed my eyes and thought "Oh what a life this is, why do we have to be born in the first place, and only so we can have our poor gentle flesh laid out to such impossible horrors as huge mountains and rock and empty space," and with horror I remembered the famous Zen saying, "When you get to the top of a mountain, keep climbing." The saying made my hair stand on end; it had been such cute poetry sitting on Alvah's straw mats. Now it was enough to make my heart pound and my heart bleed for being born at all. "In fact when Japhy gets to the top of that crag he *will* keep climbing, the way the wind's blowing. Well this old philosopher is staying right here," and I closed my eyes. "Besides," I thought, "rest and be kind, you don't have to prove anything." Suddenly I heard a beautiful broken yodel of a strange musical and mystical intensity in the wind, and looked up, and it was Japhy standing on top of Matterhorn peak letting out his triumphant mountain-conquering Buddha Mountain Smashing song of joy. It was beautiful. It was funny, too, up here on the not-so-funny top of California and in all that rushing fog. But I had to hand it to him, the guts, the endurance, the sweat, and now the crazy human singing: whipped cream on top of ice cream. I didn't have enough strength to answer his yodel. He ran around up there and went out of sight to investigate the little flat top of some kind (he said) that ran a few feet west and then dropped sheer back down maybe as far as I care to the sawdust floors of Virginia City. It was insane. I could hear him yelling at me but I just nudged farther in my protective nook, trembling. I looked down at the small lake where Morley was lying on his back with a blade of grass in his mouth and said out loud "Now there's the karma of these three men here: Japhy Ryder gets to his triumphant mountaintop and makes it, I almost make it and have to give up and huddle in a bloody cave, but the smartest of them all is that poet's poet lyin down there with his knees crossed to the sky chewing on a flower dreaming by a gurgling *plage,* goddammit they'll never get me up here again."

12

I really was amazed by the wisdom of Morley now: "Him with all his goddamn pictures of snowcapped Swiss Alps" I thought.

Then suddenly everything was just like jazz: it happened in one insane second or so: I looked up and saw Japhy *running down the mountain* in huge twenty-foot leaps, running, leaping, landing with a great drive of his booted heels, bouncing five feet or so, running, then taking another long crazy yelling yo-delaying sail down the sides of the world and in that flash I realized *it's impossible to fall off mountains you fool* and with a yodel of my own I suddenly got up and began running down the mountain after him doing exactly the same huge leaps, the same fantastic runs and jumps, and in the space of about five minutes I'd guess Japhy Ryder and I (in my sneakers, driving the heels of my sneakers right into sand, rock, boulders, I didn't care any more I was so anxious to get down out of there) came leaping and yelling like mountain goats or I'd say like Chinese lunatics of a thousand years ago, enough to raise the hair on the head of the meditating Morley by the lake, who said he looked up and saw us flying down and couldn't believe it. In fact with one of my greatest leaps and loudest screams of joy I came flying right down to the edge of the lake and dug my sneakered heels into the mud and just fell sitting there, glad. Japhy was already taking his shoes off and pouring sand and pebbles out. It was great. I took off my sneakers and poured out a couple of buckets of lava dust and said "Ah Japhy you taught me the final lesson of them all, you can't fall off a mountain."

"And that's what they mean by the saying, When you get to the top of a mountain keep climbing, Smith."

"Dammit that yodel of triumph of yours was the most

beautiful thing I ever heard in my life. I wish I'd a had a tape recorder to take it down."

"Those things aren't made to be heard by the people below," says Japhy dead serious.

"By God you're right, all those sedentary bums sitting around on pillows hearing the cry of the triumphant mountain smasher, they don't deserve it. But when I looked up and saw you running down that mountain I suddenly understood everything."

"Ah a little satori for Smith today," says Morley.

"What were you doing down here?"

"Sleeping, mostly."

"Well dammit I didn't get to the top. Now I'm ashamed of myself because now that I know how to come *down* a mountain I know how to go *up* and that I can't fall off, but now it's too late."

"We'll come back next summer Ray and climb it. Do you realize that this is the first time you've been mountainclimbin and you left old veteran Morley here way behind you?"

"Sure," said Morley. "Do you think, Japhy, they would assign Smith the title of Tiger for what he done today?"

"Oh sure," says Japhy, and I really felt proud. I was a Tiger.

"Well dammit I'll be a lion next time we get up here."

"Let's go men, now we've got a long, long way to go back down this scree to our camp and down that valley of boulders and then down that lake trail, wow, I doubt if we can make it before pitch dark."

"It'll be mostly okay." Morley pointed to the sliver of moon in the pinkening deepening blue sky. "That oughta light us a way."

"Let's go." We all got up and started back. Now when I went around that ledge that had scared me it was just fun and a lark, I just skipped and jumped and danced along and I had really learned that you can't fall off a mountain. Whether you *can* fall off a mountain or not I don't know, but I had learned that you can't. That was the way it struck me.

It was a joy, though, to get down into the valley and lose sight of all that open sky space underneath everything and finally, as it got graying five o'clock, about a hundred yards from the other boys and walking alone, to just pick my way singing and thinking along the little black cruds of a deer trail through the rocks, no call to think or look ahead or worry, just follow the little balls of deer crud with your eyes cast down and enjoy life. At one point I looked and saw crazy Japhy who'd climbed for fun to the top of a snow slope and skied right down to the bottom, about a hundred yards, on his boots and the final few yards on his back, yippeeing and glad. Not only that but he'd taken off his pants again and wrapped them around his neck. This pants bit of his was simply he said for comfort, which is true, besides nobody around to see him anyway, though I figured that when he went mountainclimbing with girls it didn't make any difference to him. I could hear Morley talking to him in the great lonely valley: even across the rocks you could tell it was his voice. Finally I followed my deer trail so assiduously I was by myself going along ridges and down across creekbottoms completely out of sight of them, though I could hear them, but I trusted the instinct of my sweet little millennial deer and true enough, just as it was getting dark their ancient trail took me right to the edges of the familiar shallow creek (where they stopped to drink for the last five thousand years) and there was the glow of Japhy's bonfire making the side of the big rock orange and gay. The moon was bright high in the sky. "Well that moon's gonna save our ass, we got eight miles to go downtrail boys."

We ate a little and drank a lot of tea and arranged all our stuff. I had never had a happier moment in my life than those lonely moments coming down that little deer trace and when we hiked off with our packs I turned to take a final look up that way, it was dark now, hoping to see a few dear little deer, nothing in sight, and I thanked everything up that way. It had been like when you're a little boy and have spent a whole day rambling alone in the woods and fields and on the dusk homeward walk you did it all with your eyes to the ground, scuffling, thinking, whistling, like little Indian boys must feel when they follow their striding fathers from Russian River to Shasta two hundred years ago, like little Arab boys following their fathers, their fathers' trails; that singsong little joyful solitude, nose sniffling, like a little girl pulling her little brother home on the

sled and they're both singing little ditties of their imagination
and making faces at the ground and just being themselves before they have to go in the kitchen and put on a straight face
again for the world of seriousness. "Yet what could be more serious than to follow a deer trace to get to your water?" I thought.
We got to the cliff and started down the five-mile valley of boulders, in clear moonlight now, it was quite easy to dance down
from boulder to boulder, the boulders were snow white, with
patches of deep black shadow. Everything was cleanly whitely
beautiful in the moonlight. Sometimes you could see the silver
flash of the creek. Far down were the pines of the meadow park
and the pool of the pond.

At this point my feet were unable to go on. I called Japhy and
apologized. I couldn't take any more jumps. There were blisters
not only on the bottoms but on the sides of my feet, from there
having been no protection all yesterday and today. So Japhy
swapped and let me wear his boots.

With these big lightweight protective boots on I knew I could
go on fine. It was a great new feeling to be able to jump from
rock to rock without having to feel the pain through the thin
sneakers. On the other hand, for Japhy, it was also a relief to be
suddenly lightfooted and he enjoyed it. We made double-time
down the valley. But every step was getting us bent, now, we
were all really tired. With the heavy packs it was difficult to
control those thigh muscles that you need to go *down* a mountain, which is sometimes harder than going up. And there were
all those boulders to surmount, for sometimes we'd be walking
in sand awhile and our path would be blocked by boulders and
we had to climb them and jump from one to the other then suddenly no more boulders and we had to jump down to the sand.
Then we'd be trapped in impassable thickets and had to go
around them or try to crash through and sometimes I'd get
stuck in a thicket with my rucksack, standing there cursing in
the impossible moonlight. None of us were talking. I was angry
too because Japhy and Morley were afraid to stop and rest, they
said it was dangerous at this point to stop.

"What's the difference the moon's shining, we can even
sleep."

"No, we've got to get down to that car tonight."

"Well let's stop a minute here. My legs can't take it."

"Okay, only a minute."

But they never rested long enough to suit me and it seemed to me they were getting hysterical. I even began to curse them and at one point I even gave Japhy hell: "What's the sense of killing yourself like this, you call this fun? Phooey." (Your ideas are a crock, I added to myself.) A little weariness'll change a lot of things. Eternities of moonlight rock and thickets and boulders and ducks and that horrifying valley with the two rim walls and finally it seemed we were almost out of there, but nope, not quite yet, and my legs screaming to stop, and me cursing and smashing at twigs and throwing myself on the ground to rest a minute.

"Come on Ray, everything comes to an end." In fact I realized I had no guts anyway, which I've long known. But I have joy. When we got to the alpine meadow I stretched out on my belly and drank water and enjoyed myself peacefully in silence while they talked and worried about getting down the rest of the trail in time.

"Ah don't worry, it's a beautiful night, you've driven yourself too hard. Drink some water and lie down here for about five even ten minutes, everything takes care of itself." Now I was being the philosopher. In fact Japhy agreed with me and we rested peacefully. That good long rest assured my bones I could make it down to the lake okay. It was beautiful going down the trail. The moonlight poured through thick foliage and made dapples on the backs of Morley and Japhy as they walked in front of me. With our packs we got into a good rhythmic walk and enjoying going "Hup hup" as we came to switchbacks and swiveled around, always down, down, the pleasant downgoing swinging rhythm trail. And that roaring creek was a beauty by moonlight, those flashes of flying moon water, that snow white foam, those black-as-pitch trees, regular elfin paradises of shadow and moon. The air began to get warmer and nicer and in fact I thought I could begin to smell people again. We could smell the nice raunchy tide-smell of the lake water, and flowers, and softer dust of down below. Everything up there had smelled of ice and

snow and heartless spine rock. Here there was the smell of sun-
heated wood, sunny dust resting in the moonlight, lake mud,
flowers, straw, all those good things of the earth. The trail was
fun coming down and yet at one point I was as tired as ever,
more than in that endless valley of boulders, but you could see
the lake lodge down below now, a sweet little lamp of light and
so it didn't matter. Morley and Japhy were talking a blue streak
and all we had to do was roll on down to the car. In fact suddenly, as in a happy dream, with the suddenness of waking up
from an endless nightmare and it's all over, we were striding
across the road and there were houses and there were automo-
biles parked under trees and Morley's car was sitting right there.

"From what I can tell by feeling this air," said Morley, leaning on the car as we slung our packs to the ground, "it mustn't
have froze at all last night, I went back and drained the
crankcase for nothing."

"Well maybe it did freeze." Morley went over and got motor
oil at the lodge store and they told him it hadn't been freezing at
all, but one of the warmest nights of the year.

"All that mad trouble for nothing," I said. But we didn't care.
We were famished. I said "Let's go to Bridgeport and go in one
of those lunchcarts there boy and eat hamburg and potatoes
and hot coffee." We drove down the lakeside dirt road in the
moonlight, stopped at the inn where Morley returned the blankets, and drove on into the little town and parked on the highway. Poor Japhy, it was here finally I found out his Achilles heel.
This little tough guy who wasn't afraid of anything and could
ramble around mountains for weeks alone and run down
mountains, was afraid of going into a restaurant because the
people in it were too well dressed. Morley and I laughed and
said "What's the difference? We'll just go in and eat." But
Japhy thought the place I chose looked too bourgeois and insisted on going to a more workingman-looking restaurant
across the highway. We went in there and it was a desultory
place with lazy waitresses letting us sit there five minutes without even bringing a menu. I got mad and said "Let's go to that
other place. What you afraid of, Japhy, what's the difference?
You may know all about mountains but I know about where to

eat." In fact we got a little miffed at each other and I felt bad. But he came to the other place, which was the better restaurant of the two, with a bar on one side, many hunters drinking in the dim cocktail-lounge light, and the restaurant itself a long counter and a lot of tables with whole gay families eating from a very considerable selection. The menu was huge and good: mountain trout and everything. Japhy, I found, was also afraid of spending ten cents more for a good dinner. I went to the bar and bought a glass of port and brought it to our stool seats at the counter (Japhy: "You sure you can do that?") and I kidded Japhy awhile. He felt better now. "That's what's the trouble with you Japhy, you're just an old anarchist scared of society. What difference does it make? Comparisons are odious."

"Well Smith it just looked to me like this place was full of old rich farts and the prices would be too high, I admit it, I'm scared of all this American wealth, I'm just an old bhikku and I got nothin to do with all this high standard of living, goddammit, I've been a poor guy all my life and I can't get used to some things."

"Well your weaknesses are admirable. I'll buy 'em." And we had a raving great dinner of baked potatoes and porkchops and salad and hot buns and blueberry pie and the works. We were so honestly hungry it wasn't funny and it was honest. After dinner we went into a liquor store where I bought a bottle of muscatel and the old proprietor and his old fat buddy looked at us and said "Where you boys been?"

"Climbin Matterhorn out there," I said proudly. They only stared at us, gaping. But I felt great and bought a cigar and lit up and said "Twelve thousand feet and we come down outa there with such an appetite and feelin so good that now this wine is gonna hit us just right." The old men gaped. We were all sunburned and dirty and wildlooking, too. They didn't say anything. They thought we were crazy.

We got in the car and drove back to San Francisco drinking and laughing and telling long stories and Morley really drove beautifully that night and wheeled us silently through the graying dawn streets of Berkeley as Japhy and I slept dead to the world in the seats. At some point or other I woke up like a little child and was told I was home and staggered out of the car and went across the grass into the cottage and opened my blankets and curled up and slept till late the next afternoon a completely dreamless beautiful sleep. When I woke up the next day the veins in my feet were all cleared. I had worked the blood clots right out of existence. I felt very happy.

13

When I got up the next day I couldn't help smiling thinking of Japhy standing huddled in the night outside the fancy restaurant wondering if we would be let in or not. It was the first time I'd ever seen him afraid of anything. I planned to tell him about such things, that night, when he'd be coming over. But that night everything happened. First, Alvah left and went out for a few hours and I was alone reading when suddenly I heard a bike in the yard and I looked and it was Princess.

"Where's everybody?" says she.

"How long can you stay?"

"I've got to go right away, unless I call my mother."

"Let's call."

"Okay."

We went down to the corner gas station pay phone, and she said she'd be home in two hours, and as we walked back along the sidewalk I put my arm around her waist but way around with my fingers digging into her belly and she said "*Oooh,* I can't stand that!" and almost fell down on the sidewalk and bit my shirt just as an old woman was coming our way ogling us angrily and after she passed us we clinched in a big mad passionate kiss under the trees of evening. We rushed to the cottage where she spent an hour literally spinning in my arms and Alvah walked in right in the middle of our final ministrations of the Bodhisattva. We took our usual bath together. It was great sitting in the hot tub chatting and soaping each other's backs. Poor Princess, she meant every word she said. I really felt good about her, and compassionate, and even warned her: "Now don't go wild and get into orgies with fifteen guys on a mountaintop."

Japhy came after she left, and then Coughlin came and suddenly (we had wine) a mad party began in the cottage. It started
off with Coughlin and me, drunk now, walking arm in arm
down the main drag of town carrying huge, almost impossibly
huge flowers of some kind we'd found in a garden, and a new
jug of wine, shouting haikus and hoos and satoris at everybody
we saw in the street and everybody was smiling at us. "Walked
five miles carrying huge flower," yelled Coughlin, and I liked him
now, he was deceptively scholarly looking or fatty-boomboom
looking but he was a real man. We went to visit some professor
of the English Department at U. of Cal. we knew and Coughlin
left his shoes on the lawn and danced right into the astonished
professor's house, in fact frightened him somewhat, though
Coughlin was a fairly well known poet by now. Then barefooted with our huge flowers and jugs we went back to the
cottage it was now about ten. I had just gotten some money in
the mail that day, a fellowship of three hundred bucks, so I
said to Japhy "Well I've learned everything now, I'm ready.
How about driving me to Oakland tomorrow and helping me
buy all my rucksack and gear and stuff so I can take off for
the desert?"

"Good, I'll get Morley's car and be over to get you first thing
in the morning, but right now how about some of that wine?" I
turned on the little red bandana dimbulb and we poured wine
and all sat around talking. It was a great night of talk. First
Japhy started telling his later life story, like when he was a mer-
chant seaman in New York port and went around with a dagger
on his hip, 1948, which surprised Alvah and me, and then
about the girl he was in love with who lived in California: "I
had a hardon for her three thousand miles long, goodness!"

Then Coughlin said "Tell 'em about Great Plum, Japh."

Instantly Japhy said "Great Plum Zen Master was asked
what the great meaning of Buddhism was, and he said rush
flowers, willow catkins, bamboo needles, linen thread, in other
words hang on boy, the ecstasy's general, 's what he means, ecstasy of the mind, the world is nothing but mind and what is the
mind? The mind is nothing but the world, goddammit. Then
Horse Ancestor said 'This mind is Buddha.' He also said 'No

mind is Buddha.' Then finally talking about Great Plum his boy, 'The plum is ripe.' "

"Well that's pretty interesting," said Alvah, "but Où sont les neiges d'antan?"

"Well I sort of agree with you because the trouble is these people saw the flowers like they were in a dream but dammit-all the world is *real* Smith and Goldbook and everybody carries on like it was a dream, shit, like they were themselves dreams or dots. Pain or love or danger makes you real again, ain't that right Ray like when you were scared on that ledge?"

"Everything was real, okay."

"That's why frontiersmen are always heroes and were always my real heroes and will always be. They're constantly on the alert in the realness which might as well be real as unreal, what difference does it make, Diamond Sutra says 'Make no formed conceptions about the realness of existence nor about the unrealness of existence,' or words like that. Handcuffs will get soft and billy clubs will topple over, let's go on being free anyhow."

"The President of the United States suddenly grows cross-eyed and floats away!" I yell.

"And anchovies will turn to dust!" yells Coughlin.

"The Golden Gate is creaking with sunset rust," says Alvah.

"And anchovies will turn to dust," insists Coughlin.

"Give me another slug of that jug. How! Ho! Hoo!" Japhy leaping up: "I've been reading Whitman, know what he says, *Cheer up slaves, and horrify foreign despots*, he means that's the attitude for the Bard, the Zen Lunacy bard of old desert paths, see the whole thing is a world full of rucksack wanderers, Dharma Bums refusing to subscribe to the general demand that they consume production and therefore have to work for the privilege of consuming, all that crap they didn't really want anyway such as refrigerators, TV sets, cars, at least new fancy cars, certain hair oils and deodorants and general junk you finally always see a week later in the garbage anyway, all of them imprisoned in a system of work, produce, consume, work, produce, consume, I see a vision of a great rucksack revolution thousands or even millions of young Americans wandering around with rucksacks, going up to mountains to pray, making children laugh and old men glad, making young girls happy and old girls happier, all of 'em Zen Lunatics who go about writing poems that happen to appear in their heads for no reason and also by being kind and also by strange unexpected acts keep giving visions of eternal freedom to everybody and to all living creatures, that's what I like about you Goldbook and Smith, you two guys from the East Coast which I thought was dead."

"We thought the *West* Coast was dead!"

"You've really brought a fresh wind around here. Why, do you realize the Jurassic pure granite of Sierra Nevada with the straggling high conifers of the last ice age and lakes we just saw is one of the greatest expressions on this earth, just think how truly great and wise America will be, with all this energy and exuberance and space focused into the Dharma."

"Oh"—Alvah—"balls on that old tired Dharma."

"Ho! What we need is a floating zendo, where an old Bodhisattva can wander from place to place and always be sure to find a spot to sleep in among friends and cook up mush."

" 'The boys was glad, and rested up for more, and Jack cooked mush, in honor of the door,' " I recited.

"What's that?"

"That's a poem I wrote. 'The boys was sittin in a grove of trees, listenin to Buddy explain the keys. Boys, sez he, the Dharma is a door . . . Let's see . . . Boys, I say the keys, cause there's lotsa keys, but only one door, one hive for the bees. So listen to me, and I'll try to tell all, as I heard it long ago, in the Pure Land Hall. For you good boys, with winesoaked teeth, that can't understand these words on a heath, I'll make it simpler, like a bottle of wine, and a good woodfire, under stars divine. Now listen to me, and when you have learned the Dharma of the Buddhas of old and yearned, to sit down with the truth, under a lonesome tree, in Yuma Arizony, or anywhere you be, don't thank me for tellin, what was told me, this is the wheel I'm a-turnin, this is the reason I be: Mind is the Maker, for no reason at all, for all this creation, created to fall.' "

"Ah but that's too pessimistic and like dream gucky," says Alvah, "though the rhyme is pure like Melville."

"We'll have a floatin zendo for Buddy's winesoaked boys to

come and lay up in and learn to drink tea like Ray did, learn to meditate like you should Alvah, and I'll be a head monk of a zendo with a big jar full of crickets."

"Crickets?"

"Yessir, that's what, a series of monasteries for fellows to go and monastate and meditate in, we can have groups of shacks up in the Sierras or the High Cascades or even Ray says down in Mexico and have big wild gangs of pure holy men getting together to drink and talk and pray, think of the waves of salvation can flow out of nights like that, and finally have women, too, wives, small huts with religious families, like the old days of the Puritans. Who's to say the cops of America and the Republicans and Democrats are gonna tell everybody what to do?"

"What's the crickets?"

"Big jar full of crickets, give me another drink Coughlin, about one tenth of an inch long with huge white antennae and hatch 'em myself, little sentient beings in a bottle that sing real good when they grow up. I wanta swim in rivers and drink goatmilk and talk with priests and just read Chinese books and amble around the valleys talking to farmers and their children. We've got to have mind-collecting weeks in our zendos where your mind tries to fly off like a Tinker Toy and like a good soldier you put it back together with your eyes closed except of course the whole thing is wrong. D'y'hear my latest poem Goldbook?"

"No what?"

"Mother of children, sister, daughter of sick old man, virgin your blouse is torn, hungry and barelegged, I'm hungry too, take these poems."

"Fine, fine."

"I wanta bicycle in hot afternoon heat, wear Pakistan leather sandals, shout in high voice at Zen monk buddies standing in thin hemp summer robes and stubble heads, wanta live in golden pavilion temples, drink beer, say goodbye, go Yokahama big buzz Asia port full of vassals and vessels, hope, work around, come back, go, go to Japan, come back to U.S.A., read Hakuin, grit my teeth and discipline myself all the time while getting nowhere and thereby learn . . . learn that my body and everything gets tired and ill and droopy and so find out all about Hakuyu."

"Who's Hakuyu?"

"His name meant White Obscurity, his name meant he who lived in the hills back of Northern-White-Water where I'm gonna go hiking, by God, it must be full of steep piney gorges and bamboo valleys and little cliffs."

"I'll go with you!" (me).

"I wanta read about Hakuin, who went to see this old man who lived in a cave, slept with deer and ate chestnuts and the old man told him to quit meditating and quit thinking about koans, as Ray says, and instead learn how to go to sleep and wake up, said, when you go to sleep you should put your legs together and take deep breaths and then concentrate your mind on a spot one and a half inches below your navel until you feel it get like a ball of power and then start breathing from your heels clear up and concentrate saying to yourself that that center just here is Amida's Pure Land, the center of the mind, and when you wake up you should start by consciously breathing and stretching a little and thinking the same thoughts, see, the rest of the time."

"That's what I like, see," says Alvah, "these actual signposts to something. What else?"

"The rest of the time he said don't bother about thinkin about nothin, just eat well, not too much, and sleep good, and old Hakuyu said he was three hundred friggin years old just then and figured he was good for five hundred more, by Gawd which makes me think he must still be up there if he's anybody at all."

"Or the sheepherder kicked his dog!" puts in Coughlin.

"I bet I can find that cave in Japan."

"You can't live in this world but there's nowhere else to go," laughs Coughlin.

"What's that mean?" I ask.

"It means the chair I sit in is a lion throne and the lion is walking, he roars."

"What's he say?"

"Says, Rahula! Rahula! Face of Glory! Universe chawed and swallowed!"

"Ah balls!" I yell.

"I'm goin to Marin County in a few weeks," said Japhy, "go walk a hunnerd times around Tamalpais and help purify the atmosphere and accustom the local spirits to the sound of sutra. What you think, Alvah?"

"I think it's all lovely hallucination but I love it sorta."

"Alvah, trouble with you is you don't do plenty night zazen especially when it's cold out, that's best, besides you should get married and have halfbreed babies, manuscripts, homespun blankets and mother's milk on your happy ragged mat floor like this one. Get yourself a hut house not too far from town, live cheap, go ball in the bars once in a while, write and rumble in the hills and learn how to saw boards and talk to grandmas you damn fool, carry loads of wood for them, clap your hands at shrines, get supernatural favors, take flower-arrangement lessons and grow chrysanthemums by the door, and get married for krissakes, get a friendly smart sensitive human-being gal who don't give a shit for martinis every night and all that dumb white machinery in the kitchen."

"Oh," says Alvah sitting up glad, "and what else?"

"Think of barn swallows and nighthawks filling the fields. Do you know, say Ray, since yesterday I translated another stanza of Han Shan, lissen, 'Cold Mountain is a house, without beams or walls, the six doors left and right are open, the hall is the blue sky, the rooms are vacant and empty, the East wall strikes the west wall, at the center not one thing. Borrowers don't trouble me, in the cold I build a little fire, when I'm hungry I boil up some greens, I've got no use for the kulak with his big barn and pasture . . . he just sets up a prison for himself, once in, he can't get out, think it over, it might happen to you.' "

Then Japhy picked up his guitar and got going on songs; finally I took the guitar and made up a song as I went along plucking on the strings any old way, actually drumming on them with my fingertips, drum drum drum, and sang the song of the Midnight Ghost freight train. "That's about the midnight ghost in California but you know what it made me think of Smith? Hot, very hot, bamboo growing up to forty feet out thar and whipping around in the breeze and hot and a bunch of monks are making a racket on their flutes somewhere and when they recite sutras with a steady Kwakiutl dance drumbeat and riffs on the bells and sticks it's something to hear like a big prehistoric coyote chanting. . . . Things tucked away in all you mad guys like that go back to the days when men married bears and talked to the buffalo by Gawd. Give me another drink. Keep your socks darned, boys, and your boots greased."

But as though that wasn't enough Coughlin says quite calmly crosslegged "Sharpen your pencils, straighten your ties, shine your shoes and button your flies, brush your teeth, comb your hair, sweep the floor, eat blueberry pies, open your eyes . . ."

"Eat blueberry spies is good," says Alvah fingering his lip seriously.

"Remembering all the while that I have tried very hard, but the rhododendron tree is only half enlightened, and ants and bees are communists and trolley cars are bored."

"And little Japanese boys in the F train sing Inky Dinky Parly Voo!" I yell.

"And the mountains live in total ignorance so I don't give up, take off your shoes and put 'em in your pocket. Now I've answered all your questions, too bad, give me a drink, mauvais sujet."

"Don't step on the ballsucker!" I yell drunk.

"Try to do it without stepping on the aardvark," says Coughlin. "Don't be a sucker all your life, dummy up, ya dope. Do you see what I mean? My lion is fed, I sleep at his side."

"Oh," says Alvah, "I wish I could take all this down." And I was amazed, pretty amazed, by the fast wonderful yak yak yak darts in my sleeping brain. We all got dizzy and drunk. It was a mad night. It ended up with Coughlin and me wrestling and making holes in the wall and almost knocking the little cottage down: Alvah was pretty mad the next day. During the wrestling match I practically broke poor Coughlin's leg; myself, I got a bad splinter of wood stuck an inch up into my skin and it didn't come out till almost a year later. Meanwhile, at some point, Morley appeared in the doorway like a ghost carrying two quarts of yogurt and wanting to know if we wanted some. Japhy left at about two a.m. saying he'd come back and get me in the morning for our big day outfitting me with full pack. Everything was fine with the Zen Lunatics, the nut wagon was too far away to hear us. But there was a wisdom in it all, as you'll see if you take a walk some night on a suburban street and pass house after house on both sides of the street each with the lamplight of the living room, shining golden, and inside the little blue square of the television, each living family riveting its attention on probably one show; nobody talking; silence in the yards; dogs barking at you because you pass on human feet instead of on wheels. You'll see what I mean, when it begins to appear like everybody in the world is soon going to be thinking the same way and the Zen Lunatics have long joined dust, laughter on their dust lips. Only one thing I'll say for the people watching television, the millions and millions of the One Eye: they're not hurting anyone while they're sitting in front of that Eye. But neither was Japhy. . . . I see him in future years stalking along with full rucksack, in suburban streets, passing the blue television windows of homes, alone, his thoughts the only thoughts not electrified to the Master Switch. As for me, maybe the answer was in my little Buddy poem that kept on: " 'Who played this cruel joke, on bloke after bloke, packing like a rat, across the desert flat?' asked Montana Slim, gesturing to him, the buddy of the men, in this lion's den. 'Was it God got mad, like the Indian cad, who was only a giver, crooked like the river? Gave you a garden, let it all harden, then comes the flood, and the loss of your blood? Pray tell us, good buddy, and don't make it muddy, who played this trick, on Harry and Dick, and why is so mean, this Eternal Scene, just what's the point, of this whole joint?' " I thought maybe I could find out at last from these Dharma Bums.

14

But I had my own little bangtail ideas and they had nothing to do with the "lunatic" part of all this. I wanted to get me a full pack complete with everything necessary to sleep, shelter, eat, cook, in fact a regular kitchen and bedroom right on my back,

and go off somewhere and find perfect solitude and look into
the perfect emptiness of my mind and be completely neutral
from any and all ideas. I intended to pray, too, as my only activity, pray for all living creatures; I saw it was the only decent
activity left in the world. To be in some riverbottom somewhere, or in a desert, or in mountains, or in some hut in Mexico or shack in Adirondack, and rest and be kind, and do
nothing else, practice what the Chinese call "do-nothing." I
didn't want to have anything to do, really, either with Japhy's
ideas about society (I figured it would be better just to avoid it
altogether, walk around it) or with any of Alvah's ideas about
grasping after life as much as you can because of its sweet sadness and because you would be dead some day.

When Japhy came to get me the following morning I had all
this in mind. He and I and Alvah drove to Oakland in Morley's car and went first to some Goodwill stores and Salvation
Army stores to buy various flannel shirts (at fifty cents a
crack) and undershirts. We were all hung-up on colored undershirts, just a minute after walking across the street in the
clean morning sun Japhy'd said, "You know, the earth is a
fresh planet, why worry about anything?" (which is true) now
we were foraging with bemused countenances among all
kinds of dusty old bins filled with the washed and mended
shirts of all the old bums in the Skid Row universe. I bought
socks, one pair of long woolen Scotch socks that go way up
over your knees, which would be useful enough on a cold
night meditating in the frost. And I bought a nice little canvas
jacket with zipper for ninety cents.

Then we drove to the huge Army Navy store in Oakland and
went way in the back where sleeping bags were hanging from
hooks and all kinds of equipment, including Morley's famous
air mattress, water cans, flashlights, tents, rifles, canteens, rubber boots, incredible doodas for hunters and fishermen, out of
which Japhy and I found a lot of useful little things for bhikkus.
He bought an aluminum pot holder and made me a gift of it; it
never burns you, being aluminum, and you just pluck your
pots right out of a campfire with it. He selected an excellent

duck-down used sleeping bag for me, zipping it open and ex-
amining the inside. Then a brand new rucksack, of which I was
so proud. "I'll give you my own old sleeping-bag cover," he
said. Then I bought little plastic snow glasses just for the hell of
it, and railroad gloves, new ones. I figured I had good enough
boots back home East, where I was going for Christmas, otherwise I would have bought a pair of Italian mountain boots like
Japhy had.

We drove from the Oakland store to Berkeley again to the
Ski Shop, where, as we walked in and the clerk came over,
Japhy said in his lumberjack voice "Outfittin me friends for
the Apocalypse." And he led me to the back of the store and
picked out a beautiful nylon poncho with hood, which you
put over you and even over your rucksack (making a huge
hunchbacked monk) and which completely protects you from
the rain. It can also be made into a pup tent, and can also be
used as your sleeping mat under the sleeping bag. I bought a
polybdenum bottle, with screw top, which could be used (I
said to myself) to carry honey up to the mountains. But I later
used it as a canteen for wine more than anything else, and
later when I made some money as a canteen for whisky. I also
bought a plastic shaker which came in very handy, just a tablespoon of powdered milk and a little creek water and you
shake yourself up a glass of milk. I bought a whole bunch of
food wraps like Japhy's. I was all outfitted for the Apocalypse
indeed, no joke about that; if an atom bomb should have hit
San Francisco that night all I'd have to do is hike on out of
there, if possible, and with my dried foods all packed tight
and my bedroom and kitchen on my head, no trouble in the
world. The final big purchases were my cookpots, two large
pots fitting into each other, with a handled cover that was
also the frying pan, and tin cups, and small fitted-together
cutlery in aluminum. Japhy made me another present from
his own pack, a regular tablespoon, but he took out his pliers
and twisted the handle up back and said "See, when you
wanta pluck a pot out of a big fire, just go flup." I felt like a
new man.

15

I put on my new flannel shirt and new socks and underwear and my jeans and packed the rucksack tight and slung it on and went to San Francisco that night just to get the feel of walking around the city night with it on my back. I walked down Mission Street singing merrily. I went to Skid Row Third Street to enjoy my favorite fresh doughnuts and coffee and the bums in there were all fascinated and wanted to know if I was going uranium hunting. I didn't want to start making speeches about what I was going to hunt for was infinitely more valuable to mankind in the long run than ore, but let them tell me: "Boy, all you gotta do is go to that Colorady country and take off with your pack there and a nice little Geiger counter and you'll be a millionaire." Everybody in Skid Row wants to be a millionaire.

"Okay boys," I said, "mebbe I'll do that."

"Lotsa uranium up in the Yukon country too."

"And down in Chihuahua," said an old man. "Bet any dough thar's uranium in Chihuahua."

I went out of there and walked around San Francisco with my huge pack, happy. I went over to Rosie's place to see Cody and Rosie. I was amazed to see her, she'd changed so suddenly, she was suddenly skinny and a skeleton and her eyes were huge with terror and popping out of her face. "What's the matter?"

Cody drew me into the other room and didn't want me to talk to her. "She's got like this in the last forty-eight hours," he whispered.

"What's the matter with her?"

"She says she wrote out a list of all our names and all our sins, she says, and then tried to flush them down the toilet where she works, and the long list of paper stuck in the toilet and they had to send for some sanitation character to clean up the mess and she claims he wore a uniform and was a cop and took it with him to the police station and we're all going to be arrested. She's just nuts, that's all." Cody was my old buddy who'd let me live in his attic in San Francisco years ago, an old trusted friend. "And did you see the marks on her arms?"

"Yes." I had seen her arms, which were all cut up.

"She tried to slash her wrists with some old knife that doesn't cut right. I'm worried about her. Will you watch her while I go to work tonight?"

"Oh man—"

"Oh you, oh man, don't be like that. You know what it says in the Bible, 'even unto the least of these . . . ' "

"All right but I was planning on having fun tonight."

"Fun isn't everything. You've got some responsibilities some-times, you know."

I didn't have a chance to show off my new pack in The Place. He drove me to the cafeteria on Van Ness where I got Rosie a bunch of sandwiches with his money and I went back alone and tried to make her eat. She sat in the kitchen staring at me.

"But you don't realize what this means!" she kept saying. "Now they know *everything* about you."

"Who?"

"You."

"Me?"

"You, and Alvah, and Cody, and that Japhy Ryder, all of you, and me. Everybody that hangs around The Place. We're all go-ing to be arrested tomorrow if not sooner." She looked at the door in sheer terror.

"Why'd you try to cut your arms like that? Isn't that a mean thing to do to yourself?"

"Because I don't want to live. I'm telling you there's going to be a big new revolution of police now."

"No, there's going to be a rucksack revolution," I said laugh-ing, not realizing how serious the situation was; in fact Cody and I had no sense, we should have known from her arms how far she wanted to go. "Listen to me," I began, but she wouldn't listen.

"Don't you *realize* what's happening?" she yelled staring at me with big wide sincere eyes trying by crazy telepathy to make me believe that what she was saying was absolutely *true*. She stood there in the kitchen of the little apartment with her skele-tal hands held out in supplicatory explanation, her legs braced, her red hair all frizzly, trembling and shuddering and grabbing her face from time to time.

"It's nothing but bullshit!" I yelled and suddenly I had the feeling I always got when I tried to explain the Dharma to people, Alvah, my mother, my relatives, girl friends, everybody, they never listened, they always wanted me to listen to them, *they* knew, I didn't know anything, I was just a dumb young kid and impractical fool who didn't understand the serious significance of this very important, very real world.

"The police are going to swoop down and arrest us all and not only that but we're all going to be questioned for weeks and weeks and maybe even years till they find out *all* the crimes and sins that have been committed, it's a network, it runs in every direction, finally they'll arrest everybody in North Beach and even everybody in Greenwich Village and then Paris and then finally they'll have *everybody* in jail, you don't know, it's only the beginning." She kept jumping at sounds in the hall, thinking the cops were coming.

"Why don't you listen to me?" I kept pleading, but each time I said that, she hypnotized me with her staring eyes and almost had me for a while believing in what she believed from the sheer weight of her complete dedication to the discriminations her mind was making. "But you're getting these silly convictions and conceptions out of nowhere, don't you realize all this life is just a dream? Why don't you just relax and enjoy God? God is *you*, you fool!"

"Oh, they're going to destroy you, Ray, I can see it, they're going to fetch all the religious squares too and fix them good. It's only begun. It's all tied in with Russia though they won't say it . . . and there's something I heard about the sun's rays and something about what happens while we're all asleep. Oh Ray the world will never be the same!"

"What world? What difference does it make? Please stop, you're scaring me. By God in fact you're not scaring me and I won't listen to another word." I went out, angry, bought some wine and ran into Cowboy and some other musicians and ran back with the gang to watch her. "Have some wine, put some wisdom in your head."

"No, I'm laying off the lush, all that wine you drink is rotgut, it burns your stomach out, it makes your brain dull. I can tell there's something wrong with you, you're not sensitive, you don't *realize* what's going on!"

"Oh come on."

"This is my last night on earth," she added.

The musicians and I drank up all the wine and talked, till about midnight, and Rosie seemed to be all right now, lying on the couch, talking, even laughing a bit, eating her sandwiches and drinking some tea I'd brewed her. The musicians left and I slept on the kitchen floor in my new sleeping bag. But when Cody came home that night and I was gone she went up on the roof while he was asleep and broke the skylight to get jagged bits of glass to cut her wrists, and was sitting there bleeding at dawn when a neighbor saw her and sent for the cops and when the cops ran out on the roof to help her that was it: she saw the great cops who were going to arrest us all and made a run for the roof edge. The young Irish cop made a flying tackle and just got a hold of her bathrobe but she fell out of it and fell naked to the sidewalk six flights below. The musicians, who lived downstairs in a basement pad, and had been up all night talking and playing records, heard the thud. They looked out the basement window and saw that horrible sight. "Man it broke us up, we couldn't make the gig that night." They drew the shades and trembled. Cody was asleep. . . . When I heard about it the next day, when I saw the picture in the paper showing an X on the sidewalk where she had landed, one of my thoughts was: "And if she had only listened to me . . . Was I talking so dumb after all? Are my ideas about what to do so silly and stupid and childlike? Isn't this the time now to start following what I know to be true?"

And that had done it. The following week I packed up and decided to hit the road and get out of that city of ignorance which is the modern city. I said goodbye to Japhy and the others and hopped my freight back down the Coast to L.A. Poor Rosie—she had been absolutely *certain* that the world was real and fear was real and now what was real? "At least," I thought, "she's in Heaven now, and she knows."

16

And that's what I said to myself, "I am now on the road to Heaven." Suddenly it became clear to me that there was a lot of teaching for me to do in my lifetime. As I say, I saw Japhy before I left, we wandered sadly to the Chinatown park, had a dinner in Nam Yuen's, came out, sat in the Sunday morning grass and suddenly here was this group of Negro preachers standing in the grass preaching to desultory groups of uninterested Chinese families letting their kiddies romp in the grass and to bums who cared just a little bit more. A big fat woman like Ma Rainey was standing there with her legs outspread howling out a tremendous sermon in a booming voice that kept breaking from speech to blues-singing music, beautiful, and the reason why this woman, who was such a great preacher, was not preaching in a church was because every now and then she just simply had to go *sploosh* and spit as hard as she could off to the side in the grass, "And I'm tellin you, the Lawd will take care of you if you re-cognize that you have a *new field* . . . *Yes!*"—and sploosh, she turns and spits about ten feet away a great sploosh of spit. "See," I told Japhy, "she couldn't do that in a church, that's her flaw as a preacher as far as the churches are concerned but boy have you ever heard a greater preacher?"

"Yeah," says Japhy. "But I don't like all that Jesus stuff she's talking about."

"What's wrong with Jesus? Didn't Jesus speak of Heaven? Isn't Heaven Buddha's nirvana?"

"According to your own interpretation, Smith."

"Japhy, there were things I wanted to tell Rosie and I felt suppressed by this schism we have about separating Buddhism from Christianity, East from West, what the hell difference does it make? We're all in Heaven now, ain't we?"

"Who said so?"

"Is this nirvana we're in now or ain't it?"

"It's both nirvana and samsara we're in now."

"Words, words, what's in a word? Nirvana by any other name. Besides don't you hear that big old gal calling you and

falling you you've got a *new field*, a new Buddha-field boy?"
Japhy was so pleased he wrinkled his eyes and smiled. "Whole
Buddha-fields in every direction for each one of us, and Rosie
was a flower we let wither."

"Never spoke more truly, Ray."

The big old gal came up to us, too, noticing us, especially me.
She called me darling, in fact. "I kin see from your eyes that
you understand ever word I'm sayin, darling. I want you to
know that I want you to go to Heaven and be happy. I want you
to understand ever word I'm sayin."

"I hear and understand."

Across the street was the new Buddhist temple some young
Chamber of Commerce Chinatown Chinese were trying to
build, by themselves, one night I'd come by there and, drunk,
pitched in with them with a wheelbarrow hauling sand from
outside in, they were young Sinclair Lewis idealistic forward-
looking kids who lived in nice homes but put on jeans to come
down and work on the church, like you might expect in some
Midwest town some Midwest kids with a bright-faced Richard
Nixon leader, the prairie all around. Here in the heart of the
tremendously sophisticated little city called San Francisco Chinatown they were doing the same thing but their church was the
church of Buddha. Strangely Japhy wasn't interested in the
Buddhism of San Francisco Chinatown because it was traditional Buddhism, not the Zen intellectual artistic Buddhism he
loved—but I was trying to make him see that everything was the
same. In the restaurant we'd eaten with chopsticks and enjoyed
it. Now he was saying goodbye to me and I didn't know when
I'd see him again.

Behind the colored woman was a man preacher who kept
rocking with his eyes closed saying "That's right." She said to
us "Bless both you boys for listenin to what I have to say. Remember that we know that all things woik together for good to
them that loves *God*, to them who *are* the called accordin to
His purpose. Romans eight eighteen, younguns. And there's a
new field a-waitin for ya, and be sure you live up to every one
of your obligations. Hear now?"

"Yes, ma'am, be seein ya." I said goodbye to Japhy.

I spent a few days with Cody's family in the hills. He was tremendously sad about Rosie's suicide and kept saying he had to pray for her night and day at this particular crucial moment when because she was a suicide her soul was still flitting around the surface of the earth ready for either purgatory or hell. "We got to get her in purgatory, man." So I helped him pray when I slept on his lawn at night in my new sleeping bag. During the days I took down the little poems his children recited to me, in my little breastpocket notebooks. Yoo hoo . . . yoo hoo . . . I come to you . . . Boo hoo . . . boo hoo . . . I love you . . . Bloo bloo . . . the sky is blue . . . I'm higher than you . . . boo hoo . . . boo hoo. Meanwhile Cody was saying "Don't drink so much of that old wine."

Late Monday afternoon I was at the San Jose yards and waited for the afternoon Zipper due in at four-thirty. It was its day off so I had to wait for the Midnight Ghost due in at seven-thirty. Meanwhile as soon as it got dark I cooked my can of macaroni on a little Indian fire of twigs among the deep dense weeds by the track, and ate. The Ghost was coming in. A friendly switchman told me I'd better not try to get on it as there was a yard bull at the crossing with a big flashlight who would see if anybody was riding away on it and would phone ahead of Watsonville to have them thrown off. "Now that it's winter the boys have been breaking into the sealed trucks and breaking windows and leaving bottles on the floor, wreckin that train."

I sneaked down to the East end of the yard with heavy pack slung on, and caught the Ghost as she was coming out, beyond the bull's crossing, and opened the sleeping bag and took my shoes off, put them under my wrapped-up balled-up coat and slipped in and slept beautiful joyous sleep all the way to Watsonville where I hid by the weeds till highball, got on again, and slept then all night long flying down the unbelievable coast and O Buddha thy moonlight O Christ thy starling on the sea, the sea, Surf, Tangair, Gaviota, the train going eighty miles an hour and me warm as toast in my sleeping bag flying down and going home for Christmas. In fact I only woke up at about seven o'clock in the morning when the train was slowing down into the L.A. yards and the first thing I saw, as I was putting my shoes on and getting my stuff ready to jump off, was a yard worker waving at me and yelling "Welcome to L.A.!"

But I was bound to get out of there fast. The smog was heavy, my eyes were weeping from it, the sun was hot, the air stank, a regular hell is L.A. And I had caught a cold from Cody's kids and had that old California virus and felt miserable now. With the water dripping out of reefer refrigerators I gathered up palmfuls and splashed it in my face and washed and washed my teeth and combed my hair and walked into L.A. to wait until seven-thirty in the evening when I planned to catch the Zipper firstclass freight to Yuma Arizona. It was a horrible day waiting. I drank coffee in Skid Row coffee houses, South Main Street, coffee-and, seventeen cents.

At nightfall I was lurking around waiting for my train. A bum was sitting in a doorway watching me with peculiar interest. I went over to talk to him. He said he was an ex-Marine from Paterson New Jersey and after a while he whipped out a little slip of paper he read sometimes on freight trains. I looked at it. It was a quotation from the Digha Nikaya, the words of Buddha. I smiled; I didn't say anything. He was a great voluble bum, and a bum who didn't drink, he was an idealistic hobo and said "That's all there is to it, that's what I like to do, I'd rather hop freights around the country and cook my food out of tin cans over wood fires, than be rich and have a home or work. I'm satisfied. I used to have arthritis, you know, I was in the hospital for years. I found out a way to cure it and then I hit the road and I been on it ever since."

"How'd you cure your arthritis? I got thrombophlebitis myself."

"You do? Well this'll work for you too. Just stand on your head three minutes a day, or mebbe five minutes. Every morning when I get up whether it's in a riverbottom or right on a train that's rollin along, I put a little mat on the floor and I stand on my head and count to five hundred, that's about three minutes isn't it?" He was very concerned about whether counting up to five hundred made it three minutes. That was strange. I figured he was worried about his arithmetic record in school.

"Yeah, about that."

"Just do that every day and your phlebitis will go away like my arthritis did. I'm forty, you know. Also, before you go to bed at night, have hot milk and honey, I always have a little jar of honey" (he fished one out from his pack) "and I put the milk in a can and the honey, and heat it over the fire, and drink it. Just those two things."

"Okay." I vowed to take his advice because he was Buddha. The result was that in about three months my phlebitis disappeared completely, and didn't show up ever again, which is amazing. In fact since that time I've tried to tell doctors about this but they seem to think I'm crazy. Dharma Bum, Dharma Bum. I'll never forget that intelligent Jewish ex-Marine bum from Paterson New Jersey, whoever he was, with *his* little slip of paper to read in the raw gon night by dripping reefer platforms in the nowhere industrial formations of an America that is still magic America.

At seven-thirty my Zipper came in and was being made up by the switchmen and I hid in the weeds to catch it, hiding partly behind a telephone pole. It pulled out, surprisingly fast I thought, and with my heavy fifty-pound rucksack I ran out and trotted along till I saw an agreeable drawbar and took a hold of it and hauled on and climbed straight to the top of the box to have a good look at the whole train and see where my flatcar'd be. Holy smokes goddamn and all ye falling candles of heaven smash, but as the train picked up tremendous momentum and tore out of that yard I saw it was a bloody no-good eighteen-car sealed sonofabitch and at almost twenty miles an hour it was do or die, get off or hang on to my life at eighty miles per (impossible on a boxcar top) so I had to scramble down the rungs again but first I had to untangle my strap clip from where it had got caught in the catwalk on top so by the time I was hanging from the lowest rung and ready to drop off we were going too fast now. Slinging the rucksack and holding it hard in one hand calmly and madly I stepped off hoping for the best and turned everything away and only staggered a few feet and I was safe on ground.

But now I was three miles into the industrial jungle of L.A. in mad sick sniffling smog night and had to sleep all that night by a wire fence in a ditch by the tracks being waked up all night by rackets of Southern Pacific and Santa Fe switchers bellyaching around, till fog and clear of midnight when I breathed better (thinking and praying in my sack) but then more fog and smog again and horrible damp white cloud of dawn and my bag too hot to sleep in and outside too raw to stand, nothing but horror all night long, except at dawn a little bird blessed me.

The only thing to do was to get out of L.A. According to my friend's instructions I stood on my head, using the wire fence to prevent me from falling over. It made my cold feel a little better. Then I walked to the bus station (through tracks and side streets) and caught a cheap bus twenty-five miles to Riverside. Cops kept looking at me suspiciously with that big bag on my back. Everything was far away from the easy purity of being with Japhy Ryder in that high rock camp under peaceful singing stars.

I7

It took exactly the entire twenty-five miles to get out of the smog of Los Angeles; the sun was clear in Riverside. I exulted to see a beautiful dry riverbottom with white sand and just a trickle river in the middle as we rolled over the bridge into Riverside. I was looking for my first chance to camp out for the night and try out my new ideas. But at the hot bus station a Negro saw me with my pack and came over and said he was part Mohawk and when I told him I was going back up the road to sleep in that riverbottom he said "No sir, you can't do that, cops in this town are the toughest in the state. If they see you down there they'll pull you in. Boy," said he, "I'd like to sleep outdoor too tonight but's against the law."

"This ain't India, is it," I said, sore, and walked off anyway to try it. It was just like the cop in the San Jose yards, even though it was against the law and they were trying to catch you the only thing to do was do it anyway and keep hidden. I laughed thinking what would happen if I was Fuke the Chinese sage of the ninth century who wandered around China constantly ringing his bell. The only alternative to sleeping out, hopping freights, and doing what I wanted, I saw in a vision would be to just sit with a hundred other patients in front of a nice television set in a madhouse, where we could be "supervised." I went into a supermarket and bought some concentrated orange juice and nutted cream cheese and whole wheat bread, which would make nice meals till tomorrow, when I'd hitchhike on through the other side of town. I saw many cop cruising cars and they were looking at me suspiciously: sleek, well-paid cops in brand-new cars with all that expensive radio equipment to see that no bhikku slept in his grove tonight.

At the highway woods I took one good look to make sure no cruisers were up or down the road and I dove right in the woods. It was a lot of dry thickets I had to crash through, I didn't want to bother finding the Boy Scout trail. I aimed straight for the golden sands of the riverbottom I could see up ahead. Over the thickets ran the highway bridge, no one could see me unless they stopped and got out to stare down. Like a criminal I crashed through bright brittle thickets and came out sweating and stomped ankle deep in streams and then when I found a nice opening in a kind of bamboo grove I hesitated to light a fire till dusk when no one'd see my small smoke, and make sure to keep it low embers. I spread my poncho and sleeping bag out on some dry rackety grove-bottom leaves and bamboo splitjoints. Yellow aspens filled the afternoon air with gold smoke and made my eyes quiver. It was a nice spot except for the roar of trucks on the river bridge. My head cold and sinus were bad and I stood on my head five minutes. I laughed. "What would people think if they saw me?" But it wasn't funny, I felt rather sad, in fact real sad, like the night before in that horrible fog wire-fence country in industrial L.A., when in fact I'd cried a little. After all a homeless man has reason to cry, everything in the world is pointed against him.

It got dark. I took my pot and went to get water but had to scramble through so much underbrush that when I got back to my camp most of the water had splashed out. I mixed it in my new plastic shaker with orange-juice concentrate and shook up an ice-cold orange, then I spread nutted cream cheese on the whole wheat bread and ate content. "Tonight," I thought, "I sleep tight and long and pray under the stars for the Lord to bring me to Buddhahood after my Buddhawork is done, amen." And as it was Christmas, I added "Lord bless you all and merry tender Christmas on all your rooftops and I hope angels squat there the night of the big rich real Star, amen." And then I thought, later, lying on my bag smoking, "Everything is possible. I am God, I am Buddha, I am imperfect Ray Smith, all at the same time, I am empty space, I am all things. I have all the time in the world from life to life to do what is to do, to do what is done, to do the timeless doing, infinitely perfect within, why cry, why worry, perfect like mind essence and the minds of banana peels" I added laughing remembering my poetic Zen Lunatic Dharma Bum friends of San Francisco whom I was beginning to miss now. And I added a little prayer for Rosie.

"If she'd lived, and could have come here with me, maybe I could have told her something, made her feel different. Maybe I'd just make love to her and say nothing."

I spent a long time meditating crosslegged, but the truck growl bothered me. Soon the stars came out and my little Indian fire sent up some smoke to them. I slipped in my bag at eleven and slept well, except for the bamboo joints under the leaves that caused me to turn over all night. "Better to sleep in an uncomfortable bed free, than sleep in a comfortable bed unfree." I was making up all kinds of sayings as I went along. I was started on my new life with my new equipment: a regular Don Quixote of tenderness. In the morning I felt exhilarated and meditated first thing and made up a little prayer: "I bless you, all living things, I bless you in the endless past, I bless you in the endless present, I bless you in the endless future, amen."

This little prayer made me feel good and fool good as I packed up my things and took off to the tumbling water that came down from a rock across the highway, delicious spring water to bathe my face in and wash my teeth in and drink. Then I was ready for the three-thousand-mile hitchhike to Rocky Mount North Carolina, where my mother was waiting, probably washing the dishes in her dear pitiful kitchen.

18

The current song at that time was Roy Hamilton singing "Everybody's Got a Home but Me." I kept singing that as I swung along. On the other side of Riverside I got on the highway and got a ride right away from a young couple, to an airfield five miles out of town, and from there a ride from a quiet man almost to Beaumont, California, but five miles short of it on a double-lane speed highway with nobody likely to stop so I hiked on in beautiful sparkling air. At Beaumont I ate hotdogs, hamburgers and a bag of fries and added a big strawberry shake, all among giggling high-school children. Then, the other side of town, I got a ride from a Mexican called Jaimy who said he was the son of the governor of the state of Baja California, Mexico, which I didn't believe and was a wino and had me buy him wine which he only threw up out the window as he drove: a droopy, sad, helpless young man, very sad eyes, very nice, a bit nutty. He was driving clear to Mexicali, a little off my route but good enough and far enough out toward Arizona to suit me.

At Calexico it was Christmas shopping time on Main Street with incredible perfect astonished Mexican beauties who kept getting so much better that when the first ones had re-passed they'd already become capped and thin in my mind, I was standing there looking everywhichaway, eating an ice-cream cone, waiting for Jaimy who said he had an errand and would pick me up again and take me personally into Mexicali, Mexico, to meet his friends. My plan was to have a nice cheap supper in Mexico and then roll on that night. Jaimy didn't show up, of course. I crossed the border by myself and turned sharp right at the gate to avoid the hawker street and went immediately to relieve myself of water in construction dirt but a crazy Mexican watchman with an official uniform thought it was a big infringement and said something and when I said I didn't know (No se) he said "No sabes *police*?"—the nerve of him to call the cops because I peed on his dirt ground. But I did notice afterward and felt sad, that I had watered the spot where he sat to light a small fire nights because there were wood coals piled so I moved up the muddy street feeling meek and truly sorry, with the big pack on my back, as he stared after me with his doleful stare.

I came to a hill and saw great mudflat riverbottoms with stinks and tarns and awful paths with women and burros ambling in the dusk, an old Chinese Mexican beggar caught my eye and we stopped to chat, when I told him I might go Dormiendo sleep in those flats (I was really thinking of a little beyond the flats, in the foothills) he looked horrified and, being a deafmute, he demonstrated that I would be robbed of my pack and killed if I tried it, which I suddenly realized was true. I wasn't in America any more. Either side of the border, either way you slice the boloney, a homeless man was in hot water. Where would I find a quiet grove to meditate in, to live in forever? After the old man tried to tell me his life story by signs I walked away waving and smiling and crossed the flats and narrow board bridge over the yellow water and over to the poor adobe district of Mexicali where the Mexico gaiety as ever charmed me, and I ate a delicious tin bowl of garbanzo soup with pieces of cabeza (head) and cebolla (onion) raw, having cashed a quarter at the border gate for three paper pesos and a big pile of huge pennies. While eating at the little mud street counter I dug the street, the people, the poor bitch dogs, the cantinas, the whores, the music, men goofing in the narrow road wrestling, and across the street an unforgettable beauty parlor (Salon de Belleza) with a bare mirror on a bare wall and bare chairs and one little seventeen-year-old beauty with her hair in pins dreaming at the mirror, but an old plaster bust with periwig beside her, and a big man with a mustache in a Scandinavian ski sweater picking his teeth behind and a little boy at the next mirror chair eating a banana and out on the sidewalk some little children gathered like before a movie house and I thought "Oh all Mexicali on some Saturday afternoon! Thank you O Lord for returning me my zest for life, for Thy ever-recurring forms in Thy Womb of Exuberant Fertility." All my tears weren't in vain. It'll all work out finally.

Then, strolling, I bought a hot doughnut stick, then two oranges from a girl, and re-crossed the bridge in dust of evening and headed for the border gate happy. But here I was stopped by three unpleasant American guards and my whole rucksack was searched sullenly.

"What'd you buy in Mexico?"

"Nothing."

They didn't believe me. They fished around. After fingering my wraps of leftover french fries from Beaumont and raisins and peanuts and carrots, and cans of pork and beans I made sure to have for the road, and half-loaves of whole wheat bread they got disgusted and let me go. It was funny, really; they were expecting a rucksack full of opium from Sinaloa, no doubt, or weed from Mazatlan, or heroin from Panama. Maybe they thought I'd walked all the way from Panama. They couldn't figure me out.

I went to the Greyhound bus station and bought a short ticket to El Centro and the main highway. I figured I'd catch the Arizona Midnight Ghost and be in Yuma that same night and sleep in the Colorado riverbottom, which I'd noticed long ago. But it wound up, in El Centro I went to the yards and angled around and finally talked to a conductor passing the sign to a switch engine: "Where's the Zipper?"

"It don't come through El Centro."

I was surprised at my stupidity.

"Only freight you can catch goes through Mexico, then Yuma, but they'll find you and kick you out and you'll wind up in a Mexican calaboose boy."

"I've had enough of Mexico. Thanks." So I went to the big intersection in town with the cars turning for the eastward run to Yuma and started thumbing. I had no luck for an hour. Suddenly a big truck pulled up to the side; the driver got out and fiddled with his suitcase. "You goin on East?" I asked.

"Soon as I spend a little time in Mexicali. You know anything about Mexico?"

"Lived there for years." He looked me over. He was a good old joe, fat, happy, middlewestern. He liked me.

"How about showin me around Mexicali tonight then I'll drive you to Tucson."

"Great!" We got in the truck and went right back to Mexicali on the road I'd just covered in the bus. But it was worth it to get clear to Tucson. We parked the truck in Calexico, which was quiet now, at eleven, and went over into Mexicali and I took him away from tourist-trap honkytonks and led him to the good old saloons of real Mexico where there were girls at a peso a dance and raw tequila and lots of fun. It was a big night, he danced and enjoyed himself, had his picture taken with a senorita and drank about twenty shots of tequila. Somewhere during the night we hooked up with a colored guy who was some kind of queer but was awfully funny and led us to a whorehouse and then as we were coming out a Mexican cop relieved him of his snapknife.

"That's my third knife this month those bastards stole from me," he said.

In the morning Beaudry (the driver) and I got back to the truck bleary eyes and hungover and he wasted no time and drove right straight to Yuma, not going back to El Centro, but on the excellent no-traffic Highway 98 straight a hundred miles after hitting 80 at Gray Wells. Soon we were in fact coming into Tucson. We'd eaten a slight lunch outside Yuma and now he said he was hungry for a good steak. "Only thing is these truck stops ain't got big enough steaks to suit me."

"Well you just park your truck up one of these Tucson supermarkets on the highway and I'll buy a two-inch thick T-bone and we'll stop in the desert and I'll light a fire and broil you the greatest steak of your life." He didn't really believe it but I did it. Outside the lights of Tucson in a flaming red dusk over the desert, he stopped and I lit a fire with mesquite branches, adding bigger branches and logs later, as it got dark, and when the coals were hot I tried to hold the steak over them with a spit but the spit burned so I just fried the huge steaks in their own fat in my lovely new potpan cover and handed him my jackknife and he went to it and said "Hm, om, wow, that *is* the best steak I ever et."

I'd also bought milk and we had just steak and milk, a great protein feast, squatting there in the sand as highway cars zipped by our little red fire. "Where'd you *learn* to do all these funny things?" he laughed. "And you know I say funny but there's sumpthin so durned sensible about 'em. Here I am killin myself drivin this rig back and forth from Ohio to L.A. and I make more money than you ever had in your whole life as a hobo, but you're the one who enjoys life and not only that but you do it without workin or a whole lot of money. Now who's smart, you or me?" And he had a nice home in Ohio with wife, daughter, Christmas tree, two cars, garage, lawn, lawnmower, but he couldn't enjoy any of it because he really wasn't free. It was sadly true. It didn't mean I was a better man than he was, however, he was a great man and I liked him and he liked me and said "Well I'll tell you, supposin I drive you all the way to Ohio."

"Wow, great! That'll take me just about home! I'm goin south of there to North Carolina."

"I was hesitatin at first on account of them Markell insurance men, see if they catch you ridin with me I'll lose my job."

"Oh hell . . . and ain't that somethin typical."

"It shore is, but I'll tell you sumpthin, after this steak you made for me, even though I paid for it, but you cooked it and here you are washin your dishes in sand, I'll just have to tell them to stick the job up their ass because now you're my friend and I got a right to give my friend a ride."

"Okay," I said, "and I'll pray we don't get stopped by no Markell insurance men."

"Good chance of that because it's Saturday now and we'll be in Springfield Ohio at about dawn Tuesday if I push this rig and it's their weekend off more or less."

And did he ever push that rig! From that desert in Arizona he roared on up to New Mexico, took the cut through Las Cruces up to Alamogordo where the atom bomb was first blasted and where I had a strange vision as we drove along seeing in the clouds above the Alamogordo mountains the words as if imprinted in the sky: "This Is the Impossibility of the Existence of Anything" (which was a strange place for that strange true vision) and then he batted on through the beautiful Atascadero Indian country in the uphills of New Mexico beautiful green valleys and pines and New England–like rolling meadows and then down to Oklahoma (at outside Bowie Arizona we'd had a short nap at dawn, he in the truck, me in my bag in the cold red clay with just stars blazing silence overhead and a distant coyote), in no time at all he was going up through Arkansas and eating it up in one afternoon and then Missouri and St. Louis and finally on Monday night bashing across Illinois and Indiana and into old snowy Ohio with all the cute Christmas lights making my heart joy in the windows of old farms. "Wow," I thought, "all the way from the warm arms of the senoritas of Mexicali to the Christmas snows of Ohio in one fast ride." He had a radio on his dashboard and played it booming all the way, too. We didn't talk much, he just yelled once in a while, telling an anecdote, and had such a loud voice that he actually pierced my eardrum (the left one) and made it hurt, making me jump two feet in my seat. He was great. We had a lot of good meals, too, en route, in various favorite truckstops of his, one in Oklahoma where we had roast pork and yams worthy of my mother's own kitchen, we ate and ate, he was always hungry, in fact so was I, it was winter cold now and Christmas was on the fields and food was good.

In Independence Missouri we made our only stop to sleep in a room, in a hotel at almost five dollars apiece, which was robbery, but he needed the sleep and I couldn't wait in the below-zero truck. When I woke up in the morning, on Monday, I looked out and saw all the eager young men in business suits going to work in insurance offices hoping to be big Harry Trumans some day. By Tuesday dawn he let me off in downtown Springfield Ohio in a deep cold wave and we said goodbye just a little sadly.

I went to a lunchcart, drank tea, figured my budget, went to a hotel and had one good exhausted sleep. Then I bought a bus ticket to Rocky Mount, as it was impossible to hitchhike from Ohio to North Carolina in all that winter mountain country through the Blue Ridge and all. But I got impatient and decided to hitchhike anyway and asked the bus to stop on the outskirts and walked back to the bus station to cash my ticket. They wouldn't give me the money. The upshot of my insane impatience was that I had to wait eight more hours for the next slow bus to Charleston West Virginia. I started hitchhiking out of Springfield figuring to catch the bus in a town farther down, just for fun, and froze my feet and hands standing in dismal country roads in freezing dusk. One good ride took me to a little town and there I just waited around the tiny telegraph office which served as a station, till my bus arrived. Then it was a crowded bus going slowly over the mountains all night long and in the dawn the laborious climb over the Blue Ridge with beautiful timbered country in the snow, then after a whole day of stopping and starting, stopping and starting, down out of the mountains into Mount Airy and finally after ages Raleigh where I transferred to my local bus and instructed the driver to let me off at the country road that wound three miles through the piney woods to my mother's house in Big Easonburg Woods which is a country crossroad outside Rocky Mount.

He let me off, at about eight p.m., and I walked the three miles in silent freezing Carolina road of moon, watching a jet plane overhead, her stream drifting across the face of the moon and bisecting the snow circle. It was beautiful to be back East in the snow at Christmastime, the little lights in occasional farm windows, the quiet woods, the piney barrens so naked and drear, the railroad track that ran off into the gray blue woods toward my dream.

At nine o'clock I was stomping with full pack across my mother's yard and there she was at the white tiled sink in the kitchen, washing her dishes, with a rueful expression waiting for me (I was late), worried I'd never even make it and probably thinking, "Poor Raymond, why does he always have to hitchhike and worry me to death, why isn't he like other men?" And I thought of Japhy as I stood there in the cold yard looking at her: "Why is he so mad about white tiled sinks and 'kitchen machinery' he calls it? People have good hearts whether or not they live like Dharma Bums. Compassion is the heart of Buddhism." Behind the house was a great pine forest where I would spend all that winter and spring meditating under the trees and finding out by myself the truth of all things. I was very happy. I walked around the house and looked at the Christmas tree in the window. A hundred yards down the road the two country stores made a bright warm scene in the otherwise bleak wooded void. I went to the dog house and found old Bob trembling and snorting in the cold. He whimpered glad to see me. I unleashed him and he yipped and leaped around and came into the house with me where I embraced my mother in the warm kitchen and my sister and brother-in-law came out of the parlor and greeted me, and little nephew Lou too, and I was home again.

19

They all wanted me to sleep on the couch in the parlor by the comfortable oil-burning stove but I insisted on making my room (as before) on the back porch with its six windows looking out on the winter barren cottonfield and the pine woods beyond, leaving all the windows open and stretching my good old sleeping bag on the couch there to sleep the pure sleep of winter nights with my head buried inside the smooth nylon duckdown warmth. After they'd gone to bed I put on my jacket and my earmuff cap and railroad gloves and over all that my nylon poncho and strode out in the cottonfield moonlight like a shroudy monk. The ground was covered with moonlit frost. The old cemetery down the road gleamed in the frost. The roofs of nearby farmhouses were like white panels of snow. I went through the cottonfield rows followed by Bob, a big bird dog, and little Sandy who belonged to the Joyners down the road, and a few other stray dogs (all dogs love me) and came to the edge of the forest. In there, the previous spring, I'd worn out a little path going to meditate under a favorite baby pine. The path was still there. My official entrance to the forest was still there, this being two evenly spaced young pines making kind of gate posts. I always bowed there and clasped my hands and thanked Avalokitesvara for the privilege of the wood. Then I went in, led moonwhite Bob direct to my pine, where my old bed of straw was still at the foot of the tree. I arranged my cape and legs and sat to meditate.

The dogs meditated on their paws. We were all absolutely quiet. The entire moony countryside was frosty silent, not even the little tick of rabbits or coons anywhere. An absolute cold blessed silence. Maybe a dog barking five miles away toward

Sandy Cross. Just the faintest, faintest sound of big trucks rolling out the night on 301, about twelve miles away, and of course the distant occasional Diesel baugh of the Atlantic Coast Line passenger and freight trains going north and south to New York and Florida. A blessed night. I immediately fell into a blank thoughtless trance wherein it was again revealed to me "This thinking has stopped" and I sighed because I didn't have to think any more and felt my whole body sink into a blessedness surely to be believed, completely relaxed and at peace with all the ephemeral world of dream and dreamer and the dreaming itself. All kinds of thoughts, too, like "One man practicing kindness in the wilderness is worth all the temples this world pulls" and I reached out and stroked old Bob, who looked at me satisfied. "All living and dying things like these dogs and me coming and going without any duration or self substance, O God, and therefore we can't possibly exist. How strange, how worthy, how good for us! What a horror it would have been if the world was real, because if the world was real, it would be immortal." My nylon poncho protected me from the cold, like a fitted-on tent, and I stayed a long time sitting crosslegged in the winter midnight woods, about an hour. Then I went back to the house, warmed up by the fire in the living room while the others slept, then slipped into my bag on the porch and fell asleep.

The following night was Christmas Eve which I spent with a bottle of wine before the TV enjoying the shows and the midnight mass from Saint Patrick's Cathedral in New York with bishops ministering, and doctrines glistering, and congregations, the priests in their lacy snow vestments before great official altars not half as great as my straw mat beneath a little pine tree I figured. Then at midnight the breathless little parents, my sister and brother-in-law, laying out the presents under the tree and more glorious than all the Gloria in Excelsis Deos of Rome Church and all its attendant bishops. "For after all," I thought, "Augustine was a spade and Francis my idiot brother." My cat Davey suddenly blessed me, sweet cat, with his arrival on my lap. I took out the Bible and read a little Saint Paul by the warm stove and the light of the tree, "Let him become a fool, that he may become wise," and I thought of good dear Japhy and wished he was enjoying the Christmas Eve with me. "Already are ye filled," says Saint Paul, "already are ye become rich. The saints shall judge the world." Then in a burst of beautiful poetry more beautiful than all the poetry readings of all the San Francisco Renaissances of Time: "Meats for the belly, and the belly for meats; but God shall bring to naught both it and them."

"Yep," I thought, "you pay through the nose for shortlived shows. . . ."

That week I was all alone in the house, my mother had to go to New York for a funeral, and the others worked. Every afternoon I went into the piney woods with my dogs, read, studied, meditated, in the warm winter southern sun, and came back and made supper for everybody at dusk. Also, I put up a basket and shot baskets every sundown. At night, after they went to bed, back I went to the woods in starlight or even in rain sometimes with my poncho. The woods received me well. I amused myself writing little Emily Dickinson poems like "Light a fire, fight a liar, what's the difference, in existence?" or "A watermelon seed, produces a need, large and juicy, such autocracy."

"Let there be blowing-out and bliss forevermore," I prayed in the woods at night. I kept making newer and better prayers. And more poems, like when the snow came, "Not oft, the holy snow, so soft, the holy bow," and at one point I wrote "The Four Inevitabilities: 1. Musty Books. 2. Uninteresting Nature. 3. Dull Existence. 4. Blank Nirvana, buy that boy." Or I wrote, on dull afternoons when neither Buddhism nor poetry nor wine nor solitude nor basketball would avail my lazy but earnest flesh, "Nothin to do, Oh poo! Practically blue." One afternoon I watched the ducks in the pig field across the road and it was Sunday, and the hollering preachers were screaming on the Carolina radio and I wrote: "Imagine blessing all living and dying worms in eternity and the ducks that eat 'em . . . there's your Sunday school sermon." In a dream I heard the words, "Pain, 'tis but a concubine's puff." But in Shakespeare it would say, "Ay, by my faith, that bears a frosty sound." Then suddenly one night after supper as I was pacing in the cold windy darkness of the yard I felt tremendously depressed and threw myself right on the ground and cried "I'm gonna die!" because there was nothing else to do in the cold loneliness of this harsh inhospitable earth, and instantly the tender bliss of enlightenment was like milk in my eyelids and I was warm. And I realized that this was the truth Rosie knew now, and all the dead, my dead father and dead brother and dead uncles and cousins and aunts, the truth that is realizable in a dead man's bones and is beyond the Tree of Buddha as well as the Cross of Jesus. *Believe* that the world is an ethereal flower, and ye live. I knew this! I also knew that I was the worst bum in the world. The diamond light was in my eyes.

My cat meowed at the icebox, anxious to see what all the good dear delight was. I fed him.

20

After a while my meditations and studies began to bear fruit. It really started late in January, one frosty night in the woods in the dead silence it seemed I almost heard the words said: "Everything is all right forever and forever and forever." I let out a big Hoo, one o'clock in the morning, the dogs leaped up and exulted. I felt like yelling it to the stars. I clasped my hands and prayed, "O wise and serene spirit of Awakenerhood, everything's all right forever and forever and forever and thank you thank you thank you amen." What'd I care about the tower of ghouls, and sperm and bones and dust, I felt free and therefore I *was* free.

I suddenly felt the desire to write to Warren Coughlin, who was strong in my thoughts now as I recalled his modesty and general silence among the vain screams of myself and Alvah and Japhy: "Yes, Coughlin, it's a shining now-ness and we've done it, carried America like a shining blanket into that brighter nowhere Already."

It began to get warmer in February and the ground began to melt a little and the nights in the woods were milder, my sleeps on the porch more enjoyable. The stars seemed to get wet in the sky, bigger. Under the stars I'd be dozing crosslegged under my tree and in my half-asleep mind I'd be saying "Moab? Who is Moab?" and I'd wake up with a burr in my hand, a cotton burr off one of the dogs. So, awake, I'd make thoughts like "It's all different appearances of the same thing, my drowsiness, the burr, Moab, all one ephemeral dream. All belongs to the same emptiness, glory be!" Then I'd run these words through my mind to train myself: "I am emptiness, I am not different from emptiness, neither is emptiness different from me; indeed, emptiness is me." There'd be a puddle of water with a star shining in it, I'd spit in the puddle, the star would be obliterated, I'd say "That star is real?"

I wasn't exactly unconscious of the fact that I had a good warm fire to return to after these midnight meditations, provided kindly for me by my brother-in-law, who was getting a little sick and tired of my hanging around not working. Once I told him a line from something, about how one grows through suffering, he said: "If you grow through suffering by this time I oughta be as big as the side of the house."

When I'd go to the country store to buy bread and milk the old boys there sitting around among bamboo poles and molasses barrels'd say, "What you do in those woods?"

"Oh I just go in there to study."

"Ain't you kinda old to be a college student?"

"Well I just go in there sometimes and just sleep."

But I'd watch them rambling around the fields all day looking for something to do, so their wives would think they were real busy hardworking men, and they weren't fooling me either. I knew they secretly wanted to go sleep in the woods, or just sit and do nothing in the woods, like I wasn't too ashamed to do. They never bothered me. How could I tell them that my knowing was the knowing that the substance of my bones and their bones and the bones of dead men in the earth of rain at night is the common individual substance that is everlastingly tranquil and blissful? Whether they believed it or not makes no difference, too. One night in my rain cape I sat in a regular downpour and I had a little song to go with the pattering rain on my rubber hood: "Raindrops are ecstasy, raindrops are not different from ecstasy, neither is ecstasy different from raindrops, yea, ecstasy is rain-drops, rain on, O cloud!" So what did I care what the old tobacco-chewing stickwhittlers at the crossroads store had to say about my mortal eccentricity, we all get to be gum in graves anyway. I even got a little drunk with one of the old men one time and we went driving around the country roads and I actually told him how I was sitting out in those woods meditating and he really rather understood and said he would like to try that if he had time, or if he could get up enough nerve, and had a little rueful envy in his voice. Everybody knows everything.

2 1

Spring came after heavy rains that washed everything, brown puddles were everywhere in moist, sere fields. Strong warm winds whipped snow white clouds across the sun and dry air. Golden days with beauteous moon at night, warm, one emboldened frog picking up a croak song at eleven p.m. in "Buddha Creek" where I had established my new straw sitting place under a twisted twin tree by a little opening in the pines and a dry stretch of grass and a tiny brook. There, one day, my nephew little Lou came with me and I took an object from the ground and raised it silently, sitting under the tree, and little Lou facing me asked "What's that?" and I said "That" and made a leveling motion with my hand, saying, "Tathata," repeating, "That . . . It's *that*" and only when I told him it was a pine cone did he make the imaginary judgment of the word "pine cone," for, indeed, as it says in the sutra: "Emptiness is discrimination," and he said "My head jumped out, and my brain went crooked and then my eyes started lookin like cucumbers and my hair'd a cowlick on it and the cowlick licked my chin." Then he said "Why don't I make up a poem?" He wanted to commemorate the moment.

"Okay, but make it up right away, just as you go along."

"Okay . . . 'The pine trees are wavin, the wind is tryin to whisper somethin, the birds are sayin drit-drit-drit, and the hawks are goin hark-hark-hark—' Oho, we're in for danger."

"Why?"

"Hawk—hark hark hark!"

"Then what?"

"Hark! Hark!—Nothin." I puffed on my silent pipe, peace and quiet in my heart.

I called my new grove "Twin Tree Grove," because of the two treetrunks I leaned against, that wound around each other, white spruce shining white in the night and showing me from hundreds of feet away where I was heading, although old Bob whitely showed me the way down the dark path. On that path one night I lost my juju beads Japhy'd given me, but the next day I found them right in the path, figuring, "The Dharma can't be lost, nothing can be lost, on a well-worn path."

There were now early spring mornings with the happy dogs, me forgetting the Path of Buddhism and just being glad; looking around at new little birds not yet summer fat; the dogs yawning and almost swallowing my Dharma; the grass waving, hens chuckling. Spring nights, practicing Dhyana under the cloudy moon. I'd see the truth: "Here, this, is *It*. The world as it is, is Heaven, I'm looking for a Heaven outside what there is, it's only this poor pitiful world that's Heaven. Ah, if I could realize, if I could forget myself and devote my meditations to the freeing, the awakening and the blessedness of all living creatures everywhere I'd realize what there is, *is* ecstasy."

Long afternoons just sitting in the straw until I was tired of "thinking nothing" and just going to sleep and having little flash dreams like the strange one I had once of being up in some kind of gray ghostly attic hauling up suitcases of gray meat my mother is handing up and I'm petulantly complaining: "I won't come down again!" (to do this work of the world). I felt I was a blank being called upon to enjoy the ecstasy of the endless truebody.

Days tumbled on days, I was in my overalls, didn't comb my hair, didn't shave much, consorted only with dogs and cats, I was living the happy life of childhood again. Meanwhile I wrote and got an assignment for the coming summer as a fire lookout for the U.S. Forest Service on Desolation Peak in the High Cascades in Washington state. So I figured to set out for

Japhy's shack in March to be nearer Washington for my summer job.

Sunday afternoons my family would want me to go driving with them but I preferred to stay home alone, and they'd get mad and say "What's the matter with him anyway?" and I'd hear them argue about the futility of my "Buddhism" in the kitchen, then they'd all get in the car and leave and I'd go in the kitchen and sing "The tables are empty, everybody's gone over" to the tune of Frank Sinatra's "You're Learning the Blues." I was as nutty as a fruitcake and happier. Sunday afternoon, then, I'd go to my woods with the dogs and sit and put out my hands palms up and accept handfuls of sun boiling over the palms. "Nirvana is the moving paw," I'd say, seeing the first thing I saw as I opened my eyes from meditation, that being Bob's paw moving in the grass as he dreamed. Then I'd go back to the house on my clear, pure, well-traveled path, waiting for the night when again I'd see the countless Buddhas hiding in the moonlight air.

But my serenity was finally disturbed by a curious argument with my brother-in-law; he began to resent my unshackling Bob the dog and taking him in the woods with me. "I've got too much money invested in that dog to untie him from his chain."

I said "How would you like to be tied to a chain and cry all day like the dog?"

He replied "It doesn't bother *me*" and my sister said "And *I* don't care."

I got so mad I stomped off into the woods, it was a Sunday afternoon, and resolved to sit there without food till midnight and come back and pack my things in the night and leave. But in a few hours my mother was calling me from the back porch to supper, I wouldn't come; finally little Lou came out to my tree and begged me to come back.

I had frogs in the little brook that kept croaking at the oddest times, interrupting my meditations as if by design, once at high noon a frog croaked three times and was silent the rest of the day, as though expounding me the Triple Vehicle. Now my frog croaked once. I felt it was a signal meaning the One Vehicle of Compassion and went back determined to overlook the whole thing, even my pity about the dog. What a sad and bootless dream. In the woods again that night, fingering the juju beads, I went through curious prayers like these: "My pride is hurt, that is emptiness; my business is with the Dharma, that is emptiness; I'm proud of my kindness to animals, that is emptiness; my conception of the chain, that is emptiness; Ananda's pity, even that is emptiness." Perhaps if some old Zen Master had been on the scene, he would have gone out and kicked the dog on his chain to give everybody a sudden shot of awakening. My pain was in getting rid of the conception of people and dogs anyway, and of myself. I was hurting deep inside from the sad business of trying to *deny* what was. In any case it was a tender little drama in the Sunday countryside: "Raymond doesn't want the dog chained." But then suddenly under the tree at night, I had the astonishing idea: "Everything is empty but awake! Things are empty in time and space and mind." I figured it all out and the next day feeling very exhilarated I felt the time had come to explain everything to my family. They laughed more than anything else. "But listen! No! Look! It's simple, let me lay it out as simple and concise as I can. All things are empty, ain't they?"

"Whattayou mean, empty, I'm holding this orange in my hand, ain't I?"

"It's empty, everythin's empty, things come but to go, all things made have to be unmade, and they'll have to be unmade simply *because* they were made!"

Nobody would buy even that.

"You and your Buddha, why don't you stick to the religion you were born with?" my mother and sister said.

"Everything's gone, already gone, already come and gone," I yelled. "Ah," stomping around, coming back, "and things are empty because they appear, don't they, you see them, but they're made up of atoms that can't be measured or weighed or taken hold of, even the dumb scientists know that now, there *isn't* any finding of the farthest atom so-called, things are just empty arrangements of something that seems solid appearing in the space, they ain't either big or small, near or far, true or false, they're ghosts pure and simple."

"Ghostses!" yelled little Lou amazed. He really agreed with me but he was afraid of my insistence on "Ghostses."

"Look," said my brother-in-law, "if things were empty how could I feel this orange, in fact taste it and swallow it, answer me that one."

"Your mind makes out the orange by seeing it, hearing it, touching it, smelling it, tasting it and thinking about it but without this mind, you call it, the orange would not be seen or heard or smelled or tasted or even mentally noticed, it's actually, that orange, depending on your mind to exist! Don't you see that? By itself it's a no-thing, it's really mental, it's seen only of your mind. In other words it's empty and awake."

"Well, if that's so, I still don't care." All enthusiastic I went back to the woods that night and thought, "What does it mean that I am in this endless universe, thinking that I'm a man sitting under the stars on the terrace of the earth, but actually empty and awake throughout the emptiness and awakedness of everything? It means that I'm empty and awake, that I *know* I'm empty, awake, and that there's no difference between me and anything else. In other words it means that I've become the same as everything else. It means I've become a Buddha." I really felt that and believed it and exulted to think what I had to tell Japhy now when I got back to California. "At least *he'll* listen," I pouted. I felt great compassion for the trees because we were the same thing; I petted the dogs who didn't argue with me ever. All dogs love God. They're wiser than their masters. I told that to the dogs, too, they listened to me perking up their ears and licking my face. They didn't care one way or the other as long as I was there. St. Raymond of the Dogs is who I was that year, if no one or nothing else.

Sometimes in the woods I'd just sit and stare at things themselves, trying to divine the secret of existence anyway. I'd stare at the holy yellow long bowing weeds that faced my grass sit-mat of Tathagata Seat of Purity as they pointed in all directions and hairily conversed as the winds dictated Ta Ta Ta, in gossip groups with some lone weeds proud to show off on the side, or sick ones and half-dead falling ones, the whole congregation of living weedhood in the wind suddenly ringing like bells and jumping to get excited and all made of yellow stuff and sticking to the ground and I'd think *This is it*. "Rop rop rop," I'd yell at the weeds, and they'd show windward pointing intelligent reachers to indicate and flail and finagle, some rooted in blossom imagination earth moist perturbation idea that had karmacized their very root-and-stem. . . . It was eerie. I'd fall asleep and dream the words "By this teaching the earth came to an end," and I'd dream of my Ma nodding solemnly with her whole head, umph, and eyes closed. What did I care about all the irking hurts and tedious wronks of the world, the human bones are but vain lines dawdling, the whole universe a blank mold of stars. "I am Bhikku Blank Rat!" I dreamed.

What did I care about the squawk of the little very self which wanders everywhere? I was dealing in outblownness, cut-off-ness, snipped, blownoutness, putoutness, turned-off-ness, nothing-happens-ness, gone-ness, gone-out-ness, the snapped link, nir, link, vana, snap! "The dust of my thoughts collected into a globe," I thought, "in this ageless solitude," I thought, and really smiled, because I was seeing the white light everywhere everything at last.

The warm wind made the pines talk deep one night when I began to experience what is called "Samapatti," which in Sanskrit means Transcendental Visits. I'd got a little drowsy in the mind but was somehow physically wide awake sitting erect under my tree when suddenly I saw flowers, pink worlds of walls of them, salmon pink, in the *Shh* of silent woods (obtaining nirvana is like locating silence) and I saw an ancient vision of Dipankara Buddha who was the Buddha who never said anything, Dipankara as a vast snowy Pyramid Buddha with bushy wild black eyebrows like John L. Lewis and a terrible stare, all in an old location, an ancient snowy field like Alban ("A *new* field!" had yelled the Negro preacherwoman), the whole vision making my hair rise. I remember the strange magic final cry that it evoked in me, whatever it means: *Colyalcolor*. It, the vision, was devoid of any sensation of I being myself, it was pure egolessness, just simply wild ethereal activities devoid of any wrong predicates . . . devoid of effort, devoid of mistake. "Everything's all right," I thought. "Form is emptiness and emptiness is form and we're here forever in one form or another which is empty. What the dead have accomplished, this rich silent hush of the Pure Awakened Land."

I felt like crying out over the woods and rooftops of North Carolina announcing the glorious and simple truth. Then I said "I've got my full rucksack pack and it's spring, I'm going to go southwest to the dry land, to the long lone land of Texas and Chihuahua and the gay streets of Mexico night, music coming out of doors, girls, wine, weed, wild hats, viva! What does it matter? Like the ants that have nothing to do but dig all day, I have nothing to do but do what I want and be kind and remain nevertheless uninfluenced by imaginary judgments and pray for the light." Sitting in my Buddha-arbor, therefore, in that "colyalcolor" wall of flowers pink and red and ivory white, among aviaries of magic transcendent birds recognizing my awakening mind with sweet weird cries (the pathless lark), in the ethereal perfume, mysteriously ancient, the bliss of the Buddha-fields, I saw that my life was a vast glowing empty page and I could do anything I wanted.

A strange thing happened the next day, to illustrate the true power I had gained from these magic visions. My mother had been coughing for five days and her nose was running and now her throat was beginning to hurt so much that her coughs were painful and sounded dangerous to me. I decided to go into a deep trance and hypnotize myself, reminding myself "All is empty and awake," to investigate the cause and cure of my mother's illness. Instantly, in my closed eyes, I saw a vision of a brandy bottle which then I saw to be "Heet" rubbing medicine and on top of that, superimposed like a movie fade-in, I saw a distinct picture of little white flowers, round, with small petals. I instantly got up, it was midnight, my mother was coughing in her bed, and I went and took several bowls of bachelor's buttons my sister had arranged around the house the week before and I set them outside. Then I took some "Heet" out of the medicine cabinet and told my mother to rub it on her neck. The next day her cough was gone. Later on, after I was gone hitch-hiking west, a nurse friend of ours heard the story and said "Yes, it sounds like an allergy to the flowers." During this vision and

this action I knew perfectly clearly that people get sick by utilizing physical opportunities to punish themselves because of their
self-regulating God nature, or Buddha nature, or Allah nature,
or any name you want to give God, and everything worked automatically that way. This was my first and last "miracle" because I was afraid of getting too interested in this and becoming
vain. I was a little scared too, of all the responsibility.

Everybody in the family heard of my vision and what I did
but they didn't seem to think much of it: in fact I didn't, either.
And that was right. I was very rich now, a super myriad tril-
lionaire in Samapatti transcendental graces, because of good
humble karma, maybe because I had pitied the dog and forgiven
men. But I knew now that I was a bliss heir, and that the final
sin, the worst, is righteousness. So I would shut up and just hit
the road and go see Japhy. "Don't let the blues make you bad,"
sings Frank Sinatra. On my final night in the woods, the eve of
my departure by thumb, I heard the word "star-body" concerning how things don't have to be made to disappear but to
awake, to their supremely pure truebody and star-body. I saw
there was nothing to do because nothing ever happened, nothing ever would happen, all things were empty light. So I took
off well fortified, with my pack, kissing my mother goodbye.
She had paid five dollars to have brand new thick rubber soles
with cleats put on the bottom of my old boots and now I was all
set for a summer working in the mountains. Our old country-
store friend, Buddhy Tom, a character in his own right, took
me in his vehicle out to Highway 64 and there we waved goodbye and I started hitching three thousand miles back to California. I would be home again the next Christmas.

22

Meanwhile Japhy was waiting for me in his nice little shack in
Corte Madera California. He was settled in Sean Monahan's
hermitage, a wooden cabin built behind a cypress windrow on
a steep little grassy hill also covered with eucalyptus and pine,
behind Sean's main house. The shack had been built by an old

man to die in, years ago. It was well built. I was invited to go
live there as long as I wanted, rent free. The shack had been
made habitable after years as a wreck, by Sean Monahan's
brother-in-law Whitey Jones, a good young carpenter, who had
put in burlap over the wood walls and a good woodstove and a
kerosene lamp and then never lived in it, having to go to work
out of town. So Japhy'd moved in to finish his studies and live
the good solitary life. If anybody wanted to go see him it was a
steep climb. On the floor were woven grass mats and Japhy said
in a letter "I sit and smoke a pipe and drink tea and hear the
wind beat the slender eucalyptus limbs like whips and the cypress windrow roars." He'd stay there until May 15, his sailing
date for Japan, where he had been invited by an American foun-
dation to stay in a monastery and study under a Master. "Meanwhile," wrote Japhy, "come share a wild man's dark cabin with
wine and weekend girls and good pots of food and woodfire
heat. Monahan will give us grocery bucks to fall a few trees in
his big yard and buck and split 'em out for firewood and I'll
teach you all about logging."

During that winter Japhy had hitchhiked up to his home-
country in the Northwest, up through Portland in snow, farther
up to the blue ice glacier country, finally northern Washington
on the farm of a friend in the Nooksack Valley, a week in a
berrypicker's splitshake cabin, and a few climbs around. The
names like "Nooksack" and "Mount Baker National Forest"
excited in my mind a beautiful crystal vision of snow and ice
and pines in the Far North of my childhood dreams. . . . But I
was standing on the very hot April road of North Carolina
waiting for my first ride, which came very soon from a young
high-school kid who took me to a country town called Nashville,
where I broiled in the sun a half-hour till I got a ride from a tac-
iturn but kindly naval officer who drove me clear to Greenville
South Carolina. After that whole winter and early spring of incredible peace sleeping on my porch and resting in my woods,
the stint of hitchhiking was harder than ever and more like hell
than ever. In Greenville in fact I walked three miles in the burning sun for nothing, lost in the maze of downtown back streets,
looking for a certain highway, and at one point passed a kind of

forge where colored men were all black and sweaty and covered
with coal and I cried "I'm suddenly in hell again!" as I felt the
blast of heat.

But it began to rain on the road and few rides took me into
the rainy night of Georgia, where I rested sitting on my pack
under the overhanging sidewalk roofs of old hardware stores
and drank a half pint of wine. A rainy night, no rides. When the
Greyhound bus came I hailed it down and rode to Gainesville.
In Gainesville I thought I'd sleep by the railroad tracks awhile
but they were about a mile away and just as I thought of sleeping in the yard a local crew came out to switch and saw me, so
I retired to an empty lot by the tracks, but the cop car kept circling around using its spot (had probably heard of me from the
railroad men, probably not) so I gave it up, mosquitoes anyway, and went back to town and stood waiting for a ride in the
bright lights by the luncheonettes of downtown, the cops seeing
me plainly and therefore not searching for me or worrying
about me.

But no ride, and dawn coming, so I slept in a four-dollar
room in a hotel and showered and rested well. But what feelings of homelessness and bleak, again, as the Christmas trip
East. All I had to be really proud of were my fine new thick-
soled workshoes and my full pack. In the morning, after breakfast in a dismal Georgia restaurant with revolving fans on the
ceiling and *mucho* flies, I went out on the broiling highway and
got a ride from a truckdriver to Flowery Branch Georgia, then a
few spot rides on through Atlanta to the other side at another
small town called Stonewall, where I was picked up by a big fat
Southerner with a broadbrimmed hat who reeked of whisky
and kept telling jokes and turning to look at me to see if I
laughed, meanwhile sending the car spurting into the soft
shoulders and leaving big clouds of dust behind us, so that long
before he reached his destination I begged off and said I wanted
to get off to eat.

"Heck, boy, I'll eat with ya 'n' drive ya on." He was drunk
and he drove very fast.

"Well I gotta go to the toilet," I said trailing off my voice.
The experience had bugged me so I decided, "The hell with

hitchhiking. I've got enough money to take a bus to El Paso and from there I'll hop Southern Pacific freights and be ten times safer." Besides the thought of being all the way out in El Paso Texas in that dry Southwest of clear blue skies and endless desert land to sleep in, no cops, made up my mind. I was anxious to get out of the South, out of chaingang Georgia.

The bus came at four o'clock and we were at Birmingham Alabama in the middle of the night, where I waited on a bench for my next bus trying to sleep on my arms on my rucksack but kept waking up to see the pale ghosts of American bus stations wandering around: in fact one woman streamed by like a wisp of smoke, I was definitely certain *she* didn't exist for sure. On her face the phantasmal belief in what she was doing . . . On my face, for that matter, too. After Birmingham it was soon Louisiana and then East Texas oilfields, then Dallas, then a long day's ride in a bus crowded with servicemen across the long immense waste of Texas, to the ends of it, El Paso, arriving at midnight, by now I being so exhausted all I wanted to do was sleep. But I didn't go to a hotel, I had to watch my money now, and instead I just hauled my pack to my back and walked straight for the railroad yards to stretch my bag out somewhere behind the tracks. It was then, that night, that I realized the dream that had made me want to buy the pack.

It was a beautiful night and the most beautiful sleep of my life. First I went to the yards and walked through, warily, behind lines of boxcars, and got out to the west end of the yard but kept going because suddenly I saw in the dark there was indeed a lot of desert land out there. I could see rocks, dry bushes, imminent mountains of them faintly in the starlight. "Why hang around viaducts and tracks," I reasoned, "when all I gotta do is exert a little footwork and I'll be safe out of reach of all yard cops and bums too for that matter." I just kept walking along the mainline track for a few miles and soon I was in the open desert mountain country. My thick boots walked well on the ties and rocks. It was now about one a.m., I longed to sleep off the long trip from Carolina. Finally I saw a mountain to the right I liked, after passing a long valley with many lights in it distinctly a penitentiary or prison. "Stay away from that yard, son," I thought. I went up a dry arroyo and in the starlight the sand and rocks were white. I climbed and climbed.

Suddenly I was exhilarated to realize I was completely alone and safe and nobody was going to wake me up all night long. What an amazing revelation! And I had everything I needed right on my back; I'd put fresh bus-station water in my polybdenum bottle before leaving. I climbed up the arroyo, so finally when I turned and looked back I could see all of Mexico, all of Chihuahua, the entire sand-glittering desert of it, under a late sinking moon that was huge and bright just over the Chihuahua mountains. The Southern Pacific rails run right along parallel to the Rio Grande River outside of El Paso, so from where I was, on the American side, I could see right down to the river itself separating the two borders. The sand in the arroyo was soft as silk. I spread my sleeping bag on it and took off my shoes and had a slug of water and lit my pipe and crossed my legs and felt glad. Not a sound; it was still winter in the desert. Far off, just the sound of the yards where they were kicking cuts of cars with a great *splowm* waking up all El Paso, but not me. All I had for companionship was that moon of Chihuahua sinking lower and lower as I looked, losing its white light and getting more and more yellow butter, yet when I turned in to sleep it was bright as a lamp in my face and I had to turn my face away to sleep. In keeping with my naming of little spots with personal names, I called this spot "Apache Gulch." I slept well indeed.

In the morning I discovered a rattlesnake trail in the sand but that might have been from the summer before. There were very few bootmarks, and those were hunters' boots. The sky was flawlessly blue in the morning, the sun hot, plenty of little dry wood to light a breakfast fire. I had cans of pork and beans in my spacious pack. I had a royal breakfast. The problem now was water, though, as I drank it all and the sun was hot and I got thirsty. I climbed up the arroyo investigating it further and came to the end of it, a solid wall of rock, and at the foot of it even deeper softer sand than that of the night before. I decided to camp there that night, after a pleasant day spent in old Juárez enjoying the church and streets and food of Mexico. For a while I contemplated leaving my pack hidden among rocks

but the chances were slim yet possible that some old hobo or
hunter would come along and find it so I hauled it on my back
and went down the arroyo to the rails again and walked back
three miles into El Paso and left the pack in a twenty-five-cent
locker in the railroad station. Then I walked through the city
and out to the border gate and crossed over for two pennies.

It turned out to be an insane day, starting sanely enough in
the church of Mary Guadaloupe and a saunter in the Indian
Markets and resting on park benches among the gay childlike
Mexicans but later the bars and a few too many to drink,
yelling at old mustachioed Mexican peons "Todas las granas de
arena del desierto de Chihuahua son vacuidad!" and finally I
ran into a bunch of evil Mexican Apaches of some kind who
took me to their dripping stone pad and turned me on by candlelight and invited their friends and it was all a lot of shadowy
heads by candlelight and smoke. In fact I got sick of it and remembered my perfect white sand gulch and the place where I
would sleep tonight and I excused myself. But they didn't want
me to leave. One of them stole a few things from my bag of
purchases but I didn't care. One of the Mexican boys was queer
and had fallen in love with me and wanted to go to California
with me. It was night now in Juárez; all the nightclubs were
wailing away. We went for a short beer in one nightclub which
was exclusively Negro soldiers sprawling around with senoritas
in their laps, a mad bar, with rock and roll on the jukebox, a
regular paradise. The Mexican kid wanted me to go down alleys and go "sst" and tell American boys that I knew where
there were some girls. "Then I bring them to my room, sst, *no
gurls!*" said the Mexican kid. The only place I could shake him
was at the border gate. We waved goodbye. But it was the evil
city and I had my virtuous desert waiting for me.

I walked anxiously over the border and through El Paso and
out to the railroad station, got my bag out, heaved a big sigh,
and went right on down those three miles to the arroyo, which
was easy to re-recognize in the moonlight, and on up, my feet
making that lonely thwap thwap of Japhy's boots and I realized
I had indeed learned from Japhy how to cast off the evils of the
world and the city and find my true pure soul, just as long as

I had a decent pack on my back. I got back to my camp and spread the sleeping bag and thanked the Lord for all He was giving me. Now the remembrance of the whole long evil afternoon smoking marijuana with slant-hatted Mexicans in a musty candlelit room was like a dream, a bad dream, like one of my dreams on the straw mat at Buddha Creek North Carolina. I meditated and prayed. There just isn't any kind of night's sleep in the world that can compare with the night's sleep you get in the desert winter night, providing you're good and warm in a duck-down bag. The silence is so intense that you can hear your own blood roar in your ears but louder than that by far is the mysterious roar which I always identify with the roaring of the diamond of wisdom, the mysterious roar of silence itself, which is a great Shhhh reminding you of something you've seemed to have forgotten in the stress of your days since birth. I wished I could explain it to those I loved, to my mother, to Japhy, but there just weren't any words to describe the nothingness and purity of it. "Is there a certain and definite teaching to be given to all living creatures?" was the question probably asked to beetlebrowed snowy Dipankara, and his answer was the roaring silence of the diamond.

23

In the morning I had to get the show on the road or never get to my protective shack in California. I had about eight dollars left of the cash I'd brought with me. I went down to the highway and started to hitchhike, hoping for quick luck. A salesman gave me a ride. He said "Three hundred and sixty days out of the year we get bright sunshine here in El Paso and my wife just bought a clothes dryer!" He took me to Las Cruces New Mexico and there I walked through the little town, following the highway, and came out on the other end and saw a big beautiful old tree and decided to just lay my pack down and rest anyhow. "Since it's a dream already ended, then I'm already in California, then I've already decided to rest under that tree at noon," which I did, on my back, even napping awhile, pleasantly.

Then I got up and walked over the railroad bridge, and just then a man saw me and said "How would you like to earn two dollars an hour helping me move a piano?" I needed the money and said okay. We left my rucksack in his moving storage room and went off in his little truck, to a home in the outskirts of Las Cruces, where a lot of nice middleclass people were chatting on the porch, and the man and I got out of the truck with the handtruck and the pads and got the piano out, also a lot of other furniture, then transported it to their new house and got that in and that was that. Two hours, he gave me four dollars and I went into a truckstop diner and had a royal meal and was all set for that afternoon and night. Just then a car stopped, driven by a big Texan with a sombrero, with a poor Mexican couple, young, in the back seat, the girl carrying an infant, and he offered me a ride all the way to Los Angeles for ten dollars.

I said "I'll give you all I can, which is only four."

"Well goddammit come on anyway." He talked and talked and drove all night straight through Arizona and the California desert and left me off in Los Angeles a stone's throw from my railroad yards at nine o'clock in the morning, and the only disaster was the poor little Mexican wife had spilled some baby food on my rucksack on the floor of the car and I wiped it off angrily. But they had been nice people. In fact, driving through Arizona I'd explained a little Buddhism to them, specifically karma, reincarnation, and they all seemed pleased to hear the news.

"You mean other chance to come back and try again?" asked the poor little Mexican, who was all bandaged from a fight in Juárez the night before.

"That's what they say."

"Well goddammit next time I be born I hope I ain't who I am now."

And the big Texan, if anybody better get another chance it was him: his stories all night long were about how he slugged so-and-so for such-and-such, from what he said he had knocked enough men out to form Coxie's army of avenged phantasmal grievers crawling on to Texas-land. But I noticed he was more of a big fibber than anything else and didn't believe half his stories and stopped listening at midnight. Now, nine a.m. in L.A.,

I walked to the railroad yards, had a cheap breakfast of dough-nuts and coffee in a bar sitting at the counter chatting with the Italian bartender who wanted to know what I was doing with the big rucksack, then I went to the yards and sat in the grass watching them make up the trains.

Proud of myself because I used to be a brakeman I made the mistake of wandering around the yards with my rucksack on my back chatting with the switchmen, asking about the next lo-cal, and suddenly here came a great big young cop with a gun swinging in a holster on his hip, all done up like on TV the Sheriff of Cochise and Wyatt Earp, and giving me a steely look through dark glasses orders me out of the yards. So he watches me as I go over the overpass to the highway, standing there arms akimbo. Mad, I went back down the highway and jumped over the railroad fence and lay flat in the grass awhile. Then I sat up and chewed grass, keeping low however, and waited. Soon I heard a highball blow and I knew what train was ready and I climbed over cars to my train and jumped on it as it was pulling out and rode right out of the L.A. yards lying on my back with a grass stem in my mouth right under the unforgiv-ing gaze of my policeman, who was now arms akimbo for a dif-ferent reason. In fact he scratched his head.

The local went to Santa Barbara where again I went to the beach, had a swim and some food over a fine woodfire in the sand, and came back to the yards with plenty of time to catch the Midnight Ghost. The Midnight Ghost is composed mainly of flatcars with truck trailers lashed on them by steel cables. The huge wheels of the trucks are encased in woodblocks. Since I always lay my head down right by those woodblocks, it would be goodbye Ray if there ever was a crash. I figured if it was my destiny to die on the Midnight Ghost it was my destiny. I fig-ured God had work for me to do yet. The Ghost came right on schedule and I got on a flatcar, under a truck, spread out my bag, stuck my shoes under my balled coat for a pillow, and re-laxed and sighed. Zoom, we were gone. And now I know why the bums call it the Midnight Ghost, because, exhausted, against all better judgment, I fell fast asleep and only woke up under the glare of the yard office lights in San Luis Obispo, a very dangerous situation, the train had stopped just in the wrong way. But there wasn't a soul in sight around the yard office, it was mid of night, besides just then, as I woke up from a perfect dreamless sleep the highball was going baugh baugh up front and we were already pulling out, exactly like ghosts. And I didn't wake up then till almost San Francisco in the morning. I had a dollar left and Gary was waiting for me at the shack. The whole trip had been as swift and enlightening as a dream, and I was back.

24

If the Dharma Bums ever get lay brothers in America who live normal lives with wives and children and homes, they will be like Sean Monahan.

Sean was a young carpenter who lived in an old wooden house far up a country road from the huddled cottages of Corte Madera, drove an old jalopy, personally added a porch to the back of the house to make a nursery for later children, and had selected a wife who agreed with him in every detail about how to live the joyous life in America without much money. Sean liked to take days off from his job to just go up the hill to the shack, which belonged to the property he rented, and spend a day of meditation and study of the Buddhist sutras and just brewing himself pots of tea and taking naps. His wife was Christine, a beautiful young honey-haired girl, her hair falling way down over her shoulders, who wandered around the house and yard barefooted hanging up wash and baking her own brown bread and cookies. She was an expert on making food out of nothing. The year before Japhy had made them an anniversary gift which was a huge ten-pound bag of flour, and they were very glad to receive it. Sean in fact was just an old-time patriarch; though he was only twenty-two he wore a full beard like Saint Joseph and in it you could see his pearly white teeth smiling and his young blue eyes twinkling. They already had two little daughters, who also wandered around barefooted in the house and yard and were brought up to take care of themselves. Sean's house had woven straw mats on the floor and there too when you came in you were required to take off your shoes. He had lots of books and the only extravagance was a hi-fi set so he could play his fine collection of Indian records and Flamenco records and jazz. He even had Chinese and Japanese records. The dining table was a low, black-lacquered, Japanese style table, and to eat in Sean's house you not only had to be in your socks but sitting on mats at this table, any way you could. Christine was a great one for delicious soups and fresh biscuits.

When I arrived there at noon that day, getting off the Greyhound bus and walking up the tar road about a mile, Christine immediately had me sit down to hot soup and hot bread with butter. She was a gentle creature. "Sean and Japhy are both working on his job at Sausalito. They'll be home about five."

"I'll go up to the shack and look at it and wait up there this afternoon."

"Well, you can stay down here and play records."

"Well, I'll get out of your way."

"You won't be in my way, all I'm gonna do is hang out the wash and bake some bread for tonight and mend a few things." With a wife like that Sean, working only desultorily at carpentry, had managed to put a few thousand dollars in the bank. And like a patriarch of old Sean was generous, he always insisted on feeding you and if twelve people were in the house he'd lay out a big dinner (a simple dinner but delicious) on a board outside in the yard, and always a big jug of red wine. It was a communal arrangement, though, he was strict about that: we'd make collections for the wine, and if people came, as they all did, for a long weekend, they were expected to bring food or food money. Then at night under the trees and the stars of his yard, with everybody well fed and drinking red wine, Sean would take out his guitar and sing folksongs. Whenever I got tired of it I'd climb my hill and go sleep.

After eating lunch and talking awhile to Christine, I went up the hill. It climbed steeply right at the back door. Huge ponderosas and other pines, and in the property adjoining Sean's a dreamy horse meadow with wild flowers and two beautiful bays with their sleek necks bent to the butterfat grass in the hot sun. "Boy, this is going to be greater than North Carolina woods!" I thought, starting up. In the slope of grass was where Sean and Japhy had felled three huge eucalyptus trees and had already bucked them (sawed whole logs) with a chain saw. Now the block was set and I could see where they had begun to split the logs with wedges and sledgehammers and doublebitted axes. The little trail up the hill went so steeply that you almost had to lean over and walk like a monkey. It followed a long cypress row that had been planted by the old man who had died on the hill a few years ago. This prevented the cold foggy winds from the ocean from blasting across the property unhindered. There were three stages to the climb: Sean's backyard; then a fence, forming a little pure deer park where I actually saw deer one night, five of them, resting (the whole area was a game refuge); then the final fence and the top grassy hill with its sudden hollow on the right where the shack was barely visible under trees and flowery bushes. Behind the shack, a well-built affair actually of three big rooms but only one room occupied by Japhy, was plenty of good firewood and a saw horse and axes and an outdoor privy with no roof, just a hole in the ground and a board. It was like the first morning in the world in fine yard, with the sun streaming in through the dense sea of leaves, and birds and butterflies jumping around, warm, sweet, the smell of higher-hill heathers and flowers beyond the barbed-wire fence which led to the very top of the mountain and showed you a vista of all the Marin County area. I went inside the shack.

On the door was a board with Chinese inscriptions on it; I never did find out what it meant: probably "Mara stay away" (Mara the Tempter). Inside I saw the beautiful simplicity of Japhy's way of living, neat, sensible, strangely rich without a cent having been spent on the decoration. Old clay jars exploded with bouquets of flowers picked around the yard. His books were neatly stacked in orange crates. The floor was covered with inexpensive straw mats. The walls, as I say, were lined with burlap, which is one of the finest wallpapers you can have, very attractive and nice smelling. Japhy's mat was covered with a thin mattress and a Paisley shawl over that, and at the head of it, neatly rolled for the day, his sleeping bag. Behind burlap drapes in a closet his rucksack and junk were put away from sight. From the burlap wall hung beautiful prints of old Chinese silk paintings and maps of Marin County and northwest Washington and various poems he'd written and just stuck on a nail for anybody to read. The latest poem superimposed over others on the nail said: "It started just now with a humming-bird stopping over the porch two yards away through the open door, then gone, it stopped me studying and I saw the old red-wood post leaning in clod ground, tangled in a huge bush of yellow flowers higher than my head, through which I push every time I come inside. The shadow network of the sunshine through its vines. White-crowned sparrows make tremendous singings in the trees, the rooster down the valley crows and crows. Sean Monahan outside, behind my back, reads the Dia-mond Sutra in the sun. Yesterday I read Migration of Birds. The Golden Plover and the Arctic Tern, today that big abstraction's at my door, for juncoes and the robins soon will leave, and nest-ing scrabblers will pick up all the string, and soon in hazy day of April summer heat across the hill, without a book I'll know, the seabirds'll chase spring north along the coast: they'll be nesting in Alaska in six weeks." And it was signed: "Japheth M. Ryder, Cypress-Cabin, 18:III: 56."

I didn't want to disturb anything in the house till he got back from work so I went out and lay down in the tall green grass in the sun and waited all afternoon, dreaming. But then I realized, "I might as well make a nice supper for Japhy" and I went down the hill again and down the road to the store and bought beans, saltpork, various groceries and came back and lit a fire in the woodstove and boiled up a good pot of New England beans, with molasses and onions. I was amazed at the way Japhy stored his food: just on a shelf by the woodstove: two onions, an orange, a bag of wheat germ, cans of curry powder, rice, mysterious pieces of dried Chinese seaweed, a bottle of soy sauce (to make his mysterious Chinese dishes). His salt and pepper was all neatly wrapped up in little plastic wrappers bound with elastic. There wasn't anything in the world Japhy would ever waste, or lose. Now I was introducing into his kitchen all the big substantial pork-and-beans of the world, maybe he wouldn't like it. He also had a big chunk of Christine's fine brown bread, and his bread knife was a dagger simply stuck into the board.

It got dark and I waited in the yard, letting the pot of beans keep warm on the fire. I chopped some wood and added it to the pile behind the stove. The fog began to blow in from the Pacific, the trees bowed deeply and roared. From the top of the hill you could see nothing but trees, trees, a roaring sea of trees. It was paradise. As it got cold I went inside and stoked up the fire, singing, and closed the windows. The windows were simply removable opaque plastic pieces that had been cleverly carpentered by Whitey Jones, Christine's brother, they let in light but you couldn't see anything outdoors and they cut off the cold wind. Soon it was warm in the cozy cabin. By and by I heard a "Hoo" out in the roaring sea of fog trees and it was Japhy coming back.

I went out to greet him. He was coming across the tall final grass, weary from the day's work, clomping along in his boots, his coat over his back. "Well, Smith, here you are."

"I cooked up a nice pot of beans for you."

"You did?" He was tremendously grateful. "Boy, what a relief to come home from work and don't have to cook up a meal yourself. I'm starved." He pitched right into the beans with bread and hot coffee I made in a pan on the stove, just French style brewing coffee stirred with a spoon. We had a great supper and then lit up our pipes and talked with the fire roaring. "Ray, you're going to have a great summer up on that Desolation Peak. I'll tell you all about it."

"I'm gonna have a great spring right here in this shack."

"Durn right, first thing we do this weekend is invite some nice new girls I know, Psyche and Polly Whitmore, though wait a minute, hmm. I can't invite both of them they both love me and'll be jealous. Anyway we'll have big parties every weekend, starting downstairs at Sean's and ending up here. And I'm not workin tomorrow so we'll cut some firewood for Sean. That's all he wants you to do. Though, if you wanta work on that job of ours in Sausalito next week, you can make ten bucks a day."

"Fine . . . that'll buy a lotta pork and beans and wine."

Japhy pulled out a fine brush drawing of a mountain. "Here's your mountain that'll loom over you, Hozomeen. I drew it myself two summers ago from Crater Peak. In nineteen-fifty-two I first went into that Skagit country, hitched from Frisco to Seattle and then in, with a beard just started and a bare shaved head—"

"Bare shaved head! Why?"

"To be like a bhikku, you know what it says in the sutras."

"But what did people think about you hitchhiking around with a bare shaved head?"

"They thought I was crazy, but everybody that gave me a ride I'd spin 'em the Dharmy, boy, and leave 'em enlightened."

"I shoulda done a bit of that myself hitchin out here just now. . . . I gotta tell you about my arroyo in the desert mountains."

"Wait a minute, so they put me on Crater Mountain lookout but the snow was so deep in the high country that year I worked trail for a month first in Granite Creek gorge, you'll see all those places, and then with a string of mules we made it the final seven miles of winding Tibetan rocktrail above timber line over snowfields to the final jagged pinnacles, and then climbed the cliffs in a snowstorm and I opened my cabin and cooked my first dinner while the wind howled and the ice grew on two walls in the wind. Boy, wait'll you get up there. That year my friend Jack Joseph was on Desolation, where you'll be."

"What a name, Desolation, oo, wow, ugh, wait . . ."

"He was the first lookout to go up, I got him on my radio first off and he welcomed me to the community of lookouts. Later I contacted other mountains, see they give you a two-way radio, it's almost a ritual all the lookouts chat and talk about bears they've seen or sometimes ask instructions for how to bake muffins on a woodstove and so on, and there we all were in a high world talking on a net of wireless across hundreds of miles of wilderness. It's a primitive area, where you're going boy. From my cabin I could see the lamps of Desolation after dark, Jack Joseph reading his geology books and in the day we flashed by mirror to align our firefinder transits, accurate to the compass."

"Gee, how'll I ever learn all that, I'm just a simple poet bum."

"Oh you'll learn, the magnetic pole, the pole star and the northern lights. Every night Jack Joseph and I talked: one day he got a swarm of ladybugs on the lookout that covered the roof and filled up his water cistern, another day he went for a walk along the ridge and stepped right on a sleeping bear."

"Oho, I thought *this* place was wild."

"This is nothin . . . and when the lightning storm came by, closer and closer, he called to finally say he was going off the air because the storm was too close to leave his radio on, he disappeared from sound and then sight as the black clouds swept over and the lightning danced on his hill. But as the summer passed Desolation got dry and flowery and Blakey lambs and he wandered the cliffs and I was on Crater Mountain in my jockstrap and boots hunting out ptarmigan nests out of curiosity, climbing and pooking about, gettin bit by bees. . . . Desolation's way up there, Ray, six thousand feet or so up looking into Canada and the Chelan highlands, the wilds of the Pickett range, and mountains like Challenger, Terror, Fury, Despair and the name of your own ridge is Starvation Ridge and the up-country of the Boston Peak and Buckner Peak range to the south thousands of miles of mountains, deer, bear, conies, hawks, trout, chipmunks. It'll be great for you Ray."

"I look forward to it okay. I bet no bee bites me."

Then he took out his books and read awhile, and I read too, both of us with separate oil lamps banked low, a quiet evening at home as the foggy wind roared in the trees outside and across the valley a mournful mule heehawed in one of the most tremendously heartbroken cries I've ever heard. "When that mule weeps like that," says Japhy, "I feel like praying for all sentient beings." Then for a while he meditated motionless in the full lotus position on his mat and then said "Well, time for bed." But now I wanted to tell him all the things I'd discovered that winter meditating in the woods. "Ah, it's just a lot of words," he said, sadly, surprising me. "I don't wanta hear all your word descriptions of words words words you made up all winter, man I wanta be enlightened by actions." Japhy had changed since the year before, too. He no longer had his goatee, which had re-

moved the funny merry little look of his face but left him looking gaunt and rocky faced. Also he'd cut his hair in a close crew
cut and looked Germanic and stern and above all sad. There
seemed to be some kind of disappointment in his face now, and
certainly in his soul, he wouldn't listen to my eager explana-
tions that everything was all right forever and forever and forever. Suddenly he said "I'm gonna get married, soon, I think,
I'm gettin tired of battin around like this."

"But I thought you'd discovered the Zen ideal of poverty and
freedom."

"Aw maybe I'm gettin tired of all that. After I come back
from the monastery in Japan I'll probably have my fill of it anyhow. Maybe I'll be rich and work and make a lot of money and
live in a big house." But a minute later: "And who wants to en-
slave himself to a lot of all that, though? I dunno, Smith, I'm
just depressed and everything you're saying just depresses me
further. My sister's back in town you know."

"Who's that?"

"That's Rhoda, my sister, I grew up with her in the woods in
Oregon. She's gonna marry this rich jerk from Chicago, a real
square. My father's having trouble with his sister, too, my Aunt
Noss. She's an old bitch from way back."

"You shouldn't have cut off your goatee, you used to look
like a happy little sage."

"Well I ain't happy little sage no mo' and I'm tired." He was
exhausted from a long hard day's work. We decided to go to
sleep and forget it. In fact we were a bit sad and sore at each
other. During the day I had discovered a spot by a wild rosebush in the yard where I planned to lay out my sleeping bag. I'd
covered it a foot deep with fresh pulled grass. Now, with my
flashlight and my bottle of cold water from the sink tap, I went
out there and rolled into a beautiful night's rest under the sighing trees, meditating awhile first. I couldn't meditate indoors
any more like Japhy had just done, after all that winter in the
woods of night I had to hear the little sounds of animals and
birds and feel the cold sighing earth under me before I could
rightly get to feel a kinship with all living things as being empty
and awake and saved already. I prayed for Japhy: it looked like

he was changing for the worse. At dawn a little rain pattered on my sleeping bag and I put my poncho over me instead of under me, cursing, and slept on. At seven in the morning the sun was out and the butterflies were in the roses by my head and a hummingbird did a jet dive right down at me, whistling, and darted away happily. But I was mistaken about Japhy changing. It was one of the greatest mornings in our lives. There he was standing in the doorway of the shack with a big frying pan in his hand banging on it and chanting "Buddham saranam gocchami . . . Dhammam saranam gocchami . . . Sangham saranam gocchami" and yelling "Come on, boy, your pancakes are ready! Come and get it! Bang bang bang" and the orange sun was pouring in through the pines and everything was fine again, in fact Japhy had contemplated that night and decided I was right about hewing to the good old Dharma.

25

Japhy had cooked up some good buckwheat pancakes and we had Log Cabin syrup to go with them and a little butter. I asked him what the "Gocchami" chant meant. "That's the chant they give out for the three meals in Buddhist monasteries in Japan. It means, Buddham Saranam Gocchami, I take refuge in the Buddha, Sangham, I take refuge in the church, Dhammam, I take refuge in the Dharma, the truth. Tomorrow morning I'll make you another nice breakfast, slumgullion, d'yever eat good old-fashioned slumgullion boy, 'taint nothin but scrambled eggs and potatoes all scrambled up together."

"It's a lumberjack meal?"

"There ain't no such thing as *lumber*jack, that must be a Back East expression. Up here we call 'em loggers. Come on eat up your pancakes and we'll go down and split logs and I'll show you how to handle a doublebitted ax." He took the ax out and sharpened it and showed me how to sharpen it. "And don't ever use this ax on a piece of wood that's on the ground, you'll hit rocks and blunt it, always have a log or sumpthin for a block."

I went out to the privy and, coming back, wishing to surprise

Japhy with a Zen trick I threw the roll of toilet paper through
the open window and he let out a big Samurai Warrior roar and
appeared on the windowsill in his boots and shorts with a dagger in his hand and jumped fifteen feet down into the loggy
yard. It was crazy. We started downhill feeling high. All the logs
that had been bucked had more or less of a crack in them,
where you more or less inserted the heavy iron wedge, and then,
raising a five-pound sledgehammer over your head, standing
way back so's not to hit your own ankle, you brought it down
konko on the wedge and split the log clean in half. Then you'd
sit the half-logs up on a block-log and let down with the doublebitted ax, a long beautiful ax, sharp as a razor, and fawap,
you had quarter-logs. Then you set up a quarter-log and brought
down to an eighth. He showed me how to swing the sledge and
the ax, not too hard, but when he got mad himself I noticed he
swung the ax as hard as he could, roaring his famous cry, or
cursing. Pretty soon I had the knack and was going along as
though I'd been doing it all my life.

Christine came out in the yard to watch us and called "I'll
have some nice lunch for ya."

"Okay." Japhy and Christine were like brother and sister.

We split a lot of logs. It was great swinging down the sledgehammer, all the weight clank on top of a wedge and feeling that
log give, if not the first time the second time. The smell of sawdust, pine trees, the breeze blowing over the placid mountains
from the sea, the meadowlarks singing, the butterflies in the
grass, it was perfect. Then we went in and ate a good lunch of
hotdogs and rice and soup and red wine and Christine's fresh
biscuits and sat there crosslegged and barefoot thumbing
through Sean's vast library.

"Did ya hear about the disciple who asked the Zen master
'What is the Buddha?' "

"No, what?"

" 'The Buddha is a dried piece of turd,' was the answer. The
disciple experienced sudden enlightenment."

"Simple shit," I said.

"Do you know what sudden enlightenment is? One disciple
came to a Master and answered his koan and the Master hit

him with a stick and knocked him off the veranda ten feet into a mud puddle. The disciple got up and laughed. He later became a Master himself. 'Twasn't by words he was enlightened, but by that great healthy push off the porch."

"All wallowing in mud to prove the crystal truth of compassion," I thought, I wasn't about to start advertising my "words" out loud any more to Japhy.

"Woo!" he yelled throwing a flower at my head. "Do you know how Kasyapa became the First Patriarch? The Buddha was about to start expounding a sutra and twelve hundred and fifty bhikkus were waiting with their garments arranged and their feet crossed, and all the Buddha did was raise a flower. Everybody was perturbed. The Buddha didn't say nothin. Only Kasyapa smiled. That was how the Buddha selected Kasyapa. That's known as the flower sermon, boy."

I went in the kitchen and got a banana and came out and said, "Well, I'll tell you what nirvana is."

"What?"

I ate the banana and threw the peel away and said nothing. "That's the banana sermon."

"Hoo!" yelled Japhy. "D'I ever tell you about Coyote Old Man and how him and Silver Fox started the world by stomping in empty space till a little ground appeared beneath their feet? Look at this picture, by the way. This is the famous Bulls." It was an ancient Chinese cartoon showing first a young boy going out into the wilderness with a small staff and pack, like an American Nat Wills tramp of 1905, and in later panels he discovers an ox, tries to tame it, tries to ride it, finally does tame it and ride it but then abandons the ox and just sits in the moonlight meditating, finally you see him coming down from the mountain of enlightenment and then suddenly the next panel shows absolutely nothing at all, followed by a panel showing blossoms in a tree, then the last picture you see the young boy is a big fat old laughing wizard with a huge bag on his back and he's going into the city to get drunk with the butchers, enlightened, and another new young boy is going up to the mountain with a little pack and staff.

"It goes on and on, the disciples and the Masters go through the same thing, first they have to find and tame the ox of their mind essence, and then abandon that, then finally they attain to nothing, as represented by this empty panel, then having attained nothing they attain everything which is springtime blossoms in the trees so they end up coming down to the city to get drunk with the butchers like Li Po." That was a very wise cartoon, it reminded me of my own experience, trying to tame my mind in the woods, then realizing it was all empty and awake and I didn't have to do anything, and now I was getting drunk with the butcher Japhy. We played records and lounged around smoking then went out and cut more wood.

Then as it got cool late afternoon we went up to the shack and washed and dressed up for the big Saturday night party. During the day Japhy went up and down the hill at least ten times to make phone calls and see Christine and get bread and bring up sheets for his girl that night (when he had a girl he put out clean sheets on his thin mattress on the straw mats, a ritual). But I just sat around in the grass doing nothing, or writing haikus, or watching the old vulture circling the hill. "Must be something dead around here," I figured.

Japhy said "Why do you sit on your ass all day?"

"I practice do-nothing."

"What's the difference? Burn it, my Buddhism is activity," said Japhy rushing off down the hill again. Then I could hear him sawing wood and whistling in the distance. He couldn't stop jiggling for a minute. His meditations were regular things, by the clock, he'd meditated first thing waking in the morning then he had his mid-afternoon meditation, only about three minutes long, then before going to bed and that was that. But I just ambled and dreamed around. We were two strange dissimilar monks on the same path. I took a shovel, however, and leveled the ground near the rosebush where my bed of grass was: it was a little too slanty for comfort: I fixed it just right and that night I slept well after the big wine party.

The big party was wild. Japhy had a girl called Polly Whitmore come out to see him, a beautiful brunette with a Spanish hairdo and dark eyes, a regular raving beauty actually, a mountainclimber too. She'd just been divorced and lived alone

in Millbrae. And Christine's brother Whitey Jones brought his
fiancée Patsy. And of course Sean came home from work and
cleaned up for the party. Another guy came out for the weekend, big blond Bud Diefendorf who worked as the janitor in
the Buddhist Association to earn his rent and attend classes
free, a big mild pipesmoking Buddha with all kinds of strange
ideas. I liked Bud, he was intelligent, and I liked the fact that
he had started out as a physicist at the University of Chicago
then gone from that to philosophy and finally now to philosophy's dreadful murderer, Buddha. He said "I had a dream one
time that I was sitting under a tree picking on a lute and
singing 'I ain't got no name.' I was the no-name bhikku." It
was so pleasing to meet so many Buddhists after that harsh
road hitchhiking.

Sean was a strange mystical Buddhist with a mind full of su-
perstitions and premonitions. "I believe in devils," he said.

"Well," I said, stroking his little daughter's hair, "all little
children know that everybody goes to Heaven" to which he as-
sented tenderly with a sad nod of his bearded skull. He was
very kind. He kept saying "Aye" all the time, which went with
his old boat that was anchored out in the bay and kept being
scuttled by storms and we had to row out and bail it out in the
cold gray fog. Just a little old wreck of a boat about twelve feet
long, with no cabin to speak of, nothing but a ragged hull floating in the water around a rusty anchor. Whitey Jones, Christine's brother, was a sweet young kid of twenty who never said
anything and just smiled and took ribbings without complaint.
For instance the party finally got pretty wild and the three couples took all their clothes off and danced a kind of quaint innocent polka all hand-in-hand around the parlor, as the kiddies
slept in their cribs. This didn't disturb Bud and me at all, we
went right on smoking our pipes and discussing Buddhism in
the corner, in fact that was best because we didn't have girls of
our own. And those were three well stacked nymphs dancing
there. But Japhy and Sean dragged Patsy into the bedroom and
pretended to be trying to make her, to bug Whitey, who blushed
all red, stark naked, and there were wrestlings and laughs all
around the house. Bud and I were sitting there crosslegged with

naked dancing girls in front of us and laughed to realize that it
was a mighty familiar occasion.

"Seems like in some previous lifetime, Ray," said Bud, "you
and I were monks in some monastery in Tibet where the girls
danced for us before yabyum."

"Yeh, and we were the old monks who weren't interested in
sex any more but Sean and Japhy and Whitey were the young
monks and were still full of the fire of evil and still had a lot to
learn." Every now and then Bud and I looked at all that flesh
and licked our lips in secret. But most of the time, actually, during these naked revels, I just kept my eyes closed and listened to
the music: I was really sincerely keeping lust out of my mind by
main force and gritting of my teeth. And the best way was to
keep my eyes closed. In spite of the nakedness and all it was really a gentle little home party and everybody began yawning for
time for bed. Whitey went off with Patsy, Japhy went up the
hill with Polly and took her to his fresh sheets, and I unrolled
my sleeping bag by the rosebush and slept. Bud had brought his
own sleeping bag and rolled out on Sean's straw mat floor.

In the morning Bud came up and lit his pipe and sat in the
grass chatting to me as I rubbed my eyes to waking. During the
day, Sunday, all kinds of other people came calling on the Mon-
ahans and half of them came up the hill to see the pretty shack
and the two crazy famous bhikkus Japhy and Ray. Among
them were Princess, Alvah, and Warren Coughlin. Sean spread
out a board in the yard and put out a royal table of wine and
hamburgers and pickles and lit a big bonfire and took out his
two guitars and it was really a magnificent kind of way to live
in Sunny California, I realized, with all this fine Dharma con-
nected with it, and mountainclimbing, all of them had rucksacks and sleeping bags and some of them were going hiking
that next day on the Marin County trails, which are beautiful.
So the party was divided into three parts all the time: those
in the living room listening to the hi-fi or thumbing through
books, those in the yard eating and listening to the guitar music,
and those on the hilltop in the shack brewing pots of tea and
sitting crosslegged discussing poetry and things and the Dharma
or wandering around in the high meadow to go see the children

fly kites or old ladies ride by on horseback. Every weekend was the same mild picnic, a regular classical scene of angels and dolls having a kind flowery time in the void like the void in the cartoon of the Bulls, the blossom branch.

Bud and I sat on the hill watching kites. "That kite won't go high enough, it hasn't got a long enough tail," I said.

Bud said, "Say, that's great, that reminds me of my main problem in my meditations. The reason why I can't get really high into nirvana is because my tail isn't long enough." He puffed and pondered seriously over this. He was the most serious guy in the world. He pondered it all night and the next morning said "Last night I saw myself as a fish swimming through the void of the sea, going left and right in the water without knowing the meaning of left and right, but because of my fin I did so, that is, my kite tail, so I'm a Buddhafish and my fin is my wisdom."

"That was pretty infinyte, that kyte," says I.

Throughout all these parties I always stole off for a nap under the eucalyptus trees, instead of by my rosebush, which was all hot sun all day; in the shade of the trees I rested well. One afternoon as I just gazed at the topmost branches of those immensely tall trees I began to notice that the uppermost twigs and leaves were lyrical happy dancers glad that they had been apportioned the top, with all that rumbling experience of the whole tree swaying beneath them making their dance, their every jiggle, a huge and communal and mysterious necessity dance, and so just floating up there in the void dancing the meaning of the tree. I noticed how the leaves almost looked human the way they bowed and then leaped up and then swayed lyrically side to side. It was a crazy vision in my mind but beautiful. Another time under those trees I dreamt I saw a purple throne all covered with gold, some kind of Eternity Pope or Patriarch in it, and Rosie somewhere, and at that moment Cody was in the shack yakking to some guys and it seemed that he was to the left of this vision as some kind of Archangel, and when I opened my eyes I saw it was only the sun against my eyelids. And as I say, that hummingbird, a beautiful little blue hummingbird no bigger than a dragonfly, kept making a whistling jet dive at me, definitely saying hello to me, every day, usually in the morning, and I always yelled back at him a greeting. Finally he began to hover in the open window of the shack, buzzing there with his furious wings, looking at me beadily, then, flash, he was gone. That California humming guy . . .

Though sometimes I was afraid he would drive right into my head with his long beaker like a hatpin. There was also an old rat scrambling in the cellar under the shack and it was a good thing to keep the door closed at night. My other great friends were the ants, a colony of them that wanted to come in the shack and find the honey ("Calling all ants, calling all ants, come and get your ho-ney!" sang a little boy one day in the shack), so I went out to their anthill and made a trail of honey leading them into the back garden, and they were at that new vein of joy for a week. I even got down on my knees and talked to the ants. There were beautiful flowers all around the shack, red, purple, pink, white, we kept making bouquets but the prettiest of all was the one Japhy made of just pine cones and a sprig of pine needles. It had that simple look that characterized all his life. He'd come barging into the shack with his saw and see me sitting there and say "Why did you sit around all day?"

"I am the Buddha known as the Quitter."

Then it would be when Japhy's face would crease up in that funny littleboy laugh of his, like a Chinese boy laughing, crow's tracks appearing on each side of his eyes and his long mouth cracking open. He was so pleased with me sometimes.

Everybody loved Japhy, the girls Polly and Princess and even married Christine were all madly in love with him and they were all secretly jealous of Japhy's favorite doll Psyche, who came the following weekend real cute in jeans and a little white collar falling over her black turtleneck sweater and a tender little body and face. Japhy had told me he was a bit in love with her himself. But he had a hard time convincing her to make love he had to get her drunk, once she got drinking she couldn't stop. That weekend she came Japhy made slumgullion for all the three of us in the shack then we borrowed Sean's jalopy and drove about a hundred miles up the seacoast to an isolated beach where we picked mussels right off the washed rocks of the sea and smoked them in a big woodfire covered with sea-weed. We had wine and bread and cheese and Psyche spent the whole day lying on her stomach in her jeans and sweater, saying nothing. But once she looked up with her little blue eyes and said "How oral you are, Smith, you're always eating and drinking."

"I am Buddha Empty-Eat," I said.

"Ain't she cute?" said Japhy.

"Psyche," I said, "this world is the movie of what everything is, it is one movie, made of the same stuff throughout, belonging to nobody, which is what everything is."

"Ah boloney."

We ran around the beach. At one point Japhy and Psyche were hiking up ahead on the beach and I was walking alone whistling Stan Getz's "Stella" and a couple of beautiful girls up front with their boyfriends heard me and one girl turned and said "Swing." There were natural caves on that beach where Japhy had once brought big parties of people and had organized naked bonfire dances.

Then the weekdays would come again and the parties were over and Japhy and I would sweep out the shack, wee dried bums dusting small temples. I still had a little left of my grant from last fall, in traveler's checks, and I took one and went to the supermarket down on the highway and bought flour, oatmeal, sugar, molasses, honey, salt, pepper, onions, rice, dried milk, bread, beans, black-eyed peas, potatoes, carrots, cabbage, lettuce, coffee, big wood matches for our woodstove and came staggering back up the hill with all that and a half-gallon of red port. Japhy's neat little spare foodshelf was suddenly loaded with too much food. "What we gonna do with all this? We'll have to feed all the bhikkus." In due time we had more bhikkus than we could handle: poor drunken Joe Mahoney, a friend of mine from the year before, would come out and sleep for three days and recuperate for another crack at North Beach and The Place. I'd bring him his breakfast in bed. On weekends sometimes there'd be twelve guys in the shack all arguing and yakking and I'd take some yellow corn meal and mix it with chopped onions and salt and water and pour out little johnnycake tablespoons in the hot frying pan (with oil) and provide the whole gang with delicious hots to go with their tea. In the Chinese Book of Changes a year ago I had tossed a couple of pennies to see what the prediction of my fortune was and it had come out, "You will feed others." In fact I was always standing over a hot stove.

"What does it mean that those trees and mountains out there are not magic but real?" I'd yell, pointing outdoors.

"What?" they'd say.

"It means that those trees and mountains out there are not magic but real."

"Yeah?"

Then I'd say, "What does it mean that those trees and mountains aren't real at all, just magic?"

"Oh come on."

"It means that those trees and mountains aren't real at all, just magic."

"Well which is it, goddammit!"

"What does it mean that you ask, well which is it goddammit?" I yelled.

"Well what?"

"It means that you ask well which is it goddammit."

"Oh go bury your head in your sleeping bag, bring me a cup of that hot coffee." I was always boiling big pots of coffee on the stove.

"Oh cut it out," yelled Warren Coughlin. "The chariot will wear down!"

One afternoon I was sitting with some children in the grass and they asked me "Why is the sky blue?"

"Because the sky is blue."

"I wanta know *why* the sky is blue."

"The sky is blue because you wanta know why the sky is blue."

"Blue blue you," they said.

There were also some little kids who came around throwing rocks on our shack roof, thinking it was abandoned. One afternoon, at the time when Japhy and I had a little jet-black cat, they came sneaking to the door to look in. Just as they were about to open the door I opened it, with the black cat in my arms, and said in a low voice "I am the ghost."

They gulped and looked at me and believed me and said "Yeah." Pretty soon they were over the other side of the hill. They never came around throwing rocks again. They thought I was a witch for sure.

26

Plans were being made for Japhy's big farewell party a few days before his boat sailed for Japan. He was scheduled to leave on a Japanese freighter. It was going to be the biggest party of all time, spilling out of Sean's hi-fi living room right out into the bonfire yard and up the hill and even over it. Japhy and I had had our fill of parties and were not looking forward to it too happily. But everybody was going to be there: all his girls, including Psyche, and the poet Cacoethes, and Coughlin, and Alvah, and Princess and her new boyfriend, and even the director of the Buddhist Association Arthur Whane and his wife and sons, and even Japhy's father, and of course Bud, and unspecified couples from everywhere who would come with wine and food and guitars. Japhy said "I'm gettin sick and tired of these parties. How about you and me taking off for the Marin trails after the party, it'll go on for days, we'll just bring our packs and take off for Potrero Meadows camp or Laurel Dell."

"Good."

Meanwhile, suddenly one afternoon Japhy's sister Rhoda appeared on the scene with her fiancé. She was going to be married in Japhy's father's house in Mill Valley, big reception and all. Japhy and I were sitting around in the shack in a drowsy afternoon and suddenly she was in the door, slim and blond and pretty, with her well-dressed Chicago fiancé, a very handsome man. "Hoo!" yelled Japhy jumping up and kissing her in a big passionate embrace, which she returned wholeheartedly. And the way they talked!

"Well is your husband gonna be a good bang?"

"He damn well is, I picked him out real careful, ya grunge-jumper!"

"He'd better be or you'll have to call on me!"

Then to show off Japhy started a woodfire and said "Here's what we do up in that real country up north," and dumped too much kerosene into the fire but ran away from the stove and waited like a mischievous little boy and *broom!* the stove let out a deep rumbling explosion way inside that I could feel the shock of clear across the room. He'd almost done it that time. Then he said to her poor fiancé "Well you know any good positions for honeymoon night?" The poor guy had just come back from being a serviceman in Burma and tried to talk about Burma but couldn't get a word in edgewise. Japhy was mad as hell and really jealous. He was invited to the fancy reception and he said "Can I show up nekkid?"

"Anything you want, but come."

"I can just see it now, the punchbowl and all the ladies in their lawn hats and the hi-fi playing hearts and flowers organ music and everybody wipin their eyes cause the bride is so beautiful. What you wanta get all involved in the middle class for, Rhoda?"

She said "Ah I don't care, I wanta start living." Her fiancé had a lot of money. Actually he was a nice guy and I felt sorry for him having to smile through all this.

After they left Japhy said "She won't stay with him more than six months. Rhoda's a real mad girl, she'd rather put on jeans and go hiking than sit around Chicago apartments."

"You love her, don't you?"

"You damn right, I oughta marry her myself."

"But she's your sister."

"I don't give a goddamn. She needs a real man like me. You don't know how wild she is, you weren't brought up with her in the woods." Rhoda was real nice and I wished she hadn't shown up with a fiancé. In all this welter of women I still hadn't got one for myself, not that I was trying too hard, but sometimes I felt lonely to see everybody paired off and having a good time and all I did was curl up in my sleeping bag in the rosebushes and sigh and say bah. For me it was just red wine in my mouth and a pile of firewood.

But then I'd find something like a dead crow in the deer park and think "That's a pretty sight for sensitive human eyes, and all of it comes out of sex." So I put sex out of my mind again. As long as the sun shined then blinked and shined again, I was satisfied. I would be kind and remain in solitude, I wouldn't pook about, I'd rest and be kind. "Compassion is the guide star," said Buddha. "Don't dispute with the authorities or with women. Beg. Be humble." I wrote a pretty poem addressed to all the people coming to the party: "Are in your eyelids wars, and silk . . . but the saints are gone, all gone, safe to that other." I really thought myself a kind of crazy saint. And it was based on telling myself "Ray, don't run after liquor and excitement of women and talk, stay in your shack and enjoy natural relationship of things as they are" but it was hard to live up to this with all kinds of pretty broads coming up the hill every weekend and even on weeknights. One time a beautiful brunette finally consented to go up the hill with me and we were there in the dark on my mattress day-mat when suddenly the door burst open and Sean and Joe Mahoney danced in laughing, deliberately trying to make me mad . . . either that or they really believed in my effort at asceticism and were like angels coming in to drive away the devil woman. Which they did, all right. Sometimes when I was really drunk and high and sitting crosslegged in the midst of the mad parties I really did see visions of holy empty snow in my eyelids and when I opened them I'd see all these good friends sitting around waiting for me to explain; and nobody ever considered my behavior strange, quite natural among Buddhists; and whether I opened my eyes to explain something or not they were satisfied. During that whole season, in fact, I had an overwhelming urge to close my eyes in company. I think the girls were terrified of this. "What's he always sitting with his eyes closed for?"

Little Prajna, Sean's two-year-old daughter, would come and

poke at my closed eyelids and say "Booba. Hack!" Sometimes I preferred taking her for little magic walks in the yard, holding her hand, to sitting yakking in the living room.

As for Japhy he was quite pleased with anything I did provided I didn't pull any boners like making the kerosene lamp smoke from turning the wick too far up, or failing to sharpen the ax properly. He was very stern on those subjects. "You've got to learn!" he'd say. "Dammit, if there's anything I can't stand is when things ain't done right." It was amazing the suppers he'd roust up out of his own part of the food shelf, all kinds of weeds and dry roots bought in Chinatown and he'd boil up a mess of stuff, just a little, with soy sauce, and that went on top of freshly boiled rice and was delicious indeed, eaten with chopsticks. There we were sitting in the roar of trees at dusk with our windows wide open still, cold, but going chomp-chomp on delicious home-made Chinese dinners. Japhy really knew how to handle chopsticks and shoveled it in with a will. Then I'd sometimes wash the dishes and go out to meditate awhile on my mat beneath the eucalypti, and in the window of the shack I'd see the brown glow of Japhy's kerosene lamp as he sat reading and picking his teeth. Sometimes he'd come to the door of the shack and yell "Hoo!" and I wouldn't answer and I could hear him mutter "Where the hell is he?" and see him peering out into the night for his bhikku. One night I was sitting meditating when I heard a loud crack to my right and I looked and it was a deer, coming to re-visit the ancient deer park and munch awhile in the dry foliage. Across the evening valley the old mule went with his heartbroken "Hee haw" broken like a yodel in the wind: like a horn blown by some terribly sad angel: like a reminder to people digesting dinners at home that all was not as well as they thought. Yet it was just a love cry for another mule. But that was why . . .

One night I was meditating in such perfect stillness that two mosquitoes came and sat on each of my cheekbones and stayed there a long time without biting and then went away without biting.

27

A few days before his big farewell party Japhy and I had an argument. We went into San Francisco to deliver his bike to the freighter at the pier and then went up to Skid Row in a drizzling rain to get cheap haircuts at the barber college and pook around Salvation Army and Goodwill stores in search of long underwear and stuff. As we were walking in the drizzly exciting streets ("Reminds me of Seattle!" he yelled) I got the overwhelming urge to get drunk and feel good. I bought a poorboy of ruby port and uncapped it and dragged Japhy into an alley and we drank. "You better not drink too much," he said, "you know we gotta go to Berkeley after this and attend a lecture and discussion at the Buddhist Center."

"Aw I don't wanta go to no such thing, I just wanta drink in alleys."

"But they're expecting you, I read all your poems there last year."

"I don't care. Look at that fog flyin over the alley and look at this warm ruby red port, don't it make ya feel like singing in the wind?"

"No it doesn't. You know, Ray, Cacoethes says you drink too much."

"And him with his ulcer! Why do you think he has an ulcer? Because he drank too much himself. Do I have an ulcer? Not on your life! I drink for joy! If you don't like my drinking you can go to the lecture by yourself. I'll wait at Coughlin's cottage."

"But you'll miss all that, just for some old wine."

"There's wisdom in wine, goddam it!" I yelled. "Have a shot!"

"No I won't!"

"Well then I'll drink it!" and I drained the bottle and we went back on Sixth Street where I immediately jumped back into the same store and bought another poorboy. I was feeling fine now.

Japhy was sad and disappointed. "How do you expect to become a good bhikku or even a Bodhisattva Mahasattva always getting drunk like that?"

"Have you forgotten the last of the Bulls, where he gets drunk with the butchers?"

"Ah so what, how can you understand your own mind essence with your head all muddled and your teeth all stained and your belly all sick?"

"I'm not sick, I'm fine. I could just float up into that gray fog and fly around San Francisco like a seagull. D'I ever tell you about Skid Row here, I used to live here—"

"I lived on Skid Road in Seattle myself, I know all about all that."

The neons of stores and bars were glowing in the gray gloom of rainy afternoon, I felt great. After we had our haircuts we went into a Goodwill store and fished around bins, pulling out socks and undershirts and various belts and junk that we bought for a few pennies. I kept taking surreptitious slugs of wine out of my bottle which I had wedged in my belt. Japhy was disgusted. Then we got in the jalopy and drove to Berkeley, across the rainy bridge, to the cottages of Oakland and then downtown Oakland, where Japhy wanted to find a pair of jeans that fitted me. We'd been looking all day for used jeans that would fit me. I kept giving him wine and finally he relented a little and drank some and showed me the poem he had written while I was getting my haircut in Skid Row: "Modern barber college, Smith eyes closed suffers a haircut fearing its ugliness 50 cents, a barber student olive-skinned 'Garcia' on his coat, two blond small boys one with feared face and big ears watching from seats, tell him 'You're ugly little boy & you've got big ears' he'd weep and suffer and it wouldn't even be true, the other thinfaced conscious concentrated patched bluejeans and scuffed shoes who watches me delicate, suffering child that grows hard and greedy with puberty, Ray and I with poorboy of ruby port in us rainy May day no used levis in this town, our size, and old barber college t and g crappers skidrow haircuts middleage barber careers start out now flowering."

"See," I said, "you wouldn't have even written that poem if it wasn't for the wine made you feel good!"

"Ah I would have written it anyway. You're just drinking too much all the time, I don't see how you're even going to gain enlightenment and manage to stay out in the mountains, you'll always be coming down the hill spending your bean money on wine and finally you'll end up lying in the street in the rain, dead drunk, and then they'll take you away and you'll have to be reborn a teetotalin bartender to atone for your karma." He was really sad about it, and worried about me, but I just went on drinking.

When we got to Alvah's cottage and it was time to leave for the Buddhist Center lecture I said "I'll just sit here and get drunk and wait for you."

"Okay," said Japhy, looking at me darkly. "It's your life."

He was gone for two hours. I felt sad and drank too much and was dizzy. But I was determined not to pass out and stick it out and prove something to Japhy. Suddenly, at dusk, he came running back into the cottage drunk as a hoot owl yelling "You know what happened Smith? I went to the Buddhist lecture and they were all drinking white raw saki out of teacups and everybody got drunk. All those crazy Japanese saints! You were right! It doesn't make any difference! We all got drunk and discussed prajna! It was great!" And after that Japhy and I never had an argument again.

2 8

The night of the big party came. I could practically hear the hubbubs of preparation going on down the hill and felt depressed. "Oh my God, sociability is just a big smile and a big smile is nothing but teeth, I wish I could just stay up here and rest and be kind." But somebody brought up some wine and that started me off.

That night the wine flowed down the hill like a river. Sean had put together a lot of big logs for an immense bonfire in the yard. It was a clear starry night, warm and pleasant, in May. Everybody came. The party soon became clearly divided into three parts again. I spent most of my time in the living room where we had Cal Tjader records on the hi-fi and a lot of girls were dancing as Bud and I and Sean and sometimes Alvah and his new buddy George played bongo drums on inverted cans.

Out in the yard it was a quieter scene, with the glow of the
fire and lots of people sitting on the long logs Sean had placed
around the fire, and on the board a spread fit for a king and
his hungry retinue. Here, by the fire, far from the freneticism
of the bongo-ing living room, Cacoethes held forth discussing
poetry with the local wits, in tones about like this: "Marshall
Dashiell is too busy cultivating his beard and driving his Mer-
cedes Benz around cocktail parties in Chevy Chase and up
Cleopatra's needle, O. O. Dowler is being carried around
Long Island in limousines and spending his summers shriek-
ing on St. Mark's Place, and Tough Shit Short alas success-
fully manages to be a Savile Row fop with bowler and
waistcoat, and as for Manuel Drubbing he just flips quarters
to see who'll flop in the little reviews, and Omar Tott I got
nothing to say. Albert Law Livingston is busy signing auto-
graph copies of his novels and sending Christmas cards to
Sarah Vaughan; Ariadne Jones is importuned by the Ford
Company; Leontine McGee says she's old, and who does that
leave?"

"Ronald Firbank," said Coughlin.

"I guess the only real poets in the country, outside the orbit
of this little backyard, are Doctor Musial, who's probably
muttering behind his living-room curtains right now, and Dee
Sampson, who's too rich. That leaves us dear old Japhy here
who's going away to Japan, and our wailing friend Gold-book
and our Mr. Coughlin, who has a sharp tongue. By God,
I'm the only good one here. At least I've got an honest anarchist background. At least I had frost on my nose, boots on my
feet, and protest in my mouth." He stroked his mustache.

"What about Smith?"

"Well I guess he's a Bodhisattva in its frightful aspect, 'ts
about all I can say." (Aside, sneering: "He's too drrronk all the
time.")

Henry Morley also came that night, only for a short while,
and acted very strange sitting in the background reading *Mad*
comic books and the new magazine called *Hip*, and left early
with the remark "The hotdogs are too thin, do you think that's

a sign of the times or are Armour and Swift using stray Mexicans you think?" Nobody talked to him except me and Japhy. I was sorry to see him leave so soon, he was ungraspable as a ghost, as ever. Nevertheless he had worn a brand-new brown suit for the occasion, and suddenly he was gone.

Up the hill meanwhile, where the stars nodded on trees, occasional couples were sneaking up to neck or just brought jugs of wine and guitars up and had separate little parties in our shack. It was a great night. Japhy's father finally came, after work, and he was a tight-built little tough guy just like Japhy, balding a little, but completely energetic and crazy just like his son. He immediately began dancing wild mambos with the girls while I beat madly on a can. "Go, man!" You never saw a more frantic dancer: he stood there, bending way back till he was almost falling over, moving his loins at the girl, sweating, eager, grinning, glad, the maddest father I ever saw. Just recently at his daughter's wedding he had broken up the lawn reception by rushing out on his hands and knees with a tiger skin on his back, snapping at the ladies' heels and barking. Now he took a tall almost sixfoot gal by the name of Jane and swung her around and almost knocked over the bookcase. Japhy kept wandering to all sections of the party with a big jug in his hand, his face beaming with happiness. For a while the party in the living room emptied out the bonfire clique and soon Psyche and Japhy were doing a mad dance, then Sean leaped up and whirled her around and she made as if to swoon and fell right in between Bud and me sitting on the floor drumming (Bud and I who never had girls of our own and ignored everything) and lay there a second sleeping on our laps. We puffed on our pipes and drummed on. Polly Whitmore kept hanging around the kitchen helping Christine with the cooking and even turning out a batch of delicious cookies of her own. I saw she was lonely because Psyche was there and Japhy wasn't hers so I went over to grab her by the waist but she looked at me with such fear I didn't do anything. She seemed to be terrified of me. Princess was there with her new boyfriend and she too was pouting in a corner.

I said to Japhy "What the hell you gonna do with all these broads? Ain't you gonna give me one?"

"Take whichever one you want. I'm neutral tonight."

I went out to the bonfire to hear Cacoethes' latest witticisms. Arthur Whane was sitting on a log, well dressed, necktie and suit, and I went over and asked him "Well what is Buddhism? Is it fantastic imagination magic of the lightning flash, is it plays, dreams, not even plays, dreams?"

"No, to me Buddhism is getting to know as many people as possible." And there he was going around the party real affable shaking hands with everybody and chatting, a regular cocktail party. The party inside was getting more and more frantic. I began to dance with the tall girl myself. She was wild. I wanted to sneak her up on the hill with a jug but her husband was there. Later in the night a crazy colored guy showed up and began playing bongos on his own head and cheeks and mouth and chest, whacking himself with real loud sounds, and a great beat, a tremendous beat. Everybody was delighted and declared he must be a Bodhisattva.

People of all kinds were pouring in from the city, where news of the great party was going the rounds of our bars. Suddenly I looked up and Alvah and George were walking around naked.

"What are you doing?"

"Oh, we just decided to take our clothes off."

Nobody seemed to mind. In fact I saw Cacoethes and Arthur Whane well dressed standing having a polite conversation in the firelight with the two naked madmen, a kind of serious conversation about world affairs. Finally Japhy also got naked and wandered around with his jug. Every time one of his girls looked at him he gave a loud roar and leaped at them and they ran out of the house squealing. It was insane. I wondered what would ever happen if the cops in Corte Madera got wind of this and came roarin up the hill in their squad cars. The bonfire was bright, anybody down the road could see everything that was going on in the yard. Nevertheless it was strangely not out of place to see the bonfire, the food on the board, hear the guitar players, see the dense trees swaying in the breeze and a few naked men in the party.

I talked to Japhy's father and said "What you think about Japhy bein naked?"

"Oh I don't give a damn, Japh can do anything he wants far as I'm concerned. Say where's that big old tall gal we was dancin with?" He was a pure Dharma Bum father. He had had it rough too, in his early years in the Oregon woods, taking care of a whole family in a cabin he'd built himself and all the horny-headed troubles of trying to raise crops in merciless country, and the cold winters. Now he was a well-to-do painting contractor and had built himself one of the finest houses in Mill Valley and took good care of his sister. Japhy's own mother was alone living in a rooming house in the north. Japhy was going to take care of her when he got back from Japan. I had seen a lonely letter from her. Japhy said his parents had separated with a great deal of finality but when he got back from the monastery he would see what he could do to take care of her. Japhy didn't like to talk about her, and his father of course never mentioned her at all. But I liked Japhy's father, the way he danced sweating and mad, the way he didn't mind any of the eccentric sights he saw, the way he let everybody do what they wanted anyway and went home around midnight in a shower of thrown flowers dancing off down to his car parked in the road.

Al Lark was another nice guy who was there, just kept sitting sprawled with his guitar plucking out rumbling rambling blues chords or sometimes flamenco and looking off into space, and when the party was over at three a.m. he and his wife went to sleep in sleeping bags in the yard and I could hear them goofing in the grass. "Let's dance," she said. "Ah, go to sleep!" he said.

Psyche and Japhy were sore at each other that night and she didn't want to come up the hill and honor his new white sheets and stomped off to leave. I watched Japhy going up the hill, weaving drunk, the party was over.

I went with Psyche to her car and said "Come on, why do you make Japhy unhappy on his farewell night?"

"Oh he was mean to me, the hell with him."

"Aw come on, nobody'll eat you up the hill."

"I don't care, I'm driving back to the city."

"Well, that's not nice, and Japhy told me he loved you."

"I don't believe it."

"That's the story of life," I said walking away with a huge jug of wine hooked in my forefinger and I started up the hill and heard Psyche trying to back up her car and do a U-turn in the narrow road and the back end landed in the ditch and she couldn't get out and had to sleep on Christine's floor anyway. Meanwhile Bud and Coughlin and Alvah and George were all up in the shack sprawled out in various blankets and sleeping bags on the floors. I put my bag down in the sweet grass and felt I was the most fortunate person of the lot. So the party was over and all the screaming was done and what was accomplished? I began to sing in the night, enjoying myself with the jug. The stars were blinding bright.

"A mosquito as big as Mount Sumeru is much bigger than you think!" yelled Coughlin from inside the shack, hearing me sing.

I yelled back, "A horse's hoof is more delicate than it looks!"

Alvah came running out in his long underwear and did a big dance and howled long poems in the grass. Finally we had Bud up talking earnestly about his latest idea. We had a kind of a new party up there. "Let's go down see how many gals are left!" I went down the hill rolling half the way and tried to make Psyche come up again but she was out like a light on the floor. The embers of the big bonfire were still red hot and plenty of heat was being given off. Sean was snoring in his wife's bedroom. I took some bread from the board and spread cottage cheese on it and ate, and drank wine. I was all alone by the fire and it was getting gray dawn in the East. "Boy, am I drunk!" I said. "Wake up! wake up!" I yelled. "The goat of day is butting dawn! No ifs or buts! Bang! Come on, you girls! gimps! punks! thieves! pimps! hangmen! Run!" Then I suddenly had the most tremendous feeling of the pitifulness of human beings, whatever they were, their faces, pained mouths, personalities, attempts to be gay, little petulances, feelings of loss, their dull and empty witticisms so soon forgotten: Ah, for what? I knew that the sound of silence was everywhere and therefore everything everywhere was silence. Suppose we suddenly wake up and see that what we thought to be this and that, ain't this and that at all? I staggered up the hill, greeted by birds, and looked at all the huddled sleeping figures on the floor. Who were all these strange ghosts rooted to the silly little adventure of earth with me? And who was I? Poor Japhy, at eight a.m. he got up and banged on his frying pan and chanted the "Gocchami" chant and called everybody to pancakes.

29

The party went on for days; the morning of the third day people were still sprawled about the grounds when Japhy and I sneaked our rucksacks out, with a few choice groceries, and started down the road in the orange early-morning sun of California golden days. It was going to be a great day, we were back in our element: trails.

Japhy was in high spirits. "Goddammit it feels good to get away from dissipation and go in the woods. When I get back from Japan, Ray, when the weather gets really cold we'll put on our long underwear and hitchhike through the land. Think if you can of ocean to mountain Alaska to Klamath a solid forest of fir to bhikku in, a lake of a million wild geese. Woo! You know what woo means in Chinese?"

"What?"

"Fog. These woods are great here in Marin, I'll show you Muir Woods today, but up north is all that real old Pacific Coast mountain and ocean land, the future home of the Dharma-body. Know what I'm gonna do? I'll do a new long poem called 'Rivers and Mountains Without End' and just write it on and on on a scroll and unfold on and on with new surprises and always what went before forgotten, see, like a river, or like one of them real long Chinese silk paintings that show two little men hiking in an endless landscape of gnarled old trees and mountains so high they merge with the fog in the upper silk void. I'll spend three thousand years writing it, it'll be packed full of information on soil conservation, the Tennessee Valley Authority, astronomy, geology, Hsuan Tsung's travels, Chinese painting theory, reforestation, Oceanic ecology and food chains."

"Go to it, boy." As ever I strode on behind him and when we

began to climb, with our packs feeling good on our backs as though we were pack animals and didn't feel right without a burden, it was that same old lonesome old good old thwap thwap up the trail, slowly, a mile an hour. We came to the end of the steep road where we had to go through a few houses built near steep bushy cliffs with waterfalls trickling down, then up to a high steep meadow, full of butterflies and hay and a little seven a.m. dew, and down to a dirt road, then to the end of the dirt road, which rose higher and higher till we could see vistas of Corte Madera and Mill Valley far away and even the red top of Golden Gate Bridge.

"Tomorrow afternoon on our run to Stimson Beach," said Japhy, "you'll see the whole white city of San Francisco miles away in the blue bay. Ray, by God, later on in our future life we can have a fine free-wheeling tribe in these California hills, get girls and have dozens of radiant enlightened brats, live like Indians in hogans and eat berries and buds."

"No beans?"

"We'll write poems, we'll get a printing press and print our own poems, the Dharma Press, we'll poetize the lot and make a fat book of icy bombs for the booby public."

"Ah the public ain't so bad, they suffer too. You always read about some tarpaper shack burning somewhere in the Middlewest with three little children perishing and you see a picture of the parents crying. Even the kitty was burned. Japhy, do you think God made the world to amuse himself because he was bored? Because if so he would have to be mean."

"Ho, who would you mean by God?"

"Just Tathagata, if you will."

"Well it says in the sutra that God, or Tathagata, doesn't himself emanate a world from his womb but it just appears due to the ignorance of sentient beings."

"But he emanated the sentient beings and their ignorance too. It's all too pitiful. I ain't gonna rest till I find out *why*, Japhy, *why*."

"Ah don't trouble your mind essence. Remember that in pure Tathagata mind essence there is no asking of the question why and not even any significance attached to it."

"Well, then nothing's really happening, then."

He threw a stick at me and hit me on the foot.

"Well, that didn't happen," I said.

"I really don't know, Ray, but I appreciate your sadness about the world. 'Tis indeed. Look at that party the other night. Everybody wanted to have a good time and tried real hard but we all woke up the next day feeling sorta sad and separate. What do you think about death, Ray?"

"I think death is our reward. When we die we go straight to nirvana Heaven and that's that."

"But supposing you're reborn in the lower hells and have hot redhot balls of iron shoved down your throat by devils."

"Life's already shoved an iron foot down *my* mouth. But I don't think that's anything but a dream cooked up by some hysterical monks who didn't understand Buddha's peace under the Bo Tree or for that matter Christ's peace looking down on the heads of his tormentors and forgiving them."

"You really like Christ, don't you?"

"Of course I do. And after all, a lot of people say he is Maitreya, the Buddha prophesied to appear after Sakyamuni, you know, Maitreya means 'Love' in Sanskrit and that's all Christ talked about was love."

"Oh, don't start preaching Christianity to me, I can just see you on your deathbed kissing the cross like some old Karamazov or like our old friend Dwight Goddard who spent his life as a Buddhist and suddenly returned to Christianity in his last days. Ah that's not for me, I want to spend hours every day in a lonely temple meditating in front of a sealed statue of Kwannon which no one is ever allowed to see because it's too powerful. Strike hard, old diamond!"

"It'll all come out in the wash."

"You remember Rol Sturlason my buddy who went to Japan to study those rocks of Ryoanji. He went over on a freighter named *Sea Serpent* so he painted a big mural of a sea serpent and mermaids on a bulkhead in the messhall to the delight of the crew who dug him like crazy and all wanted to become Dharma Bums right there. Now he's climbing up holy Mount Hiei in Kyoto through a foot of snow probably, straight up where there are no trails, steep steep, through bamboo thickets and twisty pine like in brush drawings. Feet wet and lunch forgot, that's the way to climb."

"What are you going to wear in the monastery, anyway?"

"Oh man, the works, old T'ang Dynasty style things long black floppy with huge droopy sleeves and funny pleats, make you feel real Oriental."

"Alvah says that while guys like us are all excited about being real Orientals and wearing robes, actual Orientals over there are reading surrealism and Charles Darwin and mad about Western business suits."

"East'll meet West anyway. Think what a great world revolution will take place when East meets West finally, and it'll be guys like us that can start the thing. Think of millions of guys all over the world with rucksacks on their backs tramping around the back country and hitchhiking and bringing the word down to everybody."

"That's a lot like the early days of the Crusades, Walter the Penniless and Peter the Hermit leading ragged bands of believers to the Holy Land."

"Yeah but that was all such European gloom and crap, I want my Dharma Bums to have springtime in their hearts when the blooms are girling and the birds are dropping little fresh turds surprising cats who wanted to eat them a moment ago."

"What are you thinking about?"

"Just makin up poems in my head as I climb toward Mount Tamalpais. See up there ahead, as beautiful a mountain as you'll see anywhere in the world, a beautiful shape to it, I really love Tamalpais. We'll sleep tonight way around the back of it. Take us till late afternoon to get there."

The Marin country was much more rustic and kindly than the rough Sierra country we'd climbed last fall: it was all flowers, flowers, trees, bushes, but also a great deal of poison oak by the side of the trail. When we got to the end of the high dirt road we suddenly plunged into the dense redwood forest and went along following a pipeline through glades that were so deep the fresh morning sun barely penetrated and it was cold and damp. But the odor was pure deep rich pine and wet logs. Japhy was all talk this morning. He was like a little kid again now that he was out on the trail. "The only thing wrong with that monastery shot in Japan for me, is, though for all their intelligence and good intentions, the Americans out there, they have so little real sense of America and who the people are who really dig Buddhism here, and they don't have any use for poetry."

"Who?"

"Well, the people who are sending me out there and finance things. They spend their good money fixing elegant scenes of gardens and books and Japanese architecture and all that crap which nobody will like or be able to use anyway but rich American divorcees on Japanese cruises and all they really should do is just build or buy an old Jap house and vegetable garden and have a place there for cats to hang out in and be Buddhists, I mean have a real flower of something and not just the usual American middleclass fuggup with appearances. Anyway I'm looking forward to it, oh boy I can just see myself in the morning sitting on the mats with a low table at my side, typing on my portable, and my hibachi nearby with a pot of hot water on it keeping hot and all my papers and maps and pipe and flashlight neatly packed away and outside plum trees and pines with snow on the boughs and up on Mount Hieizan the snow getting deep and sugi and hinoki all around, them's redwoods, boy, and cedars. Little tucked-away temples down the rocky trails, cold mossy ancient places where frogs croak, and inside small statues and hanging buttery lamps and gold lotuses and paintings and ancient incense-soaked smells and lacquer chests with statues." His boat was leaving in two days. "But I'm sad too about leaving California . . . s'why I wanted to take one last long look at it today with ya, Ray."

We came up out of the gladey redwood forest onto a road, where there was a mountain lodge, then crossed the road and dipped down again through bushes to a trail that probably nobody even knew was there except a few hikers, and we were in Muir Woods. It extended, a vast valley, for miles before us. An old logger road led us for two miles then Japhy got off and scrambled up the slope and got onto another trail nobody dreamed was there. We hiked on this one, up and down along a

tumbling creek, with fallen logs again where you crossed the
creek, and sometimes bridges that had been built Japhy said by
the Boy Scouts, trees sawed in half the flat surface for walking.
Then we climbed up a steep pine slope and came out to the
highway and went up the side of a hill of grass and came out in
some outdoor theater, done up Greek style with stone seats all
around a bare stone arrangement for four-dimensional presen-
tations of Aeschylus and Sophocles. We drank water and sat
down and took our shoes off and watched the silent play from
the upper stone seats. Far away you could see the Golden Gate
Bridge and the whiteness of San Francisco.

Japhy began to shriek and hoot and whistle and sing, full of
pure gladness. Nobody around to hear him. "This is the way
you'll be on top of Mount Desolation, this summer, Ray."

"I'll sing at the top of my voice for the first time in my life."

"If anybody hears ya it'll just be the conies, or maybe a critic
bear. Ray that Skagit country where you're going is the greatest
place in America, that snaky river running back through gorges
and into its own unpeopled watershed, wet snowy mountains
fading into dry pine mountains and deep valleys like Big Beaver
and Little Beaver with some of the best virgin stands of red
cedar left in the world. I keep thinking of my abandoned Crater
Mountain Lookout house sitting up there with nobody but the
conies in the howling winds, getting old, the conies down in
their furry nests deep under boulders, and warm, eating seeds or
whatever they eat. The closer you get to real matter, rock air fire
and wood, boy, the more spiritual the world is. All these people
thinking they're hardheaded materialistic practical types, they
don't know shit about matter, their heads are full of dreamy
ideas and notions." He raised his hand. "Listen to that quail
calling."

"I wonder what everybody's doing back at Sean's."

"Well they're all up now and starting on that sour old red
wine again and sitting around talking nothing. They should
have all come with us and learnt something." He picked up his
pack and started off. In a half-hour we were in a beautiful
meadow following a dusty little trail over shallow creeks and
finally we were at Potrero Meadows camp. It was a National

Forest camp with a stone fireplace and picnic tables and everything but no one would be there till the weekend. A few miles
away, the lookout shack on top of Tamalpais looked right down
on us. We undid our packs and spent a quiet late afternoon dozing in the sun or Japhy ran around looking at butterflies and
birds and making notes in his notebook and I hiked alone down
the other side, north, where a desolate rocky country much like
the Sierras stretched out toward the sea.

At dusk Japhy lit a good big fire and started supper. We were
very tired and happy. He made a soup that night that I shall
never forget and was really the best soup I'd eaten since I was a
lionized young author in New York eating lunch at the Cham-
bord or in Henri Cru's kitchen. This was nothing but a couple
of envelopes of dried pea soup thrown into a pot of water with
fried bacon, fat and all, and stirred till boiling. It was rich, real
pea taste, with that smoky bacon and bacon fat, just the thing
to drink in the cold gathering darkness by a sparkling fire. Also
while pooking about he'd found puffballs, natural mushrooms,
not the umbrella type, just round grapefruit-size puffs of white
firm meat, and these he sliced and fried in bacon fat and we had
them on the side with fried rice. It was a great supper. We
washed the dishes in the gurgling creek. The roaring bonfire
kept the mosquitoes away. A new moon peeked down through
the pine boughs. We rolled out our sleeping bags in the meadow
grass and went to bed early, bone weary.

"Well Ray," said Japhy, "pretty soon I'll be far out to sea and
you'll be hitchhiking up the coast to Seattle and on through the
Skagit country. I wonder what'll happen to all of us."

We went to sleep on this dreamy theme. During the night I
had a vivid dream, one of the most distinct dreams I ever had, I
clearly saw a crowded dirty smoky Chinese market with beggars and vendors and pack horses and mud and smokepots and
piles of rubbish and vegetables for sale in dirty clay pans on the
ground and suddenly from the mountains a ragged hobo, a little seamed brown unimaginable Chinese hobo, had come down
and was just standing at the end of the market, surveying it with
an expressionless humor. He was short, wiry, his face leathered

hard and dark red by the sun of the desert and the mountains; his clothes were nothing but gathered rags; he had a pack of leather on his back; he was barefooted. I had seen guys like that only seldom, and only in Mexico, maybe coming into Monterrey out of those stark rock mountains, beggars who probably live in caves. But this one was a Chinese twice-as-poor, twice-as-tough and infinitely mysterious tramp and it was Japhy for sure. It was the same broad mouth, merry twinkling eyes, bony face (a face like Dostoevsky's death mask, with prominent eyebrow bones and square head); and he was short and compact like Japhy. I woke up at dawn, thinking "Wow, is *that* what'll happen to Japhy? Maybe he'll leave that monastery and just disappear and we'll never see him again, and he'll be the Han Shan ghost of the Orient mountains and even the Chinese'll be afraid of him he'll be so raggedy and beat."

I told Japhy about it. He was already up stoking the fire and whistling. "Well don't just lay there in your sleeping bag pullin your puddin, get up and fetch some water. Yodelayhee hoo! Ray, I will bring you incense sticks from the coldwater temple of Kiyomizu and set them one-by-one in a big brass incense bowl and do the proper bows, how's about that. That was some dream you had. If that's me, then it's me. Ever weeping, ever youthful, hoo!" He got out the hand-ax from the rucksack and hammered at boughs and got a crackling fire going. There was still mist in the trees and fog on the ground. "Let's pack up and take off and dig Laurel Dell camp. Then we'll hike over the trails down to the sea and swim."

"Great." On this trip Japhy had brought along a delicious combination for hiking energy: Ry-Krisp crackers, good sharp Cheddar cheese a wedge of that, and a roll of salami. We had this for breakfast with hot fresh tea and felt great. Two grown men could live two days on that concentrated bread and that salami (concentrated meat) and cheese and the whole thing only weighed about a pound and a half. Japhy was full of great ideas like that. What hope, what human energy, what truly American optimism was packed in that neat little frame of his! There he was clomping along in front of me on the trail and shouting back "Try the meditation of the trail, just walk along looking at the trail at your feet and don't look about and just fall into a trance as the ground zips by."

We arrived at Laurel Dell camp at about ten, it was also supplied with stone fireplaces with grates, and picnic tables, but the surroundings were infinitely more beautiful than Potrero Meadows. Here were the real meadows: dreamy beauties with soft grass sloping all around, fringed by heavy deep green timber, the whole scene of waving grass and brooks and nothing in sight.

"By God, I'm gonna come back here and bring nothing but food and gasoline and a primus and cook my suppers smokeless and the Forest Service won't even know the difference."

"Yeah, but if they ever catch you cooking away from these stone places they put you out, Smith."

"But what would I do on weekends, join the merry picnickers? I'd just hide up there beyond that beautiful meadow. I'd stay there forever."

"And you'd only have two miles of trail down to Stimson Beach and your grocery store down there." At noon we started for the beach. It was a tremendously grinding trip. We climbed way up high on meadows, where again we could see San Francisco far away, then dipped down into a steep trail that seemed to fall directly down to sea level; you had sometimes to run down the trail or slide on your back, one. A torrent of water fell down at the side of the trail. I went ahead of Japhy and began swinging down the trail so fast, singing happily, I left him behind about a mile and had to wait for him at the bottom. He was taking his time enjoying the ferns and flowers. We stashed our rucksacks in the fallen leaves under bushes and hiked freely down the sea meadows and past seaside farmhouses with cows browsing, to the beach community, where we bought wine in a grocery store and stomped on out into the sand and the waves. It was a chill day with only occasional flashes of sun. But we were making it. We jumped into the ocean in our shorts and swam swiftly around then came out and spread out some of our salami and Ry-Krisp and cheese on a piece of paper in the sand and drank wine and talked. At one point I even took a nap.

Japhy was feeling very good. "Goddammit, Ray, you'll never know how happy I am we decided to have these last two days hiking. I feel good all over again. I *know* somethin good's gonna come out of all this!"

"All what?"

"I dunno—out of the way we feel about life. You and I ain't out to bust anybody's skull, or cut someone's throat in an economic way, we've dedicated ourselves to prayer for all sentient beings and when we're strong enough we'll really be able to do it, too, like the old saints. Who knows, the world might wake up and burst out into a beautiful flower of Dharma everywhere."

After dozing awhile he woke up and looked and said, "Look at all that water out there stretching all the way to Japan." He was getting sadder and sadder about leaving.

3 0

We started back and found our packs and went back up that trail that had dropped straight down to sea level, a sheer crawling handgrasping climb among rocks and little trees that exhausted us, but finally we came out on a beautiful meadow and climbed it and again saw all San Francisco in the distance. "Jack London used to walk this trail," said Japhy. We proceeded along the south slope of a beautiful mountain that afforded us a view of the Golden Gate and even of Oakland miles away for hours on end as we trudged. There were beautiful natural parks of serene oaks, all golden and green in the late afternoon, and many wild flowers. Once we saw a fawn standing at a nub of grass, staring at us with wonder. We came down off this meadow down deep into a redwood forest then up again, again so steeply that we were cursing and sweating in the dust. Trails are like that: you're floating along in a Shakespearean Arden paradise and expect to see nymphs and fluteboys, then suddenly you're struggling in a hot broiling sun of hell in dust and nettles and poison oak . . . just like life. "Bad karma automatically produces good karma," said Japhy, "don't cuss so much and come on, we'll soon be sitting pretty on a flat hill."

The last two miles of the hill were terrible and I said "Japhy there's one thing I would like right now more than anything in the world—more than anything I've ever wanted all my life." Cold dusk winds were blowing, we hurried bent with our packs on the endless trail.

"What?"

"A nice big Hershey bar or even a little one. For some reason or other, a Hershey bar would save my soul right now."

"There's your Buddhism, a Hershey bar. How about moonlight in an orange grove and a vanilla ice-cream cone?"

"Too cold. What I need, want, pray for, yearn for, dying for, right now, is a Hershey bar . . . with nuts." We were very tired and trudging along home talking like two children. I kept repeating and repeating about my good old Hershey bar. I really meant it. I needed the energy anyway, I was a little woozy and needed sugar, but to think of chocolate and peanuts all melting in my mouth in that cold wind, it was too much.

Soon we were climbing over the corral fence that led to the horse meadow over our shack and then climbing over the barbed-wire fence right in our yard and trudging down the final twenty feet of high grass past my rosebush bed to the door of the good old little shack. It was our last night home together. We sat sadly in the dark shack taking off our boots and sighing. I couldn't do anything but sit on my feet, sitting on my feet took the pain out of them. "No more hikes for me forever," I said.

Japhy said "Well we still have to get supper and I see where we used up everything this weekend. I'll have to go down the road to the supermarket and get some food."

"Oh, man, aren't you tired? Just go to bed, we'll eat tomorrow." But he sadly put on his boots again and went out. Everybody was gone, the party had ended when it was found that Japhy and I had disappeared. I lit the fire and lay down and even slept awhile and suddenly it was dark and Japhy came in and lit the kerosene lamp and dumped the groceries on the table, and among them were three bars of Hershey chocolate just for me. It was the greatest Hershey bar I ever ate. He'd also brought my favorite wine, red port, just for me.

"I'm leaving, Ray, and I figured you and me might celebrate a little. . . ." His voice trailed off sadly and tiredly. When Japhy was tired, and he often wore himself out completely hiking or working, his voice sounded far-off and small. But pretty soon he roused his resources together and began cooking a supper and singing at the stove like a millionaire, stomping around in his boots on the resounding wood floor, arranging bouquets of flowers in the clay pots, boiling water for tea, plucking on his guitar, trying to cheer me up as I lay there staring sadly at the burlap ceiling. It was our last night, we both felt it.

"I wonder which one of us'll die first," I mused out loud. "Whoever it is, come on back, ghost, and give 'em the key."

"Ha!" He brought me my supper and we sat crosslegged and chomped away as on so many nights before: just the wind furying in the ocean of trees and our teeth going chomp chomp over good simple mournful bhikku food. "Just think, Ray, what it was like right here on this hill where our shack stands thirty thousand years ago in the time of the Neanderthal man. And do you realize that they say in the sutras there was a Buddha of that time, Dipankara?"

"The one who never said anything!"

"Can't you just see all those enlightened monkey men sitting around a roaring woodfire around their Buddha saying nothing and knowing everything?"

"The stars were the same then as they are tonight."

Later that night Sean came up and sat crosslegged and talked briefly and sadly with Japhy. It was all over. Then Christine came up with both children in her arms, she was a good strong girl and could climb hills with great burdens. That night I went to sleep in my bag by the rosebush and rued the sudden cold darkness that had fallen over the shack. It reminded me of the early chapters in the life of Buddha, when he decides to leave the Palace, leaving his mourning wife and child and his poor father and riding away on a white horse to go cut off his golden hair in the woods and send the horse back with the weeping servant, and embarks on a mournful journey through the forest to find the truth forever. "Like as the birds that gather in the trees of afternoon," wrote Ashvhaghosha almost two thousand years ago, "then at nightfall vanish all away, so are the separations of the world."

The next day I figured to give Japhy some kind of strange little going-away gift and didn't have much money or any ideas particularly so I took a little piece of paper about as big as a thumbnail and carefully printed on it: MAY YOU USE THE DIAMONDCUTTER OF MERCY and when I said goodbye to him at the pier I handed it to him, and he read it, put it right in his pocket, and said nothing.

The last thing he was seen doing in San Francisco: Psyche had finally melted and written him a note saying "Meet me on your ship in your cabin and I'll give you what you want," or words to that effect, so that was why none of us went on board to see him off in his cabin, Psyche was waiting there for a final passionate love scene. Only Sean was allowed to go aboard and hover around for whatever was going to happen. So after we all waved goodbye and went away, Japhy and Psyche presumably made love in the cabin and then she began to cry and insist she wanted to go to Japan too and the captain ordered everybody off but she wouldn't get off and the last thing was: the boat was pulling away from the pier and Japhy came out on deck with Psyche in his arms and threw her clean off the boat, he was strong enough to throw a girl ten feet, right on the pier, where Sean helped catch her. And though it wasn't exactly in keeping with the diamondcutter of mercy it was good enough, he wanted to get to that other shore and get on to his business. His business was with the Dharma. And the freighter sailed away out the Golden Gate and out to the deep swells of the gray Pacific, westward across. Psyche cried, Sean cried, everybody felt sad.

Warren Coughlin said "Too bad, he'll probably disappear into Central Asia marching about on a quiet but steady round from Kashgar to Lanchow via Lhasa with a string of yaks selling popcorn, safety-pins, and assorted colors of sewing-thread and occasionally climb a Himalaya and end up enlightening the Dalai Lama and all the gang for miles around and never be heard of again."

"No he won't," I said, "he loves us too much."

Alvah said, "It all ends in tears anyway."

3 1

Now, as though Japhy's finger were pointing me the way, I started north to my mountain.

It was the morning of June 18, 1956. I came down and said goodbye to Christine and thanked her for everything and walked down the road. She waved from the grassy yard. "It's going to be lonely around here with everybody gone and no big huge parties on weekends." She really enjoyed everything that had gone on. There she was standing in the yard barefooted, with little barefooted Prajna, as I walked off along the horse meadow.

I had an easy trip north, as though Japhy's best wishes for me to get to my mountain that could be kept forever, were with me. On 101 I immediately got a ride from a teacher of social studies, from Boston originally, who used to sing on Cape Cod and had fainted just yesterday at his buddy's wedding because he'd been fasting. When he left me off at Cloverdale I bought my supplies for the road: a salami, Cheddar cheese wedge, Ry-Krisp and also some dates for dessert, all put away neatly in my foodwrappers. I still had peanuts and raisins left over from our last hike together. Japhy had said, "I won't be needing those peanuts and raisins on that freighter." I recalled with a twinge of sadness how Japhy was always so dead serious about food, and I wished the whole world was dead serious about food instead of silly rockets and machines and explosives using everybody's food money to blow their heads off anyway.

I hiked about a mile after eating my lunch in back of a garage, up to a bridge on the Russian River, where, in gray gloom, I was stuck for as much as three hours. But suddenly I got an unexpected short ride from a farmer with a tic that made his face twitch, with his wife and boy, to a small town, Preston, where a truckdriver offered me a ride all the way to Eureka ("Eureka!" I yelled) and then he got talking to me and said "Goldang it I get lonesome driving this rig, I want someone to talk to all night, I'll take you all the way to Crescent City if you want." This was a little off my route but farther north than

Eureka so I said okay. The guy's name was Ray Breton, he drove me two hundred and eighty miles all night in the rain, talking ceaselessly about his whole life, his brothers, his wives, sons, his father and at Humboldt Redwood Forest in a restaurant called Forest of Arden I had a fabulous dinner of fried shrimp with huge strawberry pie and vanilla ice cream for dessert and a whole pot of coffee and he paid for the whole works. I got him off talking about his troubles to talk about the Last Things and he said, "Yeah, those who're good stay in Heaven, they've been in Heaven from the beginning," which was very wise.

We drove through the rainy night and arrived at Crescent City at dawn in a gray fog, a small town by the sea, and parked the truck in the sand by the beach and slept an hour. Then he left me after buying me a breakfast of pancakes and eggs, probably sick and tired of paying for all my meals, and I started walking out of Crescent City and over on an eastward road, Highway 199, to get back to big-shot 99 that would shoot me to Portland and Seattle faster than the more picturesque but slower coast road.

Suddenly I felt so free I began to walk on the wrong side of the road and sticking out my thumb from that side, hiking like a Chinese Saint to Nowhere for no reason, going to my mountain to rejoice. Poor little angel world! I suddenly didn't care any more, I'd walk all the way. But just because I was dancing along on the wrong side of the road and didn't care, anybody began to pick me up immediately, a goldminer with a small caterpillar up front being hauled by his son, and we had a long talk about the woods, the Siskiyou Mountains (through which we were driving, toward Grants Pass Oregon), and how to make good baked fish, he said, just by lighting a fire in the clean yellow sand by a creek and then burying the fish in the hot sand after you've scraped away the fire and just leaving it there a few hours then taking it out and cleaning it of sand. He was very interested in my rucksack and my plans.

He left me off at a mountain village very similar to Bridgeport California where Japhy and I had sat in the sun. I walked out a mile and took a nap in the woods, right in the heart of the

Siskiyou Range. I woke up from my nap feeling very strange in the Chinese unknown fog. I walked on the same way, wrong side, got a ride at Kerby from a blond used-car dealer to Grants Pass, and there, after a fat cowboy in a gravel truck with a malicious grin on his face deliberately tried to run over my rucksack in the road, I got a ride from a sad logger boy in a tin hat going very fast across a great swooping up and down dream valley thruway to Canyonville, where, as in a dream, a crazy store-truck full of gloves for sale stopped and the driver, Ernest Petersen, chatting amiably all the way and insisting that I sit on the seat that faced him (so that I was being zoomed down the road backward) took me to Eugene Oregon. He talked about everything under the sun, bought me two beers, and even stopped at several gas stations and hung out displays of gloves. He said, "My father was a great man, his saying was 'There are more horses' asses than horses in this world.'" He was a mad sports fan and timed outdoor track meets with a stopwatch and rushed around fearlessly and independently in his own truck defying local attempts to get him in the unions.

At red nightfall he bade me farewell near a sweet pond outside Eugene. There I intended to spend the night. I spread my bag out under a pine in a dense thicket across the road from cute suburban cottages that couldn't see me and wouldn't see me because they were all looking at television anyway, and ate my supper and slept twelve hours in the bag, waking up only once in the middle of the night to put on mosquito repellent.

At morning I could see the mighty beginnings of the Cascade Range, the northernmost end of which would be my mountain on the skirt of Canada, four hundred more miles north. The morning brook was smoky because of the lumber mill across the highway. I washed up in the brook and took off after one short prayer over the beads Japhy had given me in Matterhorn camp: "Adoration to emptiness of the divine Buddha bead."

I immediately got a ride on the open highway from two tough young hombres to outside Junction City where I had coffee and walked two miles to a roadside restaurant that looked better and had pancakes and then walking along the highway rocks, cars zipping by, wondering how I'd ever get to Portland let alone Seattle, I got a ride from a little funny lighthaired housepainter with spattered shoes and four pint cans of cold beer who also stopped at a roadside tavern for more beer and finally we were in Portland crossing vast eternity bridges as draws went up behind us to allow crane barges through in the big smoky river city scene surrounded by pine ridges. In downtown Portland I took the twenty-five-cent bus to Vancouver Washington, ate a Coney Island hamburger there, then out on the road, 99, where a sweet young mustached one-kidney Bodhisattva Okie picked me up and said "I'm s'proud I picked you up, someone to talk to," and everywhere we stopped for coffee he played the pinball machines with dead seriousness and also he picked up all hitchhikers on the road, first a big drawling Okie from Alabama then a crazy sailor from Montana who was full of crazed intelligent talk and we balled right up to Olympia Washington at eighty m.p.h. then up Olympic Peninsula on curvy woodsroads to the Naval Base at Bremerton Washington where a fifty-cent ferry ride was all that separated me from Seattle!

We said goodbye and the Okie bum and I went on the ferry, I paid his fare in gratitude for my terrific good luck on the road, and even gave him handfuls of peanuts and raisins which he devoured hungrily so I also gave him salami and cheese.

Then, while he sat in the main room, I went topdeck as the ferry pulled out in a cold drizzle to dig and enjoy Puget Sound. It was one hour sailing to the Port of Seattle and I found a half-pint of vodka stuck in the deck rail concealed under a *Time* magazine and just casually drank it and opened my rucksack and took out my warm sweater to go under my rain jacket and paced up and down all alone on the cold fog-swept deck feeling wild and lyrical. And suddenly I saw that the Northwest was a great deal more than the little vision I had of it of Japhy in my mind. It was miles and miles of unbelievable mountains grooking on all horizons in the wild broken clouds, Mount Olympus and Mount Baker, a giant orange sash in the gloom over the Pacificward skies that led I knew toward the Hokkaido Siberian desolations of the world. I huddled against the bridgehouse hearing the Mark Twain talk of the skipper and the wheelman inside. In

the deepened dusk fog ahead the big red neons saying: PORT OF
SEATTLE. And suddenly everything Japhy had ever told me about
Seattle began to seep into me like cold rain, I could feel it and
see it now, and not just think it. It was exactly like he'd said:
wet, immense, timbered, mountainous, cold, exhilarating, chal-
lenging. The ferry nosed in at the pier on Alaskan Way and immediately I saw the totem poles in old stores and the ancient
1880-style switch goat with sleepy firemen chug chugging up
and down the waterfront spur like a scene from my own dreams,
the old Casey Jones locomotive of America, the only one I ever
saw that old outside of Western movies, but actually working
and hauling boxcars in the smoky gloom of the magic city.

I immediately went to a good clean skid row hotel, the Hotel
Stevens, got a room for the night for a dollar seventy-five and
had a hot tub bath and a good long sleep and in the morning I
shaved and walked out First Avenue and accidentally found all
kinds of Goodwill stores with wonderful sweaters and red underwear for sale and I had a big breakfast with five-cent coffee
in the crowded market morning with blue sky and clouds scud-
ding overhead and waters of Puget Sound sparkling and dancing
under old piers. It was real true Northwest. At noon I checked
out of the hotel, with my new wool socks and bandanas and
things all packed in gladly, and walked out to 99 a few miles
out of town and got many short rides.

Now I was beginning to see the Cascades on the northeast
horizon, unbelievable jags and twisted rock and snow-covered
immensities, enough to make you gulp. The road ran right
through the dreamy fertile valleys of the Stilaquamish and the
Skagit, rich butterfat valleys with farms and cows browsing under that tremendous background of snow-pure heaps. The further north I hitched the bigger the mountains got till I finally
began to feel afraid. I got a ride from a fellow who looked like
a bespectacled careful lawyer in a conservative car, but turned
out he was the famous Bat Lindstrom the hardtop racing cham-
pion and his conservative automobile had in it a souped-up motor that could make it go a hundred and seventy miles an hour.
But he just demonstrated it by gunning it at a red light to let me
hear the deep hum of power. Then I got a ride from a lumberman

who said he knew the forest rangers where I was going and said "The Skagit Valley is second only to the Nile for fertility." He left me off at Highway 1-G, which was the little highway to 17-A that wound into the heart of the mountains and in fact would come to a dead-end as a dirt road at Diablo Dam. Now I was really in the mountain country. The fellows who picked me up were loggers, uranium prospectors, farmers, they drove me through the final big town of Skagit Valley, Sedro Woolley, a farming market town, and then out as the road got narrower and more curved among cliffs and the Skagit River, which we'd crossed on 99 as a dreaming belly river with meadows on both sides, was now a pure torrent of melted snow pouring narrow and fast between muddy snag shores. Cliffs began to appear on both sides. The snow-covered mountains themselves had disappeared, receded from my view, I couldn't see them any more but now I was beginning to feel them more.

32

In an old tavern I saw an old decrepit man who could hardly move around to get me a beer behind the bar, I thought "I'd rather die in a glacial cave than in an eternity afternoon room of dust like this." A Min 'n' Bill couple left me off at a grocery store in Sauk and there I got my final ride from a mad drunk fastswerving dark long-sideburned guitar-playing Skagit Valley wrangler who came to a dusty flying stop at the Marblemount Ranger Station and had me home.

The assistant ranger was standing there watching. "Are you Smith?"

"Yeah."

"That a friend of yours?"

"No, just a ride he gave me."

"Who does he think he is speeding on government property."

I gulped, I wasn't a free bhikku any more. Not until I'd get to my hideaway mountain that next week. I had to spend a whole week at Fire School with whole bunches of young kids, all of us in tin hats which we wore either straight on our heads or as I did at a rakish tilt, and we dug fire lines in the wet woods or felled trees or put out experimental small fires and I met the oldtimer ranger and onetime logger Burnie Byers, the "lumberjack" that Japhy was always imitating with his big deep funny voice.

Burnie and I sat in his truck in the woods and discussed Japhy. "It's a damn shame Japhy ain't come back this year. He was the best lookout we ever had and by God he was the best trailworker *I* ever seen. Just eager and anxious to go climbin around and so durn cheerful, I ain't never seen a better kid. And he wasn't afraid of nobody, he'd just come right out with it. That's what I like, cause when the time comes when a man can't say whatever he pleases I guess that'll be when I'm gonna go up in the backcountry and finish my life out in a lean-to. One thing about Japhy, though, wherever he'll be all the resta his life, I don't care how old he gets, he'll always have a good time." Burnie was about sixty-five and really spoke very paternally about Japhy. Some of the other kids also remembered Japhy and wondered why he wasn't back. That night, because it was Burnie's fortieth anniversary in the Forest Service, the other rangers voted him a gift, which was a brand new big leather belt. Old Burnie was always having trouble with belts and was wearing a kind of cord at the time. So he put on his new belt and said something funny about how he'd better not eat too much and everybody applauded and cheered. I figured Burnie and Japhy were probably the two best men that had ever worked in this country.

After Fire School I spent some time hiking up the mountains in back of the Ranger Station or just sitting by the rushing Skagit with my pipe in my mouth and a bottle of wine between my crossed legs, afternoons and also moonlit nights, while the other kids went beering at local carnivals. The Skagit River at Marblemount was a rushing clear snowmelt of pure green; above, Pacific Northwest pines were shrouded in clouds; and further beyond were peak tops with clouds going right through them and then fitfully the sun would shine through. It was the work of the quiet mountains, this torrent of purity at my feet. The sun shined on the roils, fighting snags held on. Birds scouted over the water looking for secret smiling fish that only occasionally suddenly leaped flying out of the water and arched their backs and fell in again into water that rushed on and obliterated their loophole, and everything was swept along. Logs and snags came floating down at twenty-five miles an hour. I figured if I should try to swim across the narrow river I'd be a half-mile downstream before I kicked to the other shore. It was a river wonderland, the emptiness of the golden eternity, odors of moss and bark and twigs and mud, all ululating mysterious visionstuff before my eyes, tranquil and everlasting nevertheless, the hillhairing trees, the dancing sunlight. As I looked up the clouds assumed, as I assumed, faces of hermits. The pine boughs looked satisfied washing in the waters. The top trees shrouded in gray fog looked content. The jiggling sunshine leaves of Northwest breeze seemed bred to rejoice. The upper snows on the horizon, the trackless, seemed cradled and warm. Everything was everlastingly loose and responsive, it was all everywhere beyond the truth, beyond emptyspace blue. "The mountains are mighty patient, Buddha-man," I said out loud and took a drink. It was coldish, but when the sun peeped out the tree stump I was sitting on turned into a red oven. When I went back in the moonlight to my same old tree stump the world was like a dream, like a phantom, like a bubble, like a shadow, like a vanishing dew, like a lightning's flash.

Time came finally for me to be packed up into my mountain. I bought forty-five dollars' worth of groceries on credit in the little Marblemount grocery store and we packed that in the truck, Happy the muleskinner and I, and drove on up the river to Diablo Dam. As we proceeded the Skagit got narrower and more like a torrent, finally it was crashing over rocks and being fed by side-falls of water from heavy timbered shores, it was getting wilder and craggier all the time. The Skagit River was dammed back at Newhalem, then again at Diablo Dam, where a giant Pittsburgh-type lift took you up on a platform to the level of Diablo Lake. There'd been a gold rush in the 1890s in this country, the prospectors had built a trail through the solid rock cliffs of the gorge between Newhalem and what was now Ross Lake, the final dam, and dotted the drainages of Ruby Creek, Granite Creek, and Canyon Creek with claims that never paid off. Now most of this trail was under water anyway. In 1919 a fire had raged in the Upper Skagit and all the country around Desolation, my mountain, had burned and burned for two months and filled the skies of northern Washington and British Columbia with smoke that blotted out the sun. The government had tried to fight it, sent a thousand men in with pack string supply lines that then took three weeks from Marblemount fire camp, but only the fall rains had stopped that blaze and the charred snags, I was told, were still standing on Desolation Peak and in some valleys. That was the reason for the name: Desolation.

"Boy," said funny old Happy the muleskinner, who still wore his old floppy cowboy hat from Wyoming days and rolled his own butts and kept making jokes, "don't be like the kid we had a few years ago up on Desolation, we took him up there and he was the greenest kid I ever saw, I packed him into his lookout and he tried to fry an egg for supper and broke it and missed the friggin fryingpan and missed the stove and it landed on his boot, he didn't know whether to run shit or go blind and when I left I told him not to flog his damn dummy too much and the sucker says to me 'Yes sir, yes sir.'"

"Well I don't care, all I want is to be alone up there this summer."

"You're sayin that now but you'll change your tune soon enough. They all talk brave. But then you get to talkin to yourself. That ain't so bad but don't start *answerin* yourself, son." Old Happy drove the pack mules on the gorge trail while I rode the boat from Diablo Dam, to the foot of Ross Dam where you could see immense dazzling openings of vistas that showed the Mount Baker National Forest mountains in wide panorama around Ross Lake that extended shiningly all the way back to Canada. At Ross Dam the Forest Service floats were lashed a little way off from the steep timbered shore. It was hard sleeping on those bunks at night, they swayed with the float and the log and the wave combined to make a booming slapping noise that kept you awake.

The moon was full the night I slept there, it was dancing on the waters. One of the lookouts said "The moon is right on the mountain, when I see that I always imagine I see a coyote silhouettin."

Finally came the gray rainy day of my departure to Desolation Peak. The assistant ranger was with us, the three of us were going up and it wasn't going to be a pleasant day's horseback riding in all that downpour. "Boy, you shoulda put a couple quarts of brandy in your grocery list, you're gonna need it up there in the cold," said Happy looking at me with his big red nose. We were standing by the corral, Happy was giving the animals bags of feed and tying it around their necks and they were chomping away unmindful of the rain. We came plowing to the log gate and bumped through and went around under the immense shrouds of Sourdough and Ruby mountains. The waves were crashing up and spraying back at us. We went inside to the pilot's cabin and he had a pot of coffee ready. Firs on steep banks you could barely see on the lake shore were like ranged ghosts in the mist. It was the real Northwest grim and bitter misery.

"Where's Desolation?" I asked.

"You ain't about to see it today till you're practically on top of it," said Happy, "and then you won't like it much. It's snowin and hailin up there right now. Boy, ain't you sure you didn't sneak a little bottle of brandy in your pack somewheres?" We'd already downed a quart of blackberry wine he'd bought in Marblemount.

"Happy when I get down from this mountain in September I'll buy you a whole quart of scotch." I was going to be paid good money for finding the mountain I wanted.

"That's a promise and don't you forget it." Japhy had told me a lot about Happy the Packer, he was called. Happy was a good man; he and old Burnie Byers were the best oldtimers on the scene. They knew the mountains and they knew pack animals and they weren't ambitious to become forestry supervisors either.

Happy remembered Japhy too, wistfully. "That boy used to know an awful lot of funny songs and stuff. He shore loved to go out loggin out trails. He had himself a Chinee girlfriend one time down in Seattle, I seen her in his hotel room, that Japhy I'm tellin you he shore was a grunge-jumper with the women."

I could hear Japhy's voice singing gay songs with his guitar as the wind howled around our barge and the gray waves plashed up against the windows of the pilot house.

"And this is Japhy's lake, and these are Japhy's mountains," I thought, and wished Japhy were there to see me doing everything he wanted me to do.

In two hours we eased over to the steep timbered shore eight miles uplake and jumped off and lashed the float to old stumps and Happy whacked the first mule, and she scampered off the wood with her doublesided load and charged up the slippery bank, legs thrashing and almost falling back in the lake with all my groceries, but made it and went off clomping in the mist to wait on the trail for her master. Then the other mules with batteries and various equipment, then finally Happy leading the way on his horse and then myself on the mare Mabel and then Wally the assistant ranger.

We waved goodbye to the tugboat man and started up a sad and dripping party in a hard Arctic climb in heavy foggy rain up narrow rocky trails with trees and underbrush wetting us clean to the skin when we brushed by. I had my nylon poncho tied around the pommel of the saddle and soon took it out and put it over me, a shroudy monk on a horse. Happy and Wally didn't put on anything and just rode wet with heads bowed. The horse slipped occasionally in the rocks of the trail. We went on and on, up and up, and finally we came to a snag that had fallen across the trail and Happy dismounted and took out his doublebitted ax and went to work cursing and sweating and hacking out a new shortcut trail around it with Wally while I was delegated to watch the animals, which I did in a rather comfortable way sitting under a bush and rolling a cigarette. The mules were afraid of the steepness and roughness of the shortcut trail and Happy cursed at me "Goddammit it grab 'im by the hair and drag 'im up here." Then the mare was afraid. "Bring up that mare! You expect me to do everything around here by myself?"

We finally got out of there and climbed on up, soon leaving the shrubbery and entering a new alpine height of rocky meadow with blue lupine and red poppy feathering the gray mist with lovely vaguenesses of color and the wind blowing hard now and with sleet. "Five thousand feet now!" yelled Happy from up front, turning in the saddle with his old hat furling in the wind, rolling himself a cigarette, sitting easy in his saddle from a whole lifetime on horses. The heather wildflower drizzly meadows wound up and up, on switchback trails, the wind getting harder all the time, finally Happy yelled: "See that big rock face up thar?" I looked up and saw a goopy shroud of gray rock in the fog, just above. "That's another thousand feet though you might think you can reach up and touch it. When we get there we're almost in. Only another half hour after that."

"You sure you didn't bring just a *little* extry bottle of brandy boy?" he yelled back a minute later. He was wet and miserable but he didn't care and I could hear him singing in the wind. By and by we were up above timberline practically, the meadow gave way to grim rocks and suddenly there was snow on the ground to the right and to the left, the horses were slowshing in a sleety foot of it, you could see the water holes their hoofs left, we were really way up there now. Yet on all sides I could see nothing but fog and white snow and blowing mists. On a clear day I would have been able to see the sheer drops from the side of the trail and would have been scared for my horse's slips of hoof; but now all I saw were vague intimations of treetops way below that looked like little clumps of grasses. "O Japhy," I thought, "and there you are sailing across the ocean safe on a ship, warm in a cabin, writing letters to Psyche and Sean and Christine."

The snow deepened and hail began to pelt our red weather-beaten faces and finally Happy yelled from up ahead "We're almost there now." I was cold and wet: I got off the horse and simply led her up the trail, she grunted a kind of groan of relief to be rid of the weight and followed me obediently. She already had quite a load of supplies, anyway. "There she is!" yelled Happy and in the swirled-across top-of-the-world fog I saw a funny little peaked almost Chinese cabin among little pointy firs and boulders standing on a bald rock top surrounded by snowbanks and patches of wet grass with tiny flowers.

I gulped. It was too dark and dismal to like it. "This will be my home and restingplace all summer?"

We trudged on to the log corral built by some old lookout of the thirties and tethered the animals and took down the packs. Happy went up and took the weather door off and got the keys and opened her up and inside it was all gray dank gloomy muddy floor with rain-stained walls and a dismal wooden bunk with a mattress made of ropes (so as not to attract lightning) and the windows completely impenetrable with dust and worst of all the floor littered with magazines torn and chewed up by mice and pieces of groceries too and uncountable little black balls of rat turd.

"Well," said Wally showing his long teeth at me, "it's gonna take you a long time to clean up this mess, hey? Start in right now by taking all those leftover canned goods off the shelf and running a wet soapy rag over that filthy shelf." Which I did, and I had to do, I was getting paid.

But good old Happy got a roaring woodfire going in the potbelly stove and put on a pot of water and dumped half a can of coffee in it and yelled "Ain't nothing like real strong coffee, up in this country boy we want coffee that'll make your hair stand on end."

I looked out the windows: fog. "How high are we?"

"Six thousand and a half feet."

"Well how can I see any fires? There's nothing but fog out there."

"In a couple of days it'll all blow away and you'll be able to see for a hundred miles in every direction, don't worry."

But I didn't believe it. I remembered Han Shan talking about the fog on Cold Mountain, how it never went away; I began to appreciate Han Shan's hardihood. Happy and Wally went out with me and we spent some time putting up the anemometer pole and doing other chores, then Happy went in and started a crackling supper on the stove frying Spam with eggs. We drank coffee deep, and had a rich good meal. Wally unpacked the two-way battery radio and contacted Ross Float. Then they curled up in their sleeping bags for a night's rest, on the floor, while I slept on the damp bunk in my own bag.

In the morning it was still gray fog and wind. They got the animals ready and before leaving turned and said to me, "Well, do you still like Desolation Peak?"

And Happy: "Don't forget what I told ya about answerin your own questions now. And if a bar comes by and looks in your window just close your eyes."

The windows howled as they rode out of sight in the mist among the gnarled rock-top trees and pretty soon I couldn't see them any more and I was alone on Desolation Peak for all I knew for eternity, I was sure I wasn't going to come out of there alive anyway. I was trying to see the mountains but only occasional gaps in the blowing fog would reveal distant dim shapes. I gave up and went in and spent a whole day cleaning out the mess in the cabin.

At night I put on my poncho over my rain jacket and warm clothing and went out to meditate on the foggy top of the world. Here indeed was the Great Truth Cloud, Dharmamega, the ultimate goal. I began to see my first star at ten, and suddenly some of the white mist parted and I thought I saw mountains, immense black gooky shapes across the way, stark black and white with snow on top, so near, suddenly, I almost jumped. At eleven I could see the evening star over Canada, north way, and thought I could detect an orange sash of sunset behind the fog but all this was taken out of my mind by the sound of pack rats scratching at my cellar door. In the attic little diamond mice skittered on black feet among oats and bits of rice and old rigs left up there by a generation of Desolation losers. "Ugh, ow," I thought, "will I get to like this? And if I don't, how do I get to leave?" The only thing was to go to bed and stick my head under the down.

In the middle of the night while half asleep I had apparently opened my eyes a bit, and then suddenly I woke up with my hair standing on end, I had just seen a huge black monster standing in my window, and I looked, and it had a star over it, and it was Mount Hozomeen miles away by Canada leaning over my backyard and staring in my window. The fog had all blown away and it was perfect starry night. What a mountain! It had that same unmistakable witches' tower shape Japhy had given it in his brush drawing of it that used to hang on the burlap wall in the flowery shack in Corte Madera. It was built with a kind of winding rock-ledge road going around and around, spiraling to the very top where a perfect witches' tower peakied up and pointed to all infinity. Hozomeen, Hozomeen, the most mournful mountain I ever seen, and the most beautiful as soon as I got to know it and saw the Northern Lights behind it reflecting all the ice of the North Pole from the other side of the world.

33

Lo, in the morning I woke up and it was beautiful blue sunshine sky and I went out in my alpine yard and there it was, everything Japhy said it was, hundreds of miles of pure snow-covered rocks and virgin lakes and high timber, and below, instead of the world, I saw a sea of marshmallow clouds flat as a roof and extending miles and miles in every direction, creaming all the valleys, what they call low-level clouds, on my 6600-foot pinnacle it was all far below me. I brewed coffee on the stove and came out and warmed my mist-drenched bones in the hot sun of my little woodsteps. I said "Tee tee" to a big furry cony and he calmly enjoyed a minute with me gazing at the sea of clouds. I made bacon and eggs, dug a garbage pit a hundred yards down the trail, hauled wood and identified landmarks with my panoramic and firefinder and named all the magic rocks and clefts, names Japhy had sung to me so often: Jack Mountain, Mount Terror, Mount Fury, Mount Challenger, Mount Despair, Golden Horn, Sourdough, Crater Peak, Ruby, Mount Baker bigger than the world in the western distance, Jackass Mountain, Crooked Thumb Peak, and the fabulous names of the creeks: Three Fools, Cinnamon, Trouble, Lightning and Freezeout. And it was all mine, not another human pair of eyes in the world were looking at this immense cycloramic universe of matter. I had a tremendous sensation of its dreamlikeness which never left me all that summer and in fact grew and grew, especially when I stood on my head to circulate my blood, right on top of the mountain, using a burlap bag for a head mat, and then the mountains looked like little bubbles hanging in the void upsidedown. In fact I realized they were upsidedown and I was upsidedown! There was nothing here to hide the fact of gravity holding us all intact upsidedown against a surface globe of earth in infinite empty space. And suddenly I realized I was truly alone and had nothing to do but feed myself and rest and amuse myself, and nobody could criticize. The little flowers grew everywhere around the rocks, and no one had asked them to grow, or me to grow.

In the afternoon the marshmallow roof of clouds blew away in patches and Ross Lake was open to my sight, a beautiful cerulean pool far below with tiny toy boats of vacationists, the boats themselves too far to see, just the pitiful little tracks they left rilling in the mirror lake. You could see pines reflected up-sidedown in the lake pointing to infinity. Late afternoon I lay in the grass with all that glory before me and grew a little bored and thought "There's nothing there because I don't care." Then I jumped up and began singing and dancing and whistling through my teeth far across Lightning Gorge and it was too im-mense for an echo. Behind the shack was a huge snowfield that would provide me with fresh drinking water till September, just a bucket a day let melt in the house, to dip into with a tin cup, cold ice water. I was feeling happier than in years and years, since childhood, I felt deliberate and glad and solitary. "Buddy-o, yiddam, diddam dee," I sang, walking around kicking rocks. Then my first sunset came and it was unbelievable. The moun-tains were covered with pink snow, the clouds were distant and frilly and like ancient remote cities of Buddhaland splendor, the wind worked incessantly, whish, whish, booming at times, rat-tling my ship. The new moon disk was prognathic and secretly funny in the pale plank of blue over the monstrous shoulders of haze that rose from Ross Lake. Sharp jags popped up from be-hind slopes, like childhood mountains I grayly drew. Some-where, it seemed, a golden festival of rejoicement was taking place. In my diary I wrote, "Oh I'm happy!" In the late day peaks I saw the hope. Japhy had been right.

As darkness enveloped my mountain and soon it would be night again and stars and Abominable Snowman stalking on Hozomeen, I started a cracking fire in the stove and baked delicious rye muffins and mixed up a good beef stew. A high west wind buffeted the shack, it was well built with steel rods going down into concrete pourings, it wouldn't blow away. I was satisfied. Every time I'd look out the windows I'd see alpine firs with snowcapped backgrounds, blinding mists, or the lake below all riffled and moony like a toy bathtub lake. I made myself a little bouquet of lupine and mountain posies and put them in a coffee cup with water. The top of Jack Mountain was done in by silver clouds. Sometimes I'd see flashes of lightning far away, illuminating suddenly the unbelievable horizons. Some mornings there was fog and my ridge, Starvation Ridge, would be milkied over completely.

On the dot the following Sunday morning, just like the first, daybreak revealed the sea of flat shining clouds a thousand feet below me. Every time I felt bored I rolled another cigarette out of my can of Prince Albert; there's nothing better in the world than a roll-your-own deeply enjoyed without hurry. I paced in the bright silver stillness with pink horizons in the west, and all the insects ceased in honor of the moon. There were days that were hot and miserable with locusts of plagues of insects, winged ants, heat, no air, no clouds, I couldn't understand how the top of a mountain in the North could be so hot. At noon the only sound in the world was the symphonic hum of a million insects, my friends. But night would come and with it the mountain moon and the lake would be moonlaned and I'd go out and sit in the grass and meditate facing west, wishing there were a Personal God in all this impersonal matter. I'd go out to my snowfield and dig out my jar of purple Jello and look at the white moon through it. I could feel the world rolling toward the moon. At night while I was in my bag, the deer would come up from the lower timber and nibble at leftovers in tin plates in the yard: bucks with wide antlers, does, and cute little fawns looking like otherworldly mammals on another planet with all that moonlight rock behind them.

Then would come wild lyrical drizzling rain, from the south, in the wind, and I'd say "The taste of rain, why kneel?" and I'd say "Time for hot coffee and a cigarette, boys," addressing my imaginary bhikkus. The moon became full and huge and with it came Aurora Borealis over Mount Hozomeen ("Look at the void and it is even stiller," Han Shan had said in Japhy's translation); and in fact I was so still all I had to do was shift my crossed legs in the alpine grass and I could hear the hoofs of deers running away somewhere. Standing on my head before bedtime on that rock roof of the moonlight I could indeed see that the earth was truly upsidedown and man a weird vain beetle full of strange ideas walking around upsidedown and boasting, and I could realize that man remembered why this dream of planets and plants and Plantagenets was built out of the primordial essence. Sometimes I'd get mad because things didn't work out well, I'd spoil a flapjack, or slip in the snowfield while getting water, or one time my shovel went sailing down into the gorge, and I'd be so mad I'd want to bite the mountaintops and would come in the shack and kick the cupboard and hurt my toe. But let the mind beware, that though the flesh be bugged, the circumstances of existence are pretty glorious.

All I had to do was keep an eye on all horizons for smoke and run the two-way radio and sweep the floor. The radio didn't bother me much; there were no fires close enough for me to report ahead of anybody else and I didn't participate in the lookout chats. They dropped me a couple of radio batteries by parachute but my own batteries were still in good shape.

One night in a meditation vision Avalokitesvara the Hearer and Answerer of Prayer said to me "You are empowered to remind people that they are utterly free" so I laid my hand on myself to remind myself first and then felt gay, yelled "Ta," opened my eyes, and a shooting star shot. The innumerable worlds in the Milky Way, *words*. I ate my soup in little doleful bowlfuls and it tasted much better than in some vast tureen . . . my Japhy pea-and-bacon soup. I took two-hour naps every afternoon, waking up and realizing "none of this ever happened" as I looked around my mountaintop. The world was upsidedown hanging in an ocean of endless space and here were all these people sitting in theaters watching movies, down there in the world to which I would return. . . . Pacing in the yard at dusk, singing "Wee Small Hours," when I came to the lines "when the whole wide world is fast asleep" my eyes filled with tears. "Okay world," I said, "I'll love ya." In bed at night, warm and happy in my bag on the good hemp bunk, I'd see my table and my clothes in the moonlight and feel, "Poor Raymond boy, his day is so sorrowful and worried, his reasons are so ephemeral, it's such a haunted and pitiful thing to have to live" and on this I'd go to sleep like a lamb. Are we fallen angels who didn't want to believe that nothing *is* nothing and so were born to lose our loved ones and dear friends one by one and finally our own life, to see it proved? . . . But cold morning would return, with clouds billowing out of Lightning Gorge like giant smoke, the lake below still cerulean neutral, and empty space the same as ever. O gnashing teeth of earth, where would it all lead to but some sweet golden eternity, to prove that we've all been wrong, to prove that the proving itself was nil . . .

34

August finally came in with a blast that shook my house and augured little augusticity. I made raspberry Jello the color of rubies in the setting sun. Mad raging sunsets poured in seafoams of cloud through unimaginable crags, with every rose tint of hope beyond, I felt just like it, brilliant and bleak beyond words. Everywhere awful ice fields and snow straws; one blade of grass jiggling in the winds of infinity, anchored to a rock. To the East, it was gray; to the north, awful; to the west, raging mad, hard iron fools wrestling in the groomian gloom; to the south, my father's mist. Jack Mountain, his thousand-foot rock hat overlooked a hundred football fields of snow. Cinnamon Creek was an eyrie of Scottish fog. Shull lost itself in the Golden Horn of Bleak. My oil lamp burned in infinity. "Poor gentle flesh," I realized, "there is no answer." I didn't know anything any more, I didn't care, and it didn't matter, and suddenly I felt really free. Then would come really freezing mornings, cracking fire, I'd chop wood with my hat on (earmuff cap), and would feel lazy and wonderful indoors, fogged in by icy clouds. Rain, thunder in the mountains, but in front of the stove I read my Western magazines. Everywhere snowy air and woodsmoke. Finally the snow came, in a whirling shroud from Hozomeen by Canada, it came surling my way sending radiant white heralds through which I saw the angel of light peep, and the wind rose, dark low clouds rushed up as out of a forge, Canada was a sea of meaningless mist; it came in a general fanning attack advertised by the sing in my stovepipe; it rammed it, to absorb my old blue sky view which had been all thoughtful clouds of gold; far, the rum dum dum of Canadian thunder; and to the south another vaster darker storm closing in like a pincer; but Hozomeen mountain stood there returning the attack with a surl of silence. And nothing could induce the gay golden horizons far northeast where there was no storm, to change places with Desolation. Suddenly a green and rose rainbow shafted right down into Starvation Ridge not three hundred yards away from my door, like a bolt, like a pillar: it came among steaming clouds and orange sun turmoiling.

> What is a rainbow, Lord?
> A hoop
> For the lowly.

It hooped right into Lightning Creek, rain and snow fell simultaneous, the lake was milkwhite a mile below, it was just too crazy. I went outside and suddenly my shadow was ringed by the rainbow as I walked on the hilltop, a lovely-haloed mystery making me want to pray. "O Ray, the career of your life is like a raindrop in the illimitable ocean which is eternal awakenerhood. Why worry ever any more? Write and tell Japhy that." The storm went away as swiftly as it came and the late afternoon lake-sparkle blinded me. Late afternoon, my mop drying on the rock. Late afternoon, my bare back cold as I stood above the world in a snowfield digging shovelsful into a pail. Late afternoon, it was I not the void that changed. Warm rose dusk, I meditated in the yellow half moon of August. Whenever I heard thunder in the mountains it was like the iron of my mother's love. "Thunder and snow, how we shall go!" I'd sing. Suddenly came the drenching fall rains, all-night rain, millions of acres of Bo-trees being washed and washed, and in my attic millennial rats wisely sleeping.

Morning, the definite feel of autumn coming, the end of my job coming, wild windy cloud-crazed days now, a definite golden look in the high noon haze. Night, made hot cocoa and sang by the woodfire. I called Han Shan in the mountains: there was no answer. I called Han Shan in the morning fog: silence, it said. I called: Dipankara instructed me by saying nothing. Mists blew by, I closed my eyes, the stove did the talking. "Woo!" I yelled, and the bird of perfect balance on the fir point just moved his tail; then he was gone and distance grew immensely white. Dark wild nights with hint of bears: down in my garbage pit old soured solidified cans of evaporated milk bitten into and torn apart by mighty behemoth paws: Avalokitesvara the Bear. Wild cold fogs with awesome holes. On my calendar I ringed off the fifty-fifth day.

My hair was long, my eyes pure blue in the mirror, my skin tanned and happy. All night gales of soaking rain again, autumn rain, but I warm as toast in my bag dreaming of long infantry-scouting movements in the mountains; cold wild morning with high wind, racing fogs, racing clouds, sudden bright suns, the pristine light on hill patches and my fire roaring with three big logs as I exulted to hear Burnie Byers over the radio telling all his lookouts to come down that very day. The season was over. I paced in the windy yard with cup of coffee forked in my thumb singing "Blubbery dubbery the chipmunk's in the grass." There he was, my chipmunk, in the bright clear windy sunny air staring on the rock; hands clasping he sat up straight, some little oat between his paws; he nibbled, he darted away, the little nutty lord of all he surveyed. At dusk, big wall of clouds from the north coming in. "Brrr," I said. And I'd sing "Yar, but my she was yar!" meaning my shack all summer, how the wind hadn't blown it away, and I said "Pass pass pass, that which passes through everything!" Sixty sunsets had I seen revolve on

that perpendicular hill. The vision of the freedom of eternity was
mine forever. The chipmunk ran into the rocks and a butterfly
came out. It was as simple as that. Birds flew over the shack re-
joicing; they had a mile-long patch of sweet blueberries all the
way down to the timberline. For the last time I went out to the
edge of Lightning Gorge where the little outhouse was built right
on the precipice of a steep gulch. Here, sitting every day for sixty
days, in fog or in moonlight or in sunny day or in darkest night,
I had always seen the little twisted gnarly trees that seemed to
grow right out of the midair rock.

And suddenly it seemed I saw that unimaginable little Chinese bum standing there, in the fog, with that expressionless
humor on his seamed face. It wasn't the real-life Japhy of rucksacks and Buddhism studies and big mad parties at Corte
Madera, it was the realer-than-life Japhy of my dreams, and he
stood there saying nothing. "Go away, thieves of the mind!" he
cried down the hollows of the unbelievable Cascades. It was
Japhy who had advised me to come here and now though he
was seven thousand miles away in Japan answering the meditation bell (a little bell he later sent to my mother in the mail, just
because she was my mother, a gift to please her) he seemed to
be standing on Desolation Peak by the gnarled old rocky trees
certifying and justifying all that was here. "Japhy," I said out
loud, "I don't know when we'll meet again or what'll happen in
the future, but Desolation, Desolation, I owe so much to Desolation, thank you forever for guiding me to the place where I
learned all. Now comes the sadness of coming back to cities
and I've grown two months older and there's all that humanity
of bars and burlesque shows and gritty love, all upsidedown in
the void God bless them, but Japhy you and me forever we
know, O ever youthful, O ever weeping." Down on the lake
rosy reflections of celestial vapor appeared, and I said "God, I
love you" and looked up to the sky and really meant it. "I have
fallen in love with you, God. Take care of us all, one way or the
other."

To the children and the innocent it's all the same.

And in keeping with Japhy's habit of always getting down on
one knee and delivering a little prayer to the camp we left, to

the one in the Sierra, and the others in Marin, and the little prayer of gratitude he had delivered to Sean's shack the day he sailed away, as I was hiking down the mountain with my pack I turned and knelt on the trail and said "Thank you, shack." Then I added "Blah," with a little grin, because I knew that shack and that mountain would understand what that meant, and turned and went on down the trail back to this world.